UNDER SUSPICION . . .

UNDER SIEGE . . .

Zack reached down and pulled another file folder out of the box. Normally he thought of this as the fact-finding portion of his pretrial preparation. Right now it felt like little more than reading over and over about a cold-blooded multiple murder performed by a calculating butcher.

Terry shuffled through some papers until he found what looked like one of the police reports. "Let's see. He fired off somewhere in the neighborhood of one hundred twenty rounds, using an illegally modified AK-47, which was found five feet from him in the hallway."

Zack inhaled sharply. "He fired a hundred and twenty bullets?" He pulled out a few photos from a box at his feet. "No wonder the place looks like somebody went at it with a chain saw."

"Have you seen the video yet?"

"What video?" Zack asked.

"It's in the box with the other thing," Terry responded helpfully, rummaging around in a carton Zack hadn't gotten to yet. "I peeked at it a little last night," he said, handing the tape to Zack. "I don't recommend popcorn."

Premeditated Murder

Ed Gaffney

A Dell Book

PREMEDITATED MURDER
A Dell Book / June 2005

Published by
Bantam Dell
A Division of Random House, Inc.
New York, New York

ISBN 0-440-24194-4

Printed in the United States of America
Published simultaneously in Canada

www.bantamdell.com

OPM 10 9 8 7 6 5 4 3 2 1

This book is dedicated to Attorneys Don Bronstein, Derege Demissie, Beth Eisenberg, Tom Hagar, Dave Nathanson, John Osler, Jim Pingeon, Mary Anne Rathmann, Rick Rathmann, Matthew Robinowitz, Eric Ruben, Brownlow Speer, Leslie Walker, Tanis Yanetti, and countless other lawyers in Massachusetts and throughout the United States for their work defending and protecting the constitutional rights of people who are too poor to hire attorneys. You are true patriots.

ACKNOWLEDGMENTS

First, thanks to my editor, Kate Miciak, for your brilliant suggestions, enthusiastic support, and expert guidance. I am very lucky—and thrilled—to be working with you.

And thanks to my agent, Steve Axelrod, who had the insight to introduce me (and Zack and Terry) to Kate.

Thanks also to the entire Bantam Dell team for all of their hard work helping this first-time author.

For their help with research, thank you to the remarkably knowledgeable Michelle Gomez, Tina Trevaskis, and especially Kathy Lague, who did the scary stuff.

Thanks to my fearless first-draft readers: my brothers, Steve and John Gaffney, Deede Bergeron, and English experts Fred and Lee Brockmann (who read the second draft, too!).

Special thanks to Eric Ruben, whose passion and humor are the inspiration for Terry.

Thanks to everyone in the Tribe for their boundless support.

And finally, to my partner forever, Suz Brockmann, thanks for too many things to try to list. I can't wait to see what we do next. I love you.

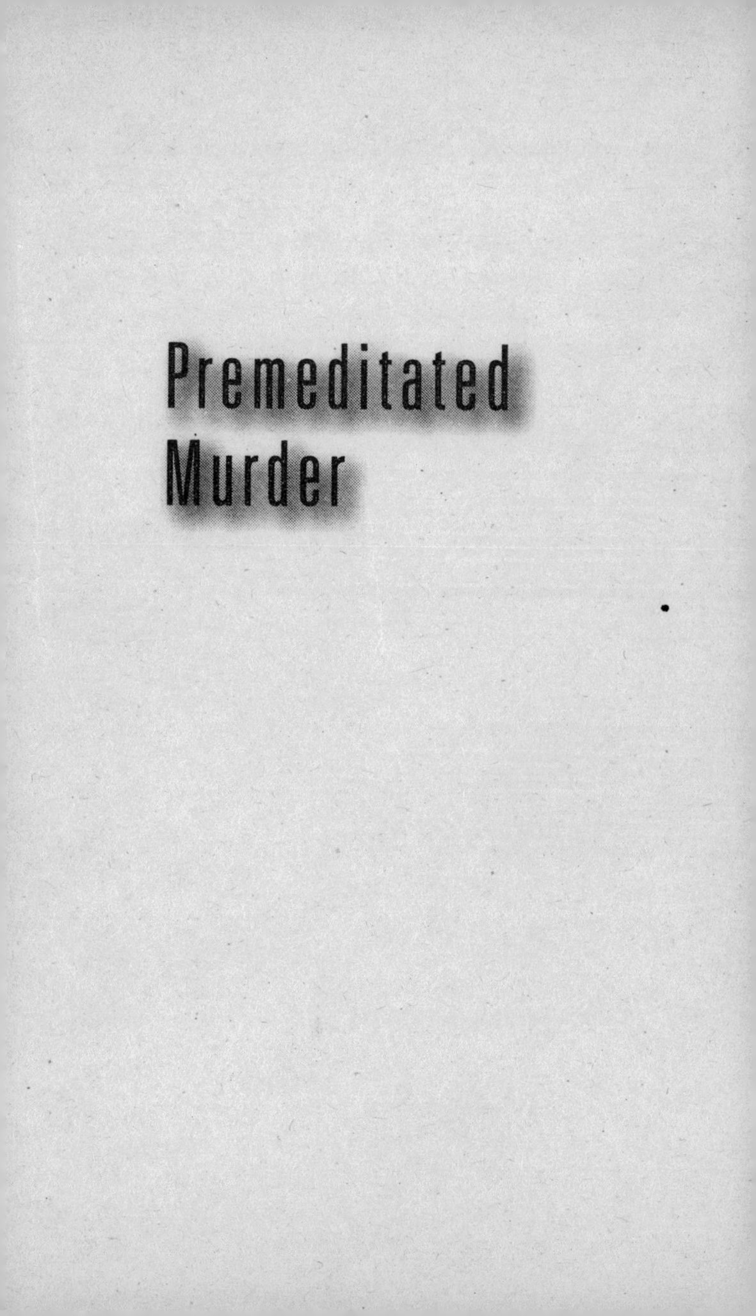

Premeditated Murder

PROLOGUE

Northampton, Massachusetts

WHEN AHMAD EL AMIN TURNED THE CORNER and headed down the street toward his apartment, raw panic knotted his stomach. From a block away, he could see a fleet of police cars and ambulances and fire trucks all with colored strobe lights flashing madly, scattered across the sidewalks and street. It was impossible to know exactly what building the authorities were occupying, but then he saw them bring a stretcher out of his apartment house. It was carrying a corpse in a black body bag. Then another stretcher emerged, with another dead body.

Then another.

There had been an attack. They had been discovered. He had to escape. It would be a disaster if he was captured, or if the trunk of his car was searched. He immediately turned around and walked in the opposite direction, back toward his car, away from the chaos.

He was going to assume the worst; he'd head to the emergency meeting place to wait. If any of the others managed to escape and showed up in the next twenty-four hours, that would be best.

But if not, he'd mourn them, and then carry on

alone. It would be a more difficult mission, but he would not fail. He would take his place with the blessed ones who had already died fighting this holy war.

With God's help, the blood of the infidels would flow like a river.

ONE

CAPTAIN LITTLE: *And, Mr. Thompkins, while you were waiting in the apartment across the hallway, what were you thinking?*

MR. THOMPKINS: *I wasn't really thinking much of anything. I was just watching their door, waiting for it to open.*

Q: *Well, what did you think was going to happen when it opened?*

A: *I thought that I was going to walk in and start shooting.*

(Transcript of Massachusetts State Police Interview of Calvin Thompkins, January 14, Page 8)

January 15—Northampton, Massachusetts

ATTORNEY TERRY TALLACH WATCHED WITH disbelief as Hampshire County Superior Court Officer Gloria Blainey squeezed the handcuffs around his wrists and then took hold of his left elbow. "Let's go," she said.

If this had been Terry's fantasy world, Gloria would have been an adventurous twenty-three-year-old, wearing stiletto heels and stockings, and leading him to her bedroom.

In the painfully real world, however, Gloria was a sixty-something grandmother of four, wearing dark blue Reeboks and thick socks, and leading him to the courthouse lockup because the worst judge in Massachusetts had decided to break Terry's balls.

It was the perfect ending to the perfect case—a thirty-nine-dollar-per-hour court-appointed criminal assignment with an idiot for a client.

Terry was representing James O'Toole, a squeaky-voiced kid with a limp, already a veteran of several guilty pleas to a variety of misdemeanors, who had been charged with the armed and masked robbery of a grocery store. The prosecution's case rested on the testimony of three eyewitnesses who emphatically identified O'Toole—despite the mask—because of his limp and his distinctive voice. And in case anybody cared, there were fingerprints, too. Conviction was inevitable. After which Judge Richard Cottonwood would impose a life-destroying sentence.

O'Toole had told Terry that he had spent the night with his girlfriend, and with the unwavering certainty available only to the profoundly stupid, declared that he was sure to be acquitted on the basis of her testimony. A significant flaw in that plan was that despite looking for this dream witness for weeks, Terry couldn't find her.

So in the days leading up to the trial, Terry engaged in many hours of hard negotiating, during which he cobbled together a plea bargain which would result in O'Toole getting a reasonable sentence.

Of course, O'Toole, being an idiot, refused the deal. Bringing them to the last day of trial with nothing to their case except the testimony of the defendant—a man who walked and talked funny, standing accused of a serious crime committed by a man who, well, walked and talked funny.

But then, that morning, just as Terry was entering the courthouse for the final act of the farce, a young woman identifying herself as the girlfriend's sister came up to him and said that she would testify that O'Toole had been with her sister on the night of the robbery.

So Terry called her as a witness.

Which is when things kind of went south with the Big Dick.

Richard Cottonwood never let a defendant call a witness who was not on the witness list—reason number 324 why the judge was a turd. The official rules of criminal procedure required that before the trial, the defense lawyer and the prosecutor exchange lists of witnesses that they expected to testify. But every once in a while, somebody needed to call a witness who wasn't on the list. Judges hated it, but usually allowed it, if you could show them a good reason. Not Dick Cottonwood, though. The word across the state was that in over thirty years on the bench, Cottonwood had never let a defendant call a witness who wasn't on the list.

Never. What an ass.

But Terry called the girlfriend's sister anyway, even though he knew that Cottonwood wouldn't let her testify. Terry figured that he'd have the opportunity to explain why the witness was important, so that on appeal, O'Toole had at least a chance at getting a new trial.

But instead of letting Terry make a statement as to why he needed to call the witness, Judge Cottonwood just said, "This witness was not on the list. Call another one."

"Your Honor," Terry had responded, "I'd like to come to sidebar to give an offer of proof as to the purpose—"

"That's not necessary," interrupted the judge. "Are you going to call another witness, or is the defense resting?"

"I'm sorry, Your Honor," Terry persisted, "but I need to insist on coming to sidebar in order to make a record—"

"You'll insist on nothing in my courtroom, Mr. Tallach," said the judge. "And I order you to call your next witness."

"But, Your Honor—" Terry said, only to be interrupted again.

"Mr. Tallach," the judge said, "listen carefully to me. You will either call another witness or you will tell me that the defense rests. If you do anything—and I mean anything—else, I will hold you in contempt of court."

Terry laughed. "You're going to throw me in the can for trying to defend my client?" he asked.

"Apparently I am," the judge replied. "The court finds you in contempt, and instructs the court officers to take you into custody immediately. Court is in recess."

And now Gloria and her partner, Big Tony Z, were escorting Terry down the back stairs to the holding cell in the courthouse basement. They stopped at the entrance, Gloria undid the cuffs, Terry walked inside, and the heavy door clanged shut behind him.

The bare, concrete floor was painted gray. An ancient sink with a rust stain beneath the single cold-water spigot was the only thing hanging on the puke-yellow cinder-block walls. The place smelled like stale sweat and urine. Terry stared through the bars at Big Tony. Incarceration wasn't all it was cracked up to be.

"I already called Zack," Big Tony told him. "He'll be here in a few minutes."

Zack Wilson was Terry's closest friend, and the best lawyer he knew. They'd met in high school, and were now law partners. Although there were times, like these, when Terry wondered if Zack doubted the wisdom of that arrangement.

It wasn't that Terry was a bad lawyer. Far from it. He worked hard for his clients—even the worst of the deadbeats.

It was just that his style was different from Zack's. Terry was kind of dark, and bulky, and in your face. If you needed a brawler on your side of a criminal trial, Terry Tallach was your guy.

Zack, on the other hand, was more like a golden boy—lean, athletic-looking, fair-skinned, blond. He walked into a room, and you'd swear that somebody had actually turned up the lights. It was weird. He didn't dress very well, and he wasn't even that good-looking, but somehow, people were drawn to him. Especially women. And children.

And juries.

And Zack was smart, too. But in a way that people appreciated, not in a way that pissed them off. The combination made him a terrific attorney. Whether he was terrific enough to get Terry out of this jackpot was an open question, though. A very important open question. Being locked in a shithole sucked.

After what seemed like hours, but was probably more like forty-five minutes, Tony took a phone call; thirty seconds later the elevator bell rang, and then Zack's voice was greeting Gloria and Tony. Another minute passed, it sounded like Zack said, "Let me tell him," and then Zack came around the corner.

As usual, he somehow managed to carry himself like he owned the place, even if the place happened to be a dungeon prison cell. He was wearing his default expression—a warm, genuine smile that managed not only to be all-inclusive but to radiate a message which everyone around him read loud and clear: Things were already pretty darn good, and they were just about to get better. Gloria was shuffling along behind him, probably to ask him to marry one of her daughters.

Before Zack even reached the cell, he began to speak. "The good news is that we just got assigned the biggest and most important criminal case Northampton has ever seen."

If he was waiting for a response, he was going to wait for a while. That wasn't the good news Terry was looking for.

"The better news is that Gloria tells me it's meat loaf night."

Aw, fuck. Zack couldn't get him out. He was screwed.

And then Gloria moved past Zack and started putting her key into the lock. Zack continued. "But the best news of all is that you won't be around here for dinner."

January 30—Washington, D.C.

"EXCUSE ME, MR. PRESIDENT. YOU'RE NEEDED IN the Oval Office . . ."

Matt Ferguson tried to hide his relief as his body man, Carlos Oliveira, interrupted his meal. Matt stood, and suddenly the entire table full of dignitaries jumped to its feet. "Please stay seated, everyone," Matt said. "You'll have to excuse me for a moment." He tried to look disappointed. "Some business has come up that needs my attention. I shouldn't be long."

And with that, he and Carlos made their temporary escape.

Forty-five minutes earlier, the band started playing "Hail to the Chief," and a ballroom full of people decked out in monkey suits and evening gowns started to applaud. Matt continuously marveled at what a big deal people could make out of dinner, if they really put their minds to it. And when he stole a look at the long line of V.I.P.s he had to greet before he took his seat, he was reminded for about the fiftieth time that day how much he missed Sammy, and how glad he would be when she returned from helping their daughter move into her new place.

He was also glad that he had grabbed a few slices of pizza before dinner, because over the past months Matt had learned that the first forty-five minutes of every official state dinner consisted of stale toasts, small talk, and a smaller salad. He'd barely taken two bites of his appetizer when Carlos arrived.

As they walked down the long corridor toward the West Wing, a portrait of Thomas Jefferson came into view. They turned a corner and passed a painting of Abraham Lincoln. Six months ago, the idea that one of these days somebody might stick a picture of Matt in a White House corridor would have been crazy.

But that was before the phone rang on that summer night and changed his and Sammy's lives forever.

"Colonel Ferguson? This is White House Chief of Staff Vernon Browning. President Graham has asked me to call you to see if you would be willing to meet with him on an urgent matter concerning additional service for the country."

Talk about understatements.

"What's going on?" Matt said now, as he and Carlos walked together.

"I don't know, sir. Mr. Browning just said that I should ask you to come back to the office. He said something about a development in East Africa that you should know about."

Over the past two weeks, rebel forces had been amassing in the western provinces of Kenya, not far from its capital city, Nairobi. A civil war looked imminent. Months of drought and the resulting famine had already put a great deal of pressure on the recently elected government of President Mwanga. Not to mention the new strain of malaria that had been sweeping through the population like wildfire.

And if that wasn't enough, there were reports that Mwanga might use chemical weapons if a rebellion did break out.

They were still a minute or two away from the office. Matt looked over at the young man walking beside him. "You know, I haven't had a chance to talk to your father for quite a while. How's he doing?"

Carlos's father, José, had been Matt's staff sergeant in Vietnam, and had saved his life more times than either could remember.

"Poppy's fine, sir. He's still running the shop with Mom." Carlos smiled. "She says even though he complains about that kind of work making him soft, that just means that he likes it there."

"I'm glad to hear it. Give him my best, the next time you speak to him. And if he's ever in Washington, you know he's got a standing invitation to visit the White House, right?"

"Yes, sir. I've told him."

"Good," Matt said, and meant it, as they reached the area outside the Oval Office.

As always, CNN was playing on a television set mounted on the wall. Another former heavyweight boxing champ was going bankrupt, and Mitchell Stanton, a federal judge in Michigan, committed suicide yesterday. Matt was going to have to check into that.

Chief of Staff Vernon Browning was waiting for him

in the Oval Office. Impeccably dressed, as usual, in a gray suit, starched white shirt, and dark tie, Browning said, "Good evening, Mr. President. I'm sorry I had to interrupt your dinner . . ."

The thin, fifty-something political powerhouse worked very hard at his job, which included about a hundred thousand different functions, among them to organize the White House staff, to help prioritize the avalanche of information flowing into the Oval Office, and to advise the President. Browning was remarkably good at his work. Matt felt extremely fortunate that he'd been willing to stay on after President Graham's death.

"I owe you one, Vernon," Matt replied. "You know how I hate those things." He and the Chief of Staff sat down across from each other in the center of the room. "What's up?"

Browning opened a folder that he had been holding, glanced down at some notes, and then looked back up at Matt. "Mr. President, we have good intelligence that several thousand Tanzanian troops have been mobilized and are now gathering at the Kenyan border. And we suspect that more troops will be joining them soon. They appear to be trying to do this covertly, but it won't be a secret for long."

"So Kenya doesn't know about this yet?" Matt asked.

"That's right, sir. President Mwanga is meeting with several other African heads of state at the U.N. over the next few days. As soon as he hears about this, he'll fly back home, the Kenyan Ambassador to the U.N. will request an emergency meeting of the Security Council, and they'll appeal to us to send them anything you can imagine—peacekeepers, advisors, troops, weapons. You name it, they'll want it."

Matt nodded. "If I were in their shoes, I'd probably be looking around for a hand, too. Mwanga's on the verge of fighting a two-front war using an army that's about half the size of the Rhode Island National Guard." He paused. The guy running Kenya before Mwanga had been connected to a Russian thug who was infamous for supplying just about anything to anyone—including weapons to radical third-world countries that were barely safe in the hands of the most stable governments. "We never learned whether Mwanga ever got hold of any of those chemical weapons we were worrying about last year, did we?"

"No, sir," Browning replied.

"Okay," Matt said, standing up and walking behind his desk. The Chief of Staff rose, too. "I'll need a briefing here in an hour. I want Defense, State, the Chairman of the Joint Chiefs, the National Security Advisor, and Homeland Security there. Half of them are probably at the dinner."

"Secretary of Defense Maisenbacher is still out of the country," Vernon said.

"Never mind," Matt said. "Rusty will cover it." The Chairman of the Joint Chiefs of Staff, General Russell Levine, had been a classmate of Matt's at West Point; Rusty Levine was about the only friend Matt had among his senior advisors.

"Very good, Mr. President," Vernon replied, heading toward the door to his adjoining office. But just before he reached it, he turned back. "Would you like Kenny and Adrienne at the meeting, sir?"

Ken Stoutland and Adrienne Tippins were the administration's top political advisors. Most of the time, the pair seemed more worried about approval ratings polls than whether Matt was actually doing something right. At a time like this, Matt needed them about as much as a case of hives.

"I don't think so, Vernon," he answered. "What's the Navy got in the area?"

Browning thought for a moment. "The Kitty Hawk Battle Group is off the west coast of India."

"Okay," Matt said. "Tell General Levine that in about ninety minutes I expect he'll want to order an amphibious assault group to detach and head for the coast of Kenya."

"Yes, sir, Mr. President."

As soon as Browning left the Oval Office, Matt picked up the phone and hit the intercom. "Carlos, can you please send my regrets to the table at dinner? Something urgent has come up. And then bring me the latest briefing notes on East Africa."

"Yes, sir," the young man replied.

"One more thing," Matt continued. "If you can find me a chicken salad sandwich and a Coke, that would be great. And grab something for yourself, too. It's going to be a late night."

TWO

THE CLERK: *Defendant, please rise.*

Members of the jury, harken to the indictments returned against this defendant by the grand inquest by the body of the County of Hampshire.

Indictment 79443, Calvin Thompkins.

At the Superior Court begun and holden at the City of Northampton within and for the County of Hampshire, on the first Monday in February in this year, the Grand Jurors for the Commonwealth of Massachusetts on their oath present that Calvin Thompkins, on or about the 14th day of January at Northampton, in the County of Hampshire aforesaid, did assault and beat Rudolf Lange with intent to murder the said Rudolf Lange and by such assault and beating did kill and murder the said Rudolf Lange . . . the said John Bercher . . . the said Marc Nathenson . . . Mitchell Nathenson . . . Marianne Duhamel . . . Helene Ghazi.

Against the peace of said Commonwealth and contrary to the form of the statute.

To these indictments, members of the jury, the defendant has pleaded not guilty and for trial thereof he has placed himself upon the country, which country you are.

You are now sworn to try the issues.

(Trial Volume II, Pages 212–213)

January 30—Northampton, Massachusetts

ZACK WAS HAVING A SINGLE-PARENT MOMENT.

He was sitting on the couch in the living room, playing "I'm Being Somebody" with his four-year-old son. Which at the moment consisted of Zack watching Justin run back and forth in front of the coffee table in only a pair of little white underpants, giggling like a maniac and waving his skinny arms back and forth over his head with two fingers on each hand raised in the peace sign. Or was it the victory sign?

Was it okay to burst into the laughter that Zack could barely hold back? Or would that hurt the little guy's feelings?

What in the world was he doing trying to be this boy's father?

It wasn't that he doubted his love for Justin. Four years ago, the arrival of the baby with the raven black hair and dark eyes had transformed Zack's life into something much more meaningful than he had ever imagined possible. He would do anything for his son. Absolutely anything.

The problem was that there were so many times, like now, when Zack really didn't have a clue *what* to do.

Was running around in underwear like a lunatic healthy for a four-year-old boy? Twenty years from now, would Justin be lying on some shrink's couch, explaining that he was a homeless, jobless, friendless loser because when he was four his father let him run around in tighty whities pretending—Zack looked over at his mostly naked son—well, whatever he was pretending?

"C'mon, Daddy, I'm *being* somebody!" Justin shouted with glee, coming to a complete halt directly in front of the couch, arms above head, fingers in the *V*. "Guess who am I being!"

"Um," Zack said, stalling, searching his completely empty mind for anything to say. "Richard Nixon?"

Justin obviously had no idea what Zack was talking about, but that didn't stop him from wrapping his arms around himself like he always did when he was having fun, exploding into laughter, running around the coffee table, and jumping into Zack's arms. "No, silly, I'm SpongeBob *Square*Pants!" he hollered, completely delighted. "I guess you are not the luckiest big winner!"

"I guess I'm not," replied Zack, hugging the little boy. "Are you ready for some bathroom work before bed?"

"Yes, I am," said Justin. "And I have a surprise for you, too, Daddy! C'mon!"

Zack let Justin tug him by the hand down the endless hall of their recently purchased, way too old, way too big, way too falling-apart house to the bathroom nearest Justin's bedroom. The boy opened the door and said with excitement, "Remember how you said I could help paint?"

Zack could merely stare.

In a mere forty-five minutes, using his play paints, Justin had managed to paint the entire bathroom—or at least as much as he could reach—fire-engine red.

Except the toilet seat.

For that, he had chosen black.

The Massachusetts Board of Bar Overseers suspended Criminal Defense Attorney Zachary Wilson for three months effective immediately for "engaging in behavior which had the appearance of impropriety." Mr. Wilson was sanctioned for entering the Hampshire County Superior Courthouse in Northampton with a glossy black paint ring on his ass . . .

"Didn't I do a good job, Daddy?" Justin asked.

Zack was afraid that if he even tried to speak, he

would burst into laughter, which just wasn't fair to Justin. The boy would think Zack was mocking something he obviously cared about. And contrary to the overriding philosophy of Zack's own chronically angry father, punishment was out of the question. This was clearly an honest mistake. Zack *had* told Justin earlier that day that he could help paint. Little did he imagine . . .

"This is, uh, amazing," Zack choked out with a smile. "Tell you what. Why don't we use the bathroom at the front of the house for now, just to make sure all of the paint is super-dry before we do anything in here, okay?"

"Okay!" said Justin, scampering off down the hall.

Christ, Zachary, you must really dislike your mother and me. You finally start acting like an adult and buy a house, and the first thing you do is let that child you took in paint it like a brothel.

Did somebody with a crappy childhood have any business trying to raise a little boy as a single parent? While handling a huge multiple murder case?

Earlier that day, before Terry's mess with Judge Cottonwood, Zack had gotten a call from Judge Baumgartner, who was in charge of assigning lawyers to represent indigent defendants charged with serious felony charges. There had been a multiple homicide at a building in Northampton. Six victims. The cops picked up a guy at the scene they thought was the shooter.

Ever since the judge had described the case to Zack, the usual questions had been running through his mind.

Did the defendant make any statements? Were there any eyewitnesses? Any survivors of the attack? Was a weapon found at the scene? Did the defendant have a history of mental illness? Were drugs involved? How much time passed between the shooting and the cops' arrival on the scene? Was there an alibi defense? What was the defendant's relationship with the victims?

And then a new one popped in: Did the victims suffer before they died?

Where had that come from?

Anyway, five minutes into the conversation, it started to become clear why Judge Baumgartner had called Zack. This was going to be the first case that the Commonwealth was going to try under the Governor's new crime bill. The state was going to go for the death penalty on this one.

And that was just great. Most lawyers and judges had a hard enough time getting the system to work right without the distraction of television cameras in the courtroom and reporters lurking behind every bathroom door. And there was nothing like the possibility of a death sentence to make the media come running. The fact that if this guy got convicted he was going to be the first person executed in Massachusetts in about fifty years made it a virtual certainty that this trial was going to be the biggest media event in Northampton's recent history. Hooray for Hollywood.

Worse still, Fran O'Neill, Northampton's elected District Attorney, had been waiting for a case like this for his whole life. There was no way O'Neill was going to let someone else handle it. The limelight would be irresistible.

And that's really why the judge had called. Baumgartner needed Zack in the courtroom because he knew Zack didn't care about what a trial would do for his wallet, or the front page of *USA Today*, or just about anything except getting the guy a fair trial. With the prospect of overbearing press coverage, and Fran O'Neill strutting around like a bad TV character, the trial was going to need a well-grounded defense attorney if there was any hope for justice to elbow its way into the courtroom.

Zack tucked Justin into bed, returned to the couch with a beer, clicked on the TV to catch a little of the Celtics game, and tried to take his mind off the Thompkins case. He was going to be meeting with the client tomorrow—a man who was recovering from a couple of bullet wounds suffered during an attack in which he probably murdered six UMass students.

Was defending Thompkins something a good father would do? How were the fathers of the six victims feeling right now? Zack didn't even want to think about how he'd feel if out of nowhere he received a phone call saying that Justin had been murdered by some madman with a machine gun.

Paul Pierce hit a jumper, putting the Celts up by four. Zack took a swig of beer.

He wasn't big on self-doubt. He knew that he was a good lawyer, and he also knew that it was important to protect the constitutional rights of all criminal defendants—even those guilty of the most horrible crimes.

The problem was that right now, Zack seemed to be much more interested in the victims and their families than in the defendant. And that made him wonder if he was the right lawyer for this case.

Hell, was he the right lawyer for *any* criminal case?

Pierce blocked a shot and then fired a half-court pass starting a fast break that ended in an easy layup. Zack's beer was gone, and the Celts were up by twelve. When had that happened?

And how was Zack ever going to be able to explain to Justin what he did for a living? Right now, the little boy was too young to take a serious interest in Zack's work, but Justin was a smart and curious guy. It wouldn't be long before the hard questions started to come.

Daddy, wasn't it wrong for your client to hurt people?

Daddy, if your client hurt people and did a crime, how come you want the jury to say not guilty?

Daddy, what happens if one of your clients hurts me?

By the time that Zack focused again on the basketball game, it was over. But he didn't even bother to check who won before turning off the TV. He just kept thinking about tomorrow's meeting with Calvin Thompkins. How was he going to handle this case?

Washington, D.C.

ABOUT FIVE MINUTES INTO THE BRIEFING, Matt had a hunch how the Tanzania-Kenya thing was going to play out. Fifteen minutes in, he was sure.

First, Katie Francks, the Director of Homeland Security, and Aaron Miller, the National Security Advisor, confirmed that there was good reason to believe that despite his public denials, President Mwanga of Kenya had inherited some rudimentary chemical weapons from the last regime. This poison would kill a lot of innocent civilians as well as soldiers if used against the rebels or to repel troops invading from Tanzania.

And it would pose a nightmarish terrorist threat anywhere in the world if it found its way into the wrong hands.

Then Miller confirmed what they all knew in the first place—that there were plenty of wrong hands located in East Africa, and that civil or any other kind of war in Kenya would greatly increase the chances that those weapons either would be used or would go missing.

That's why Tanzania was stirring. It was panicking about those chemical weapons.

"At this point, sir, it looks like the Tanzanians are planning to race the rebels to Nairobi." Rusty Levine, the Chairman of the Joint Chiefs of Staff, might as well have been reading Matt's mind.

"What are we looking at as far as timing goes?" Matt asked.

"Well, sir, the Tanzanian army isn't ready to move yet," the general answered, "but it can be in less than two days. The rebels could go at any time." He paused. "In my opinion, the situation is extremely volatile."

No shit.

Bob Butler from State had verified that the heads of both Kenya and Tanzania, as well as the Secretary-General, would be at U.N. Headquarters in New York City all day tomorrow.

"Who's in contact with the rebels?" asked Matt.

"The Ugandan government, sir," replied Butler. "I've delivered your message to Prime Minister Jackson. The rebels should already have it."

"And will Jackson also be at the U.N. tomorrow?" Matt asked.

"Yes, sir," said Butler. "He's hosting a reception tomorrow evening at their embassy in New York."

"Good," Matt said. He turned to the Chairman of the Joint Chiefs. "Rusty, how soon can we be in position off the coast of Kenya?"

"About forty-eight hours from when I give the order, Mr. President."

"Okay," Matt said, standing. The entire room stood with him. "General Levine, please consider the order given. I want an amphibious assault group in position as soon as possible. And don't bother trying to disguise your movements." He might have been the commander in chief of the most powerful military force on the earth, but he was still the new guy when it came to the international scene. For a while, he was going to have to go out of his way to make sure that people believed him when he said the kinds of things he was certain to say tomorrow.

Matt turned to the rest of the group. "Thank you all for coming on such short notice. It's pretty clear to me that I've got to get to New York tomorrow to see if I can work this thing out while everyone is in the same place, and before things get too far out of hand. Depending on what happens, I may need to meet with you again tomorrow after I return, so please stay available. Vernon will be in touch."

Matt returned to his desk and picked up the phone to call for Carlos. He needed to check one more bit of background information before he spoke to Mwanga, but when he looked up, he was surprised to see that rather than file out with the others, his Chief of Staff had stayed behind.

"Mr. President—may I make a suggestion?"

"Of course."

"I'd like you to meet with your political advisors before deciding on a course of action," Browning said. "I can have Kenny and Adrienne here in—"

When Matt interrupted him, he was careful to keep his voice even. It was late, and he knew that the lifelong politician was merely doing his job. But while there was a time and a place for politics, it was not here, and it was not now. "Whether this is a political decision or not," Matt said, "I've already made it, Vernon."

The Chief of Staff smiled and spread his hands. "With all due respect, sir, I don't see the harm in getting a political perspective—"

Matt interrupted him again. "I realize that you

never expected me to be in this position, and God knows, I never expected it myself. But in situations like this, we need to have an understanding. Early in my career as a military officer, I came to peace with the fact that there were going to be people who disagreed with my decisions." He walked around the desk to look directly down into Browning's face. Matt was about six inches taller than the politician. "And I came to peace with the fact that there were even going to be people who disagreed with the way I made my decisions. But, Mr. Chief of Staff, for better or worse, when I tell you that I've made a decision, the decision has been made." He let that hang there for a minute. "Now, I'm going to need to review a few things before I turn in. Carlos will run them down for me. I expect that you've got some calls to make before tomorrow's trip?"

Browning looked like someone had just swiped his lunch money. Matt felt a little sorry for him, but if there was any question about who was going to decide how to handle this problem, that needed to end immediately. A weak commander was worse than no commander at all. For better or worse, Matt was in charge, and he owed it to the American people to act like it.

"Very good, sir," the thin man said. "I'll get right on it."

It wasn't until he was lying in bed, an hour later, that Matt realized he had forgotten entirely to ask his Chief of Staff about that dead federal judge.

THREE

VOIR DIRE EXAMINATION BY THE COURT

Q: *Good morning.*

A: *Good morning.*

Q: *You raised your hand to what question?*

A: *The question about forming an opinion about the case.*

Q: *All right.*

A: *I definitely formed an opinion.*

Q: *And what is your opinion?*

A: *I found—he's guilty, as far as I'm concerned. I mean, I saw that from the TV reports, back when they arrested him.*

THE COURT: *Okay. You are excused.*

COURT OFFICER: *Juror 2–13.*

VOIR DIRE EXAMINATION BY THE COURT

Q: *Good morning.*

A: *Good morning.*

Q: *Did you raise your hand to any questions?*

A: *No.*

Q: *Have you been exposed to any news media coverage of any kind concerning this case?*

A: *Yes.*

Q: *Okay. When?*

A: *Back when it happened, I guess. A few months ago?*

Q: *Okay. And what do you recall about that coverage? Was it newspaper, television? Both? Radio?*

A: *Newspaper and television.*

Q: *And what do you recall about the content of the coverage itself? What do you remember of it?*

A: *Well, I remember they were reporting the shooting, and that this big black guy was arrested. And that's it.*

Q: *And nothing further?*

A: *Well, I saw some reports that the trial was coming up, but that's it.*

Q: *And based on what you have seen, you still believe that you remain fair and impartial?*

A: *Yes.*

(Sidebar conference.)

THE COURT: *I find this juror stands indifferent.*

MR. O'NEILL: *The Commonwealth is content, Your Honor.*

MR. WILSON: *The defendant challenges, Your Honor.*

THE COURT: *You are out of peremptories, Mr. Wilson.*

MR. WILSON: *Then the defendant challenges for cause, Your Honor, based on the juror's characterization of the defendant as a "big black guy."*

THE COURT: *The challenge is overruled, and the objection is noted.*

(End of sidebar conference.)

THE COURT: *All right. You, sir, will be juror number three.*

(Trial Volume II, Pages 129–133)

January 31

TERRY PUSHED HIS WAY THROUGH ZACK'S front door and said loudly enough for anyone inside the oversized old house to hear, "Number One, Northampton is too pathetic a town to have a traffic jam, so I don't know what I was just in, but whatever it was, somebody better make sure it never happens again, and Number Two"—he paused to catch a breath as Zack appeared in the front hall—"this case is barely two weeks old, and somebody already fuh"—at the last minute he saw Justin join Zack, and just barely stopped himself in time—"uh, asked the duck out to dinner. Hi, Justin."

Zack pulled him into his office and closed the door, and Terry handed him a copy of today's *Boston Post*—the worst newspaper in Massachusetts, if not the world.

The entire front page was taken up by a gigantic color photo of the mug shot of their new, scary-looking, African American client, accused multiple murderer Calvin Thompkins. Thompkins looked like he was hoping to be cast as the bad guy in some movie. Somehow, the cop who had taken the picture had managed to catch him between a scowl and a sneer, which was bad enough, but it also looked like Thompkins had a cut lip, because there was a little blood trickling out of the corner of his mouth.

It was the worst mug shot Terry had ever seen. And to top it off, the good folks at the *Post* had plastered a banner headline in gigantic type over the picture: MONSTER! Terry groaned. They weren't even out of the first inning yet, and they were already down by fifteen runs.

Zack glanced at the picture, returned the paper to Terry, and then gave him the same look he'd given him when they first met.

It was 1985, Waterbury High School, Waterbury, Rhode Island. The principal, Georgia Stephenson, was a never-say-die ex-hippie, who insisted that the school motto was What Is Your Inner Voice Saying? The school colors were purple and gold. The school football team was the Waterbury Berries. The school loser was Terry Tallach.

It was a somewhat crappy day in October, and Terry was in Mr. Overmeyer's tenth-grade chemistry class doing an astoundingly unimportant lab. There was an odd number of kids in the class, so Terry didn't have a lab partner. What a surprise.

Then the door opened, and this skinny boy with light hair came into the room, holding a pass from the main office. He had "new kid" written all over him, except, for some reason, he didn't seem to care. Overmeyer immediately stuck him with Terry at the back lab table. As the teacher returned to the front of the classroom, Terry whispered, "So, you're on quite a roll. You get the Evil Overlord for chemistry and the fat kid for a lab partner. Welcome to hell. My name's Terry, by the way."

Fifteen-year-olds always know who the disasters are, so it was a lock that the new kid was going to ignore him. Or maybe he'd first taunt him and then ignore him. It was fifty-fifty that the kid wouldn't even tell Terry his name.

But instead, a strange look came over the new kid's

face. It was a look of amused recognition, as if he and Terry were both members of a small club of people who knew that regardless of whatever anyone else said, the world was, at least a little bit, insane. And then the new kid's smile broadened, and Terry was stunned to realize that he was about to be included in a joke. Using an artificially stilted voice, the new kid said, "Hi, Terry, my name's Zack. I'm a new student in this school. What is your inner voice saying?"

And Terry, as always, blurted out the first thing that came into his head. "My inner voice is saying that the school motto should be changed to: Waterbury High School—We Will Never Stop Fucking You."

Zack now reached for a tie hanging on the back of the door and said with a shrug, "Mug shots are always bad. He can't stay on the front page forever."

"But that's not all," Terry replied. "On the way over here I called down to the courthouse to speak to Mary Beth. You know, Mary Beth, who's really good at—"

"I'm familiar with Mary Beth," Zack interrupted.

"Yeah. Okay. Well, anyway, Mary Beth just happens to be best friends with the assistant clerk who has access to the judicial assignments. So I thought I'd give Mary Beth a call to see if we could learn which judge is in line to get this one."

"And?"

"And we might as well strap our guy into the chair and juice him right now, 'cause it's the Big Dick."

Which really sucked. And not just because he'd thrown Terry in jail. Cottonwood had only been working in the western part of Massachusetts for the last eight years, but his anti-defendant reputation in criminal trials over the past three decades throughout the state was legendary. Getting a favorable ruling on something as small as an evidentiary issue was rare. But getting a favorable ruling on something big—like overruling a jury's guilty verdict—was as likely as getting hit by a bus and then struck by lightning.

While walking your dog on the moon.

And the only not-guilty verdict anyone could remember ever coming out of Cottonwood's courtroom was followed by his now-famous post-verdict freak-out, during which the judge bawled out the defendant, the lawyers, and, just for good measure, the jury, too. At least one juror left sobbing. Way to go, Dick, you asshole.

"This is going to be bad, Zack," Terry said. "That judge blows."

The doorbell rang. "That's the babysitter," Zack said, shrugging on his tired-looking jacket, which, with the shaggy hair, loosened tie, jeans, and boots, completed the I-don't-give-a-shit-what-I-look-like look.

"Are you ever going to buy some real lawyer clothes?" Terry asked as they moved toward the front door. "And by the way, you think you're ready for a haircut?"

Zack didn't even bother answering. "You think you're ready to go talk to our guy?"

"Our kill-six-people-with-a-machine-gun guy?" Terry said, following Zack out of the house. "I was born ready."

NORMALLY, TERRY HATED VISITING HOSPITALS, but the fact that Cal Thompkins's doctor was a green-eyed hottie more than made up for it. He and Zack met with the doctor before seeing Thompkins, and she told them that he had suffered two bullet wounds—one to his forearm, which had broken a bone, and one to his thigh. Both were painful, Cal had lost a good deal of blood, and the leg wound had required surgery. The extent of the nerve damage was not yet fully assessed. But there was a reasonable chance that he was going to recover fully.

Which was good news, because nobody likes to execute a defendant who isn't in tiptop shape.

Room 304 was guarded by two young state troopers who were both trying hard to look menacing. Somehow, Zack and Terry made it past them without confessing to something, and opened the door.

Calvin Thompkins wasn't just black—he was huge. The news just kept getting better.

For a guy who at one time might have been able to bench-press three hundred pounds, the man looked like shit. His dark eyes were bloodshot. He hadn't shaved in a while, and although his face looked fairly young—he was probably in his thirties or early forties—the stubble on his chin had some gray in it.

He was propped up in bed by a pile of pillows and was hooked up to a full console of machinery, including a beeping heart monitor and an IV which was dripping at least two different liquids into his right arm. His left arm was in a cast and sling. He looked like he was tilting to one side—probably trying not to put too much weight on the leg with the bullet wound. He was manacled to the bed at the ankle.

Zack walked over to introduce himself, but Thompkins spoke first.

"I'm sorry I can't stand up, or even shake your hands," the prisoner said, closing his eyes and shaking his head ruefully. "I'm Calvin Thompkins. You must be the lawyers."

Terry had expected the man's voice to be deep. Instead, it was soft and hoarse.

"That's right," Zack said. "I'm Zack Wilson, and this is Terry Tallach. The court has asked us to represent you."

"And you're here to see if you want the case, right?"

"More or less," Zack replied. "We need to find out what's involved in defending you and decide whether we can do the job. But before we start, we need to get a couple of ground rules out of the way."

"Good," Thompkins said.

"First of all," Zack began, "anything you say to us stays in this room. It's private, unless you decide to tell someone."

Thompkins nodded, but then winced, and a light sweat quickly appeared on his forehead. "Sorry. I asked the doctors not to give me the pain medicine so I could focus. Every once in a while, though, I move wrong and give myself a real good jolt." He took a shaky breath. "Go ahead."

"The other thing is that the rules of ethics prohibit us from hearing one story," Zack said, "and then putting you on the stand to tell a different one."

Terry hated when Zack did that. "Don't take that as an invitation to jerk us around, though," he interposed. "We've been doing criminal work for over ten years, and Zack and I have got extremely sensitive bullshit meters. So tell us what happened, and we'll let you know whether there's anything we can do for you. Tell us a bunch of crap, and we're out the door."

For some reason, a smile spread across the big man's face.

"And by the way, the fact that you're black is going to make this case ten times harder than it already is. Which really sucks. Just so you know," Terry added.

Thompkins's smile broadened. "You know, I can tell already that I'm really going to like you two," he said.

Maybe they were going to catch a break and find out the guy was a whack job.

"Why don't you tell us what happened?" Zack said.

"There's a lot of background leading up to this," Thompkins said. "I'm not sure where to begin. After I graduated college, I started postgraduate work at M.I.T. Should I start there?"

Background. Unbelievable. *I was born in a small log cabin*— Uh, excuse me, could you jump ahead to the part where you blow six people away? Terry started to pace.

"How about a couple of hours before you were arrested?" Zack suggested. "Let's say, start at two or three that afternoon. We'll have plenty of time to get into the background later." Thank God.

"Oh. Okay. Let's see. By two that afternoon, I was already waiting for them in the apartment across the hall. I was renting it," Thompkins explained. "I was expecting the last of them to come back at around four o'clock, so at about two, I made sure the gun was loaded and ready, and I started waiting. Since our doors were directly across the hall from each other, all I had to do was look through my peephole and I could see whenever they went in or out.

"I don't know exactly when it was, but before I was really ready, their apartment opened, and one of them, the one with the big nose, came out into the hallway. But almost as soon as he started down the hall, he must have seen one of his friends coming toward him, because suddenly he was back in front of his apartment with this other guy—a short guy with a real thick beard. So the guy with the big nose goes in, and then while the short guy starts to follow him in, I open my door. I didn't want to have to knock on their door or anything. I just wanted to blast through while it was already open.

"And that's just what happened. As soon as I got out into the hallway I started firing right into that door. The gun was incredibly loud, but I could still hear shouting and screaming—I figure from the short guy. He probably got hit from the bullets that went through the door."

Amazing. It was like attending a lecture titled "How to Commit a First-Degree Murder." Premeditation and intent were a lock—the gunman had rented the place across the hall from his victims and then waited until the door was opened before he started shooting. He planned the whole thing. The prosecution was going to have no problem with that. Self-defense, defense of others, mistaken identity—all these strategies were a joke. Either they were going to have to prove that Thompkins was crazy, or they might as well just walk him right into the execution chamber.

"That was stupid of me, of course, because when the short guy fell, it made it hard to get the door open," Cal continued. "But I kicked, and it finally gave way.

"By that time, they were running all over the place, trying to get away, or I don't know, maybe to get guns to shoot me, but the weapon I had was incredible. I just swept it back and forth across the room again and again as I walked in, hardly aiming at anyone. I didn't have to. They were just falling like they were made out of cardboard."

Maybe the guy really was nuts, talking about killing a handful of people in cold blood with no more emotion than if he were just shooting the shit with his neighbor while watering his freakin' lawn.

"Anyway, it seemed like a long time, but I bet it was only fifteen or twenty seconds before I thought I'd killed them all, and I stopped shooting. That was another stupid mistake," Cal said, smiling again. "I started going from body to body, shooting them with a little burst, just to make sure they were dead, when all of a sudden the bathroom door flies open, and this guy comes out wearing only a bathrobe, screaming 'You'll never get away with this!' and running across the room. I know it's strange, but the first thing I thought of was 'Shit, I'm not getting away with *anything*,' and then I started shooting at him. Some of the bullets must have hit this window, though, because when he went down he kind of leaned against it, and ended up crashing right through it, and falling down into the courtyard.

"Like a fool, I started to walk toward the window to look where he fell, but right about then I heard a pop, and I knew that I was dead, because I obviously hadn't killed them all. And before I could even turn I was on the floor with this burning pain in my leg. Luckily, I'd held on to my gun, and as soon as I could, I dragged myself past this table and started shooting again. The guy who shot me in the leg turned out to be the one with the big nose. I don't think that he got off another shot, so maybe the bullet that hit my arm was a ricochet. I didn't even notice it at first, because my leg hurt so bad, and I was bleeding so much.

"I dragged myself out into the hallway, and then I called 911 on my cell phone. That's when I realized my arm was shot, too. I threw the gun down the hallway a bit, so the cops wouldn't think I was going to shoot them. Then I laid down and just waited for them to come." Cal paused for a moment, in thought, then nodded. "That's exactly what happened," he decided.

The room fell dead silent except for the beep of the heart monitor. Zack looked like he hadn't moved in five minutes.

Finally, Cal turned slowly to Terry and asked, "So how's your bullshit meter?"

Terry nodded. "It's good," he answered quietly.

FOUR

Automated Voice: *January 30. Two twenty-four* A.M.

911 Operator: *Nine-one-one. This call is being recorded. What is your emergency?*

Male Voice #1: *Hello? I think there's somebody in my house. I think there are robbers . . . Somebody's inside my house.*

Operator: *There are intruders in your house right now, sir?*

Male Voice #1: *I hear—*

Male Voice #2 [in distance]: *Oh, shit! Somebody's here!*

Operator: *Who is that?*

Male Voice #1: *Oh, no.*

Male Voice #2 [in distance]: *Jack, we gotta get out of here! [Sound of door slamming.]*

Operator: *Sir, what is your location?*

[Crashing sound.]

Operator: *Sir? Sir?*

[Sound of groaning.]

Operator: *We're sending someone out to you right*

now. Can you verify your address? Sir? Can you hear me, sir?

[Sound of female crying.]

Operator: *Ma'am? Ma'am, can you hear me?*

Female Voice #1 [in distance]: *Grandpa?*

Operator: *Ma'am? If you can hear me, please pick up the telephone.*

Female Voice #1 [crying in distance]: *Grandpa?*

Operator: *Ma'am? Can you please pick up the telephone and tell me—*

Female Voice #1: *Hello?*

Operator: *Hello. This is the nine-one-one operator. Are you hurt?*

Female Voice [crying]: *No. But something's wrong with my grandfather.*

Operator. *Okay, okay. Try to calm down, okay? Can you tell me if your address is Sixteen Michaels Drive?*

Female Voice [crying]: *No. Yes. I mean yes.*

Operator: *Okay. Someone is coming right now to help you. They should be there in just a minute. Can you tell me if anyone is there besides your grandfather? He called and said that there were strangers in your house.*

Female Voice [crying]: *I don't know. I don't think so.*

Operator: *Okay. And you aren't hurt?*

Female Voice [crying]: *No, but I think my grandfather is having a heart attack.*

Operator: *Okay. Someone will be right there.*

Female Voice: *Hurry.*

Automated Voice: *January 30. Two twenty-six* A.M.

CERTIFICATE

I hereby certify that the foregoing record, consisting of two pages exclusive of this Certificate, is a true and complete transcription of the tape recording labeled "9–1–1 DPD Precinct 4, January 30, 2:24 A.M." and delivered to me by the Detroit Police Department.

In witness whereof, I have hereunto set my hand . . .

s/Regina Bedloe

January 31—Air Force One

"MR. PRESIDENT, WE'LL BE COMING UP ON lower Manhattan in just a minute or two. Should have a clear view out the left side of the plane."

"Thanks, Major," Matt answered, hanging up the phone and getting up to take a look.

Matt had specifically asked to have Air Force One's flight path changed so that he could see Ground Zero as they flew by. He made a point to see it every time he had a chance. To silently honor the sacrifice of those who died that day.

Matt was familiar with sacrifice. Hell, every soldier who had ever done a tour in Vietnam was best friends with sacrifice. Matt's staff sergeant, José, called it scrubbing the outhouse. You didn't eat well, you didn't sleep well, you got sick, you got shot at, you got injured, and sometimes you even got killed.

You were a soldier, you scrubbed the outhouse.

But the tragedy of September 11 was different. Not just because so many of the victims were civilians, but because the losses went beyond the physical and emotional injuries suffered by thousands. Beyond the devastation of that part of the Manhattan skyline that Matt watched quietly as he flew past on his way to the U.N.

America itself was a victim. The land of the free was now the land of the suspicious. It had been years since that horrible day, but personal freedoms were still far from where they'd been before 9/11.

Of course, that was the way it had to be. It didn't make a hell of a lot of sense to pretend that things could just go on as they had before. Some of the changes that the government had made after the terrorist attacks were part of an extremely painful but very important process. It wasn't easy finding the right balance between vigilance and respecting personal privacy. But it was a cold fact of life in this new era that security from the kind of terror that was unleashed on September 11 was going to cost something. From long and slow lines at airports, to metal detectors at baseball games—baseball games, for God's sake—to inspections of car trunks at parking garages, to tougher immigration policies.

Now everyone was scrubbing the outhouse. Everyone was sacrificing.

"I know it will be a sacrifice for you, Colonel, to come out of retirement so soon, but this Monday, I'd like to announce you as my choice to replace Vice President Quarters. The Vice President will be resigning before the week is out."

Matt had been to Washington plenty of times while in the service, and he'd even been to the White House a few times—once to receive the medal, and once to meet with Vernon Browning about some testimony he was going to give to Congress on a couple of the military operations that he had run.

But that was only because Matt had become a sort of short-term minor celebrity for handling a very difficult assignment in Lebanon several years ago and then found himself smack in the middle of the whole Pakistan mess when push had truly become shove, and President Graham had to act. Thanks to some excellent intel and a superior core of junior officers, that operation had also turned into an overwhelming success. The press, as always, needed somebody to put on the front page, and they picked Matt. The way they kept throwing his picture onto magazine covers and bringing up the whole Vietnam story was embarrassing.

But six months ago that had all been ancient history. So the fact that the President had wanted Matt to come to Washington was strange enough. But the fact that he wanted to name him Vice President was surreal.

For one thing, the last job in the world Matt wanted was politician. Hell, he hadn't even registered as a member of either party in the last election. He'd voted for Graham, even with his fake Hollywood smile, simply because Matt thought he was the candidate best qualified to do the job. Graham had been a senator for eight years, he had business and foreign affairs experience, and he seemed like the kind of person that could bring together a badly divided Congress.

And for another, Matt hadn't the slightest idea how to be Vice President, much less, God forbid, President of the United States.

"Mr. President, we're in our final approach. We should be on the ground in a minute or two."

But here he was anyway, on the verge of plunging headlong into an explosive United Nations, about to decide who was going to scrub the outhouse in East Africa.

Detroit, Michigan

THE FIRST THING THAT LENA TAKAMURA DID when she got off the bus in front of the Andrews Funeral Home was step into an ankle-high puddle of Detroit's famous midwinter slush. Her mother would have been comforted by the fact that the damage was minimal—Lena's thick and very practical boots were made to withstand such missteps.

What her mother wouldn't have been so comforted by was the fact that her daughter was about to attend the wake of another complete stranger. The third one in less than two weeks.

It had been a nasty winter so far, and the salt and sand that was sprinkled on the funeral home steps crunched under Lena's boots as she made her way to the door. But it was mercifully warm inside, and she unbuttoned her coat, took off her gloves, and looked for the sign that would direct her to the wake of Phillipe LeClerq.

Lena had stopped talking with her parents about this part of her work long ago. Regardless of what she said, her mother refused to believe that there was any explanation for Lena's actions except that she had been turned into a total freak by all those horror movies she had watched as a kid. Her father was more interested in learning why Lena was still living by herself in a tiny apartment in Detroit. Why couldn't she move back home and try to be a reporter in Tempe?

But to Lena, there was nowhere like metropolitan Detroit for an aspiring investigative crime reporter. The city was bursting with the kind of passionate energy that generated stories that she longed to uncover and write about.

Now if only she could actually uncover one and write about it.

It had been a year since she quit the job she had gotten right out of college, at the *Ypsilanti Sentinel*, covering boring community events in boring suburbia for boring Mr. Olafsen. At the pace things moved at the *Sentinel*, Lena figured that by the time she was about ninety years old, they'd let her cover the most recent rash of bicycle thefts.

So she'd moved to the city and become a part-time waitress, a part-time convenience store clerk, and a full-time snoop, reading obituaries and police blotters, looking for the story that would break her career wide open.

But ten funerals and sixteen wakes later, her career remained quite firmly shut.

There were about thirty people inside Salon B, where Phillipe LeClerq had been laid out. Most were adults. They stood around in small groups, talking quietly. According to the obituary, Mr. LeClerq had died suddenly and unexpectedly from a heart attack. He had been a native of Haiti. Everyone at the wake looked like they were from the Caribbean as well.

And here Lena was, a five-foot-nothing Japanese American with the roundest face in the world, about to crash the party. Cultural diversity, anyone? Just once, Lena would have liked to walk into a room and not feel like she was auditioning for the role of the spunky little Asian girl.

At the University of Michigan, it seemed like everyone else in her dorm was tall and blond and had big boobs. Okay. That wasn't exactly true. Lisa and Sherry were African American. So they were tall and dark and had big boobs.

Of course, none of that would have mattered as much if Lena had managed to find a good boyfriend. Yet somehow, she had made it though four years at a gigantic university with little more than a handful of awkward dates and the night she'd spent with Tad Spellman.

The Night of a Thousand Mistakes.

To be fair, though, if Lena hadn't met Tad, she never would have met his sister, Becca, who worked as an administrative assistant at Precinct Four, and who was Lena's closest friend and most reliable source of information. It was Becca who'd told Lena about the eleven-year-old named Giselle LeClerq who called 911 and who feverishly administered CPR to her dying grandfather until the paramedics arrived.

There had been a few recent cases of foul-ups in the 911 system, so Lena thought she'd look into the case. It was way not the hottest lead she'd ever followed, but there was something so courageous in what Giselle did that Lena wanted to meet her, even if it turned out that there was no story there. So Lena watched the obits for the funeral information.

The area around the open coffin was decorated with sprays and vases of colorful flowers, but Lena was drawn to the small table that stood off to the left on which had been placed some memorabilia, including two photos. One was of Mr. LeClerq and a gray-haired woman his age. Their arms around each other, cheek to cheek, they smiled at the camera. The obit had said that Mr. LeClerq's wife had died three years ago. And the other was a team photo of a high school state championship soccer team. From the hairstyles of the boys in the picture, it looked like it was from about thirty years ago. Mr. LeClerq was the coach.

Lena turned and saw a little girl she hoped was Giselle, sitting in the front row of chairs that had been set up in front of the casket, next to a woman who was probably her mother. Lena walked over to them.

This moment was always the worst. It was hard convincing some people that to investigate unusual or suspicious deaths was to honor those who died. Most people thought that since Lena didn't know the deceased, she didn't care about them.

Lena understood their suspicions, but her job really was an honorable one. People's lives were important, and so, therefore, were their deaths. And if there was something unusual about a death, then that needed to be understood. Anything less would cheapen the life of the deceased.

When she reached the little girl and her mother, both stood up to greet her. She cleared her throat and plunged in. "Hi, my name is Lena Takamura. I'm a freelance reporter, and when I heard about Mr. LeClerq's death, I wanted to pay my respects, and after some time has passed—"

But she never got a chance to finish. The woman turned to the little girl, hugged her, and said emphatically, "I *told* you they wouldn't get away with it." The girl smiled tentatively—she had obviously been crying and her eyes were still wet with tears. The woman then turned back to Lena and said, "My name is Rhonda LeClerq. Mr. LeClerq was my husband's father. And this is my daughter, Giselle. You can ask us anything you want to, because I know as sure as I'm standing here, those men killed Giselle's grandfather."

U.N. Headquarters, New York City, New York

IF HE HADN'T KNOWN BETTER, CARLOS WOULD have thought that President Ferguson was greeting a bunch of old friends at a reunion, not shaking hands with a room full of dignitaries he'd never met before, including two who were about fifteen minutes from starting a war with each other.

The atmosphere in the conference room of the U.N. Secretary-General was so tense Carlos could barely breathe. It was swarming with important people—government officials, advisors, military officers, U.N. diplomats and translators—all just milling around, talking to each other. Just from looking, it was impossible to know who was ignorant of the situation and who knew just how dangerous things were.

The Secretary-General, a gray-haired man who looked a little like Carlos's grandfather, was speaking to the Ugandan Prime Minister, a small man with the whitest teeth Carlos had ever seen, and the President of Tanzania, who was flanked by two grim men in military uniforms.

President Mwanga of Kenya was on the other side of the room. His very dark skin contrasted sharply with his bright white shirt and light tie. Mwanga looked way too young to be the president of a country, and was trying hard to look relaxed. President Ferguson walked over to him, gave him a big friendly handshake, and pulled him into a corner.

Carlos couldn't hear the conversation, but after about ten seconds, it was clear that the discussion was very one-sided. President Ferguson was talking, and President Mwanga was listening.

And then he was mopping his forehead with a handkerchief.

After only about three or four minutes, they split up. President Mwanga went to talk to someone Carlos didn't know, who immediately pulled out a cell phone and started talking. After a few seconds, he turned and nodded to President Mwanga.

Meanwhile, President Ferguson went over and whispered something to the Secretary-General. And then, like magic, everyone in the room suddenly started to be ushered outside, except the Secretary-General, President Ferguson, President Mwanga, and the rulers of Uganda and Tanzania. Just before Carlos left, President Ferguson leaned over and said into his ear, "This shouldn't take more than twenty minutes."

Actually, it turned out to be closer to ten. And then, just like that, it became a normal day for the President of the United States, and Carlos was riding with him to the airport, where they'd take Air Force One back to Washington for a full afternoon's business.

The President called the Chief of Staff from the road. "Yeah, well, after I explained the situation to President Mwanga, all of the interested parties got together and Mwanga told them that he had discovered what he suspected were chemical weapons in a munitions storage facility outside the capital, and was going to turn them over to U.N. weapons experts for identification and destruction. He also said that he was calling for elections within a month, and would need U.N. help with that, too."

The President paused for a minute and took a bite of a sandwich that had been waiting for him in the car while he listened to what Mr. Browning was saying.

"No, he sure wasn't happy. He didn't think the country was ready for elections, and he didn't want to let go of those weapons, either. But I told him that if he didn't, he should start looking around for extra guest towels, because in about two days, he was going to be hosting several thousand U.S. Marines."

Another pause.

"Yes, we'll still set up offshore, both to support the weapons inspectors and to do what we can to make sure the elections go smoothly. I figure that's the best way to make sure everybody gets something. Mwanga, the rebels, and the people of Kenya get a new shot at electing leaders without a civil war destroying the country; Tanzania doesn't have to worry about chemical weapons killing their people in droves; and we get a more stable situation in that part of the world, and destroy some very bad stuff in the bargain."

The President listened to Mr. Browning and took another bite of the sandwich.

"Yeah, well, sometimes you've just got to go with your gut, Vernon." He took a swig of his water. "And by the way, I'd like to be briefed on what happened to that judge who committed suicide in Michigan." There was a pause. "Good," he said. "I'll see you in a few hours."

Northampton, Massachusetts

"ARE YOU SURE YOU'RE OKAY WITH THIS CASE, Richard? I can probably give it to Barbara if you don't want it."

Judge Richard Cottonwood was scheduled to retire in less than a year—judges in Massachusetts were required to step down by their seventieth birthday. And for somebody who didn't really know him, they might have thought that was welcome news. After all, everyone knew that Judge Cottonwood was suffering from arthritis in his hips, and it was getting harder and harder to get through the day without the pain pills. What people didn't know was that Richard was almost entirely blind in his right eye. The doctors called it macular degeneration.

"That's all right, Harold, I'll take it," he told Baumgartner. "I might as well go out with a bang."

Judge Cottonwood was one of the Commonwealth's

most senior judges. He had been presiding over trials for more than a quarter century. His reputation as a hard-ass, especially in criminal trials, was well deserved. He was brutal on defendants. He meant to be.

"The media scrutiny is going to be intense, because this'll be the first death penalty case under the new statute. You sure you want to deal with all that?"

Professional courtesy prevented Baumgartner from coming right out and asking the question he really wanted answered, but Richard got the message. "I'll be fine," he said.

Judge Cottonwood couldn't care less that he had a reputation for having more than his share of criminal convictions reversed on appeal. Let those wimps in the Appeals Court give out new trials like candy at Halloween. He'd keep locking up scum that needed to be locked up. Period.

Right after he'd graduated from law school, he had taken a job in the Norfolk County prosecutor's office, not so much because he wanted to practice criminal law, but because he needed a job, and he didn't have particularly high grades. He worked hard, though, and developed a reputation as a solid, if uninspiring, litigator.

Then, about a week after her sixtieth birthday, his mother was raped and murdered in her apartment by some monster. Richard Cottonwood had never recovered.

From that moment, his life became a crusade against crime. He was no longer a solid litigator, he was a manic one. He surrendered completely to his feelings of vengeance, channeling them through his work as an assistant district attorney. For five years running, he got more convictions and longer sentences than anyone in his office. The next year, he was appointed to the bench, where his one-man war on crime continued.

"Okay. I'll handle the pretrial motions for you on the case," Baumgartner now said, "so you can wrap up whatever you've got going now. I think this one's going to take an awful lot of time, once it gets started."

Judge Cottonwood doubted it.

FIVE

THE COURT: *In order for the Commonwealth to prove beyond a reasonable doubt that the defendant is guilty of murder in the first degree, it must prove each of the following three elements:*

First, that the defendant committed a killing that was unlawful. That is, a killing that was not justified or excusable. A killing is justified, and therefore not murder, if authorized by law, for example, when committed during a battle of war, or by a police officer when using reasonable force to effect a lawful arrest, or when committed in self-defense . . .

Second, that the killing was committed with deliberate premeditation. That is, that the defendant thought before he acted. That he formed the plan or resolution, no matter how simple, to commit the act which killed the victim, after deliberation . . .

And third, that the killing was committed with malice aforethought. That is, that the defendant specifically intended to kill the victim . . .

(Trial Volume III, Pages 61, 63–64, 66, 71)

February 12—Northampton, Massachusetts

ZACK REACHED DOWN AND PULLED ANOTHER file folder out of the box of material that the court had ordered the Commonwealth to turn over in advance of the trial. Normally he thought of this as the fact-finding portion of his pretrial preparation. Right now it felt like little more than sitting in his office and reading over and over about a cold-blooded multiple murder performed by a calculating butcher.

Terry had come over to help, but had apparently become tired of it. He had gotten up from the table where he'd been working and was now standing at the window, fidgeting with his PDA, and occasionally looking out at the street.

"How's the reading going?" Zack asked.

"Yeah, fine," Terry replied absently. Then he turned to Zack. "You know, you never told me why you didn't introduce me to Patty Stallworth after you guys broke up senior year."

Great. Patty the gymnast. An endless source of fascination for Terry. "That was what, fifteen years ago, Elvis," Zack said, turning back to the files on his desk. "I think you're probably going to need to let that go."

"I still bear the scars of that disappointment. And don't call me Elvis. You know I was right."

A few years ago, Terry and Zack had gotten into an argument about whether Elvis would be named as one of the fifty all-time movie legends. Terry had been wrong, and occasionally needed to be reminded. "I don't think so."

"Fine," Terry said, returning to his table. "But we will be returning to the topic of Ms. Stallworth one of these days, Counselor." After a moment passed, he said, "Did I tell you I spoke to the doctor? She said that Cal should be well enough for us to go see him again later this week."

Zack looked up. "They ever find out what happened to him?"

"She just said it was a combination of a bad infection in his leg and some other complications from the wound in his arm."

Cal Thompkins had ended their last meeting early because he'd started to feel ill. By late that night, his temperature had climbed to over 104 degrees. He'd spent the next five days in intensive care and the next fifteen too weak to visit with anyone.

"I even got a chance to talk to Cal for a second about an insanity defense," Terry continued.

Talk about long shots. Juries were incredibly skeptical about insanity as a defense, especially to murder. But it was rapidly looking like it was the only strategy they could use. What sane person would gun down six strangers?

"Oh, yeah?" Zack asked, glancing up at a drawing taped to the wall that Justin had given him yesterday. It was either a house or a potato with a chimney. "What'd he say?"

"He said he'd go through an evaluation, but don't get your hopes up. He says he knew exactly what he was doing, he wasn't insane, and he doesn't want to say he was insane. He just wants to tell his story to the jury and let them decide. Course, that pretty much proves he's nuts, as far as I'm concerned," Terry said. "Or dumb as dirt. Maybe M.I.T.'s slipping."

Zack shook his head. "Boy. If he doesn't plead insanity, I don't know how we're going to argue this thing."

"Well, we can't very well say that he didn't fuck the duck, because let's face it—he fucked it good. So if he won't let us say he was crazy, I guess that leaves us with 'But I can explain.' "

"Great."

On the list of things juries loved to hear defendants say, "I was insane" was only slightly below "But I can explain." Zack had heard some dandies.

"I had to shoot him. He wouldn't give me his money."

"I didn't think anybody would be home."

"My brother told me it would be easy. We were gonna be in and out of there in two seconds. Nobody was supposed to get hurt."

"So I shot him. Big deal. I been shot before. Twice."

"I was so drunk I had no idea how hard I hit him."

"What was I supposed to do? He called my girl a slut."

What could possibly explain the machine-gun shooting of six college students? Zack looked back at the file. There had to be something else. "What about the gun that guy used to shoot Thompkins? Was it registered?"

Terry shuffled through some papers until he found what looked like one of the police reports. "Let's see. It was a nine-millimeter handgun, completely legal. He got off one shot, which hit Cal in the leg." Terry flipped through some other reports. "Meanwhile, Mr. M.I.T. fired off somewhere in the neighborhood of one hundred twenty rounds, using an illegally modified AK-47, which was found five feet from him in the hallway. Good thing we have gun control," he muttered, continuing to scan the report.

Zack inhaled sharply. "He fired a hundred and twenty bullets?"

"Go big or stay home."

Zack pulled out a few photos from a box at his feet and studied them. "No wonder the place looks like somebody went at it with a chain saw."

"Have you seen the video yet?"

"What video?" Zack asked.

"It's in the box with the other thing," Terry responded helpfully, rummaging around in a carton Zack hadn't gotten to yet. "I peeked at it a little last night," he said, handing a tape to Zack. "I don't recommend popcorn."

Zack brought the tape over to the VCR he had set up in his office and started it. Then he turned the TV on and watched with Terry as the screen flashed to life.

Like most of the police videos Zack had seen, the camera operator wasn't trying to do anything but slowly sweep over everything, stopping on important details. The idea was to try to give the viewer a sense of the whole scene, something that even the best still photos often failed to do.

This whole scene looked like the set of a silent horror movie. Lifeless, bloody bodies, mutilated by multiple wounds, were strewn across the floor and furniture like garbage.

"The one on his back near the kitchen is Marc Nathenson," Terry said, as an image came into view of a skinny guy in a yellow T-shirt with his legs awkwardly bent. Marc Nathenson was wearing old-fashioned white Converse All-Stars. "He was a grad student in chemistry. Helped out in freshman chem, I guess." The camera continued to crawl around the room, stopping and zooming in on the body of a young woman sprawled facedown, one arm trapped beneath her. There was an incredible amount of blood around her. Zack was having trouble focusing. Terry seemed to be reading from some file. "The two women were both seniors. Marianne Duhamel was majoring in French, and the other one . . ." Terry kept on speaking, but the humming in Zack's ears drowned him out. He needed to concentrate. This was evidence that needed to be analyzed. He needed to do more than gape at carnage, like a motorist who slows down to watch the paramedics attend to a driver in a head-on collision.

One of the victims was wearing a silver bracelet and had apparently been drinking a Diet Pepsi.

Another had a chipped tooth.

Terry said something about a biology teaching assistant.

A third had been wearing glasses with thick black frames when he was killed. He looked a little like Elvis Costello with a tan. Slumped over the arm of a couch.

With a hole in his neck.

Zack began to sweat. He wasn't sure how much more he could take.

The screen flickered, and other images began to appear. But even when the camera turned away from the bodies, it revealed an astonishing level of violence.

The shooter's rampage was most evident in the damage to the living room. The stream of bullets had broken all of the windows, torn down curtains and shades, cut through a table, smashed a mirror and several lamps, sliced open and scattered upholstery and stuffing which was all over the place, and blasted dozens of holes in the walls and floor. There were even a few in the ceiling. In the kitchen, broken glass and dishes were on the counters and floor. What was left of the entry door was hanging by one hinge at a crazy angle. The rest had been reduced to kindling.

And blood was splattered everywhere.

Then the screen flickered again and returned to the living room. This time, the camera operator seemed to be concentrating on details that he might have missed the first time around.

A single blue-and-white running shoe, lying on its

side near the door to the kitchen next to the Nathenson brother, who had a blood-soaked baseball cap clutched in his left hand.

The bookshelf in the corner had miraculously dodged the fusillade, on which sat a college course catalog, a few dog-eared paperbacks—*Franny and Zooey, L'Etranger, The Crying of Lot 49*—and a small, passport-size photo of a dark-haired young man with a charming smile housed in a tacky frame that said "World's Greatest Uncle."

The thin white cardboard pizza box spilling slices of pepper-and-onion pizza onto the ugly green carpet, leaning against the remains of a shattered coffee table. "You've Tried All the Rest—Now Try the Best. University Pizza."

Zack turned the TV off. His hand was shaking.

"Is that it?" asked Terry.

"That's it for now," answered Zack.

Why was he transfixed by the horror? Every criminal case had victims, or destruction, or both. Anyone who practiced this kind of law had to be able to detach himself from his personal feelings of revulsion from the crime in order to do his job. But this time, Zack wasn't feeling detached. He was feeling sick.

He stood up. "I'm starting to wonder if I should have taken this one."

"Why? Just because he's guilty?"

Zack shook his head. "I don't know. I'm not sure if it's because I've got Justin now, or because I've been away from this kind of felony for so long, but—I just don't know."

"What? The guy flipped out and blew away a room full of people."

"Flipped out?" Zack retorted. "This guy didn't flip out. He waited for hours for these people. And then he shot them over and over with a hundred and twenty bullets." He paused for a moment. "Wait a minute. I'm wrong. He didn't wait for hours. He waited for *days*. He rented the place across the way so he could sit around and watch them come and go before he did it. This guy didn't just kill these people. He *executed* them. A couple of English majors, a postgrad chemistry student, a biology teaching assistant. Somebody's favorite uncle." He closed his eyes, and for some reason, the image of that single running shoe came into his mind. "Jesus Christ."

Terry shrugged. "It doesn't change the fact that he's entitled to a defense."

"I know that," Zack said. "I'm just not sure I'm going to be able . . ." His voice trailed off.

"Well, why don't we wait to hear the rest of his story?" Terry suggested. "Maybe something will come up."

Zack looked at his friend for a few seconds before picking up the next part of the file and starting to read again. "Maybe," he said.

Oak Park, Michigan

TO LENA, THE WHOLE THING SEEMED PRETTY sketchy.

According to Giselle's mother, on the very same night that Mr. LeClerq had a heart attack, his home was broken into by burglars who didn't bother to take anything of value. Despite the fact that the police said nothing of the sort happened.

Sketchy City.

But so what if Giselle's mother had some off-the-wall theory that underachiever thieves were to blame for her father-in-law's death? As long as Giselle and her mother were willing to talk to her, Lena was interested in hearing what they had to say. And she had been more than happy to meet them at Mr. LeClerq's home in Oak Park.

The first thing that Lena noticed when she walked through the front door was that Phillipe LeClerq was a lot neater than she was.

Well, okay. Just about anyone who was able to see their floor was a lot neater than Lena was. But Phillipe LeClerq was pretty exceptional.

From the tidy entryway with its little table and vase of dried flowers, to the formal dining room, with the lace tablecloth and the sideboards featuring lovely china, to the gleaming but somewhat outdated kitchen, to the living room with the surprisingly modern entertainment system, everything was clean, and everything was in its place.

But Giselle's mother was much more interested in having Lena look at the den. That's where she said that the men who broke into the house had gone. Lena checked to see the reaction of Giselle, the only witness to the supposed break-in. There was none. She could well have been the quietest girl that Lena had ever met. Maybe in a little while, she'd feel more comfortable around Lena and open up.

The den was lined with bookcases filled with books, dozens of framed rare coins—apparently Mr. LeClerq was a coin collector—and the kind of memorabilia that a well-loved high school math teacher and soccer coach accumulates over thirty years. Class pictures, yearbooks, and team photos were everywhere, as well as a few autograph-covered soccer balls, trophies, certificates, even a framed picture of Mr. LeClerq with a famous foreign soccer player that Lena's father used to talk about all the time. He had one name. Pepé, or something like that.

But the desk was clearly where Giselle's mom wanted Lena to look. There really was nothing special about it, except that for Phillipe LeClerq, it was ridiculously messy. Drawers were opened, and papers and file folders were scattered around on its surface. A computer monitor flashed a screen saver message repeatedly. *I love my granddaughter . . . I love my granddaughter . . . I love my granddaughter . . .*

Lena cleared her throat. "Is this the way you found the desk after, um, after Mr. LeClerq was taken to the hospital?" One of the file folders held the closing documents for the sale of the house to Mr. and Mrs. LeClerq back in 1971. Another held insurance information. One contained several articles on teaching strategies for kids with learning disabilities.

Giselle's mom nodded emphatically. "My husband and I came over later that day and found it just like this. We didn't touch a thing. Neither did the police," she added, with a disgusted sound. "Like I told you, they don't think anyone was here. Even though I told them that they took my father-in-law's CDs."

"You mean from the living room?" Lena asked.

"No. His computer CDs." The woman crossed her arms. "They were here on the desk."

Lena moved the mouse and the screen saver disappeared to reveal the program manager screen. "Did your father-in-law do anything unusual with his computer?" she asked.

"Not unless you call e-mailing with his family unusual."

"Did they check for fingerprints?" Lena asked.

"Oh, yeah. They spent about two minutes talking to Giselle, and then about two more minutes looking around for fingerprints and whatever, but they said they didn't find anything."

Lena turned to the little girl. "What did they say to you, Giselle?"

The girl looked up at her mother for a second, and then back to Lena. "They kept saying how brave I was, and kept asking how I knew CPR." She spoke in a small voice. "I told them I learned it from a book I read in the library."

"Wow," said Lena. "That's impressive. I don't think I knew CPR until I went to college. You know, something I was wondering was how you knew to call 911 so quickly. I know that some people—"

Giselle cut her off. "I didn't call 911. I even told the police that, 'cause they thought I called, too."

"You didn't call? But how did the ambulance know to come here?"

"Grandpa called 911 about the break-in," she replied.

"He did?" Lena said. "That's funny. I thought you called about your grandfather's heart attack."

"Nuh-uh. Like I told the police. I was already in bed. I only came downstairs because I heard the door slam. And Grandpa was on the kitchen floor, and the phone was next to him." Suddenly, her voice broke, her lip started to quiver, and a single tear ran down her cheek.

Okay. This was getting weird. When Becca had called Lena and told her about this, she'd specifically said that Giselle had called 911 because her grandfather had had a heart attack. It wasn't like Becca was making this up. She had been reading from a police report.

"How did you know your grandfather called about a break-in? Couldn't he have been calling about his heart?"

"That's what the lady on the phone told me. The 911 lady," the child replied.

"Oh," Lena said. "So you picked up the phone, and the 911 operator was already on the phone?"

"Yeah." Giselle's mother gave her a tissue, and she blew her nose loudly.

"Giselle," Lena said, "I know this is hard, but I was wondering if you remember the name of the police officer that you spoke to."

The little girl sniffed, and wiped her face with her hand, but didn't hesitate. "His name was Officer Halsey," she answered.

Lena shot a quick look at her mother, who was nodding with pride. "My girl has an amazing memory," she told Lena. "If she says it's Halsey, it's Halsey."

So Lena pulled out her cell phone and dialed Becca's number. Sometimes when they were working on a case, cops got a few things wrong.

But when Becca got back on the line and read Officer Halsey's report to Lena, it was clear that, in this case, there were more than a few things wrong. A lot more.

Northampton, Massachusetts

IT HAD TAKEN HIM TWENTY-TWO YEARS, BUT District Attorney Francis X. O'Neill was finally going to have a goddamn press conference. A real goddamn press conference.

As he peeked from behind the back door past the podium that they'd set up in the conference room, he saw that CNN, Court TV, *USA Today,* the *Globe,* the *Post,* and the *Herald,* as well as all four Boston local affiliates for the television networks, were covering him. There were others, but he couldn't tell who they were. He'd get Frieda to find out later.

He stole a quick look at his reflection in the glass of a window across the hallway. He'd gotten his hair cut two days ago, and he'd gotten a manicure yesterday. His suit was just dry-cleaned, and his tie was brand-new. He looked really good. He was ready to try the biggest murder case in Northampton history.

He stepped into the conference room, took his place at the podium, and began his new life.

Twenty-two years ago F.X. had signed on as an assistant district attorney working out of a nothing town called Orange, in the western part of Massachusetts. He'd started small, like everyone else. OUIs, minor-league assault and batteries, soliciting. All District Court cases.

The pathetic salaries and thankless work of assistant D.A.s caused such heavy turnover that after only four years, he was one of the senior members of the office. He started doing low- and mid-level felonies in the Superior Court. A few sex crimes, a bunch of robberies, some A&Bs with a dangerous weapon.

In his sixth year, he did his first murder trial, and within the next five years, he'd become one of the top prosecutors in the western counties. Just before Christmas, thirteen years ago, he'd been appointed First Assistant D.A. A stroke of good luck sent the elected D.A. to an early grave from a car accident four years after that, God rest his soul, and F.X. stepped in as acting D.A. until he was officially elected District Attorney seven years ago.

"Will you be heading the prosecution team?"

Jeez, it took 'em ten minutes to finally ask that one.

"Yes. In fact, I'll be trying the case myself. This one is too important to delegate to one of my staff. Of course, I'll have excellent help from Assistant District Attorney Stacey Ruben and Police Chief Darryl Brooks."

"Mr. O'Neill, do you have any plans to try to move into other elected offices?"

Now they were talking. He'd paid his dues in this crappy little job for long enough. He was hitting his political prime. He'd be forty-eight this November. Goddamn right he had plans.

"At the moment the only thing I'm focusing on is this trial and continuing to work to make sure that the people of the Commonwealth are fairly and aggressively represented in the criminal justice system."

"But you wouldn't rule out running for elected office in, say, a statewide contest, would you?"

F.X. flashed his most charming smile. "My mother, God rest her soul, always used to tell me, 'Never say never.' I'm just going to do the best that I can do with the job at hand, which is to aggressively prosecute this multiple-murder case, and leave the rest to another day. Thank you."

As he left the room, he leaned in to speak to Stacey. He didn't really have anything to say—he just wanted to look like he was very busy and important.

"How'd you think it went?" he asked in a low voice, taking her by the arm and leading her out of the room. He hoped his expression looked as if he were urgently handling the people's business.

"Fine, I guess," she answered.

"Good," said the district attorney, letting her arm go as soon as they left the conference room. He hurried down the hall to his office. He needed to call his wife to tell her to tape the news tonight.

Worcester, Massachusetts

EL AMIN TURNED OFF THE TELEVISION IN DISgust. The district attorney was a pompous jackass, but that was no surprise. This entire country was a farce.

It was still puzzling that there was no announcement from the authorities, foolishly trumpeting the killings of the martyrs as some major victory over so-called terrorism. Instead, their own assassin was being tried as a common criminal. The man's prison photo seemed to be in the newspapers every day. According to public opinion, he was going to be executed. Maybe he was being punished for his failure to escape before the police arrived.

It didn't matter. The preparations for this summer's attack were already under way, and a preliminary set of small tests would likely be conducted sometime in March. In April, there would probably be a few larger tests in a remote location, and by May and June, the final plans would be made, and the operation would be put into place.

This Fourth of July was going to be one that no one would forget.

SIX

DIST. ATTY. O'NEILL: *Directing your attention to what has been marked as Exhibit 33, can you identify this for us?*

MS. DEL RIO: *Yes. That is the standard lease that we use for our buildings. This was for the rental of Unit 3C, at 214 Main Street, in Northampton.*

Q: *And are you familiar with the signatures on this lease?*

A: *[Indicating.] Well, that's my signature, right there.*

Q: *And who else signed the lease?*

A: *Those were the signatures of the four men that leased the apartment: Marc Nathenson, Mitchell Nathenson, Rudolf Lange, and John Bercher.*

Q: *So you met these men?*

A: *Yes. We all met in my office and signed the lease together.*

Q: *Are you familiar with two women named Marianne Duhamel and Helene Ghazi?*

A: *No, I am not.*

Q: *So they weren't renters at your apartment complex?*

A: *Not to my knowledge.*

Q: *And directing your attention to Exhibit 34, can you identify this?*

A: *Yes. That's another lease. That one's for Unit 3B.*

Q: *At 214 Main Street?*

A: *Yes.*

Q: *And where is Unit 3B located, relative to Unit 3C?*

A: *It's right across the hall. Directly across from 3C.*

Q: *And are you familiar with the signatures on this lease?*

A: *Yes. I signed it, and the defendant, Calvin Thompkins, also signed it, too.*

Q: *And what is the term of this lease?*

A: *The term? Uh, one year.*

Q: *I mean—Strike that. What was—Was the defendant leasing Unit 3B on the date of the shooting? On January 14?*

A: *Yes, he was.*

(Trial Volume V, Page 116)

February 25—Springfield, Massachusetts

"IT SEEMED PRETTY STUPID TO ME, SPENDING all that time and energy trying to keep me alive, when all they're going to do is execute me anyway."

The two lawyers were back, and Cal figured that if they really wanted the truth, they might as well get it all.

The tall one, Terry, looked the same. Kind of like an angry bear who hadn't slept in about fifteen years. He had a pad in his hand, and a pen that he clicked continuously. The other one, though—Zack—was real different. Last time, he actually looked kind of friendly. He did a lot of the talking, and he sounded like he had an open mind. This time, he didn't say a word. And his eyes stayed cold.

"You guys must have seen pictures of the place," Cal said. "I really shot it up."

"Yeah. We came to find out what the story was on that," Terry said.

"No doubt," Cal said, sitting forward a little to get more comfortable. The IV and the monitors were gone, so now they had him cuffed to the bed not only by his ankle but also by his good wrist. He leaned forward and, using the straw, took a sip of water from the glass on the tray in front of him. His appetite was returning slowly, but he seemed to be constantly thirsty. "Any chance I might be able to get rid of the cuffs?"

"You've been accused of shooting six people to death with an AK-47," Zack said, his voice hard. "There's no chance."

Cal nodded again. This guy Zack was pissed. "All right." He sat back upright. "This whole thing started in 1998—"

Terry's eyes all but rolled back in his head. "Oh my God—1998? Are you sure?"

"Listen. You've got to hear the whole story, otherwise you'll never understand what happened in there." From the way Zack kept staring at him, it didn't look like he'd ever understand. "Either of you guys have kids?"

"Never mind about us, okay, Cal?" Terry said. "Just tell us the story." If it was possible, Zack started to look worse. Who needed a jury to hang him? Zack would take care of it all by himself.

"All right. But after I get done, you've got to be honest with me. This is a hard case. I know that. If you can't represent me, I respect that, but you've got to tell me.

Don't stay in this thing and just go through the motions. I'd rather do it myself."

Zack nodded almost imperceptibly. "That's fair," he said softly.

"And if you do take the case, when we've lost—I mean when it's over, really over, I need you to tell me. No lies, no bullshit."

"Don't worry." Zack was dead serious. "I'll tell you when it's over."

"Okay." Call shifted a bit. His arm still ached, and his hand was still numb. The doctors said something about nerve damage. "About five years ago, things were very different. I had just earned, well, let's just say an extremely large amount of money from licensing a software product to Cellcom—"

"The phone company?" Terry interrupted.

"Yeah," Cal said. "I had been working on this technology back from when I was a grad student at M.I.T.—"

"When was that?" asked Terry, clicking the pen, obviously intending at some point to check up on the facts.

"Let's see. I graduated in '93 and started postgrad right after," Cal said. *Click click.* Terry wrote something down. Zack didn't move. "Anyway, my first payment was a little more than a million dollars, and the agreement was that Cellcom was going to pay me around thirty thousand dollars per month as a minimum licensing fee. It was likely to increase as their business grew. I was set for life, basically," he said, checking to see if either believed him. Not so far.

Terry said, "Any way we can verify this?"

"Sure. My contact at Cellcom was Gina Gefardo." Clumsily, he picked up a sheet of paper with the arm in a cast and handed it to Terry. "I figured you'd want to talk to some people about me, so before you came, I wrote down some names and numbers. Sorry about the handwriting." He smiled apologetically as Terry took the paper from him. There was no reaction. Wow. "Gina can connect you with the legal department."

Terry squinted at the paper. "Who's Steve . . . Doctorow?"

"He's my—well, he *was* my financial advisor. Steve can tell you whatever you need to know about my money."

At this, Terry exchanged a look with Zack. *Financial advisor*. Terry looked like he didn't know what to think. *Crazy-ass rich black dude blew away a bunch of students. Now what do we do?* Zack's look was more like *If I had a gun with me, I might just shoot him now, and save us all a lot of aggravation.*

"So anyway, right after I got the money, we decided that we were going to take a trip to Africa."

"What?" Terry interrupted. "Who decided?" *Click click.*

"Me and my wife, Cheryl. I was married back then." Another look passed between the lawyers. Terry wrote something else down. "And I had a son. Kevin. He was five at the time. We wanted him to see a part of the world where being black was the rule, not the exception, before he started kindergarten." Cal paused for a moment. "So in the summer of '98, we took him to Kenya."

Terry's eyes flashed up. "Aw, holy shit. Don't tell me. Kenya in 1998."

Cal smiled sadly. "Yeah. On the morning of August seventh, Kevin woke up early. I'm not much of a morning person, so Cheryl decided to take him for a walk downtown to a bakery that had these sweet rolls that he loved. We were in the capital. Nairobi." Cal swallowed. This was a little harder than he thought it was going to be. "They weren't going to the embassy, they were just out for a walk." He paused. "They were right next to it when the bomb exploded." His throat ached; his words sounded thick. "The cops told me that they died instantly. But I don't know."

Terry's pen clicking stopped. Zack's ferocious mask had been replaced by something a little less hostile.

"Before the bombing, I always had something going full speed. My education, my software design, my family. But after Kenya, I just didn't care about anything. I couldn't eat, I couldn't sleep. I started drinking, first to help me get to sleep, then to numb myself when I was awake. I got so depressed I wouldn't even let anyone in the house.

"It was bad for a long time." Cal stopped to take another drink of water. "Nothing mattered to me. Absolutely nothing. I remember getting a call from a friend around that time, telling me that there had been a break in the investigation of the bombing and that they had found the people who were responsible. I didn't care. I was basically just waiting to die." He took a deep breath.

"Then, one day, I dropped a bottle of vodka in the sink by accident. And there it was. All this broken glass, right in front of me. I could just cut my wrists and be done with it."

He shook his head and laughed quietly. "Before Kevin and Cheryl got killed, if you'd ever have told me I'd be that close to suicide, I'd have told you you were crazy. But there I was, ready to do it, when this incredible wave of fatigue hit me." It was funny watching Terry listen to this. Cal doubted that the man had slept more than five hours in a row in his life. "Here I was, on the verge of killing myself, when all of a sudden, I couldn't keep my eyes open. I went into the living room, laid down on the couch, and slept for twenty-seven straight hours. Then I got up, went to the bathroom, and fell asleep for another twelve hours." Cal took another sip of water.

"Go on," Zack said, very still.

"When I woke up, I don't know. It was like something had shifted inside of me. It was really strange," Cal said. "I had this odd, calm feeling, like I finally understood what I wanted to do. And I didn't want to drink, and I didn't want to kill myself, and I didn't want to stay in my house forever." He swallowed and said, "I wanted revenge."

"So you're telling us you shot six innocent people in Massachusetts as revenge for a bombing that happened five years ago, halfway around the world," Terry said. He looked like he was ready to give up.

"Yeah, I shot them out of revenge, but they were not six innocent people. Oh, no. These were six terrorists. This was an Al Qaeda cell, right here in Northampton, Massachusetts. Cold-blooded killers. Planning to kill again."

Terry put his head in his hands. "Oh, man," he moaned.

"And you didn't report this to anyone," Zack said skeptically. "You just figured out they were terrorists, all by yourself, and then you wasted them."

Cal felt a flicker of annoyance. "Look. I didn't just check out the phone book for Arabic names and then start shooting. I'm not a fool. I'm actually a pretty smart guy. I really was postgrad at M.I.T., and I really was a software designer, all right? It took me years to find these people and confirm that they were terrorists. Remember all that money I had? I used it to hire people. Dozens of investigators in over thirty states. I traveled all over the country doing research, training for when I was going to confront them. This wasn't a half-assed, stupid mistake." He looked at each of the lawyers before he spoke again. "This was revenge. I killed these people to avenge the murder of my wife and child," he said. "They'd murdered innocent people before, and they were planning on murdering innocent people again. I'm not sorry for what I did, and I'm not going to lie about it. And if that means I'm going to get executed, then I want a trial so someone can look me in the face and say I deserve to die."

Worcester, Massachusetts

BY THE TIME POLICE SERGEANT PETE VANDER-wall arrived at the bar, it looked as if the officers who had already responded to the call to break up the fight had everything pretty much under control. The lights were still low, and the jukebox was still pounding out some lame disco hit, but the party had definitely been put on serious hold. A college-age kid was sitting at a table, holding a piece of ice to his bloody lip, while he talked to Patrolman Freddy Kramer. Freddy's partner, a rookie named Charone, was across the room, talking to another kid, who was clearly agitated. Probably the other fighter. Detectives Billy Saunders and Paula Ulanski stood near the door, speaking to a bouncer, a guy wearing a tight T-shirt with the name of the bar across the chest. *Rockets*.

The head bartender had just started to walk over to speak to Pete when all of a sudden this little tornado with a ponytail came flying out of nowhere and jumped at the guy with the split lip. Before the kid had a chance to hit back, Freddy had wrestled him away from the tiny teenage girl, and Pete quickly grabbed her from behind.

"Let me go, you asshole!" she screamed, flailing

uselessly as Pete scooped her up and moved her away from her target.

"Calm down," Pete shouted over the music, right into her ear. "I'm a police officer, and I'm way bigger than you are. Just calm down and let's figure this thing out so nobody else gets hurt, okay?"

Way bigger indeed. What was she? Fourteen? Fifteen at the most? Maybe a hundred pounds, soaking wet. She could've been one of his daughter's classmates. But she just kept kicking and flailing and screaming. Until she went limp.

Pete looked down at her skeptically. Pretending to give up was not a new method of escaping, and since seconds before she had been battling to get away, Pete assumed that she was just hoping he'd release his hold, giving her another chance to do whatever nutty thing she wanted to do next.

Then he saw the back of her head.

Dark blood matted her hair and was still oozing from her scalp. Whatever had hit her back there had hit her hard. "Hey," he said, holding her still with one hand, while turning her by the chin to face him.

Her eyes rolled back in her head.

"Paula!" he shouted, shifting his hold on the girl so he was carrying her in both arms like the baby she was as he headed for the door to the street. "I need a ride to the emergency room right now. Billy, call for more backup!"

SEVEN

Ferguson Confirmed as Vice President

In what can safely be described as the first positive news in nearly a month for President James Graham's embattled administration, Congress today overwhelmingly approved his choice of retired Colonel Matthew Ferguson as Vice President by a resounding majority in both the Senate and the House of Representatives.

Ferguson was named to replace former Vice President Wilton Quarters, who resigned last month amid a growing scandal.

Quarters had been credited by many for ensuring Graham's victory in the general election two years ago as a result of statements he made in the last week of the campaign, charging that Graham's opponent was part of a corporate group that owned and operated a company that makes pornographic movies. It is widely believed that the flurry of publicity generated by the charges moved conservative voters to vote for Graham, especially in South Carolina and Tennessee, states which gave Graham enough electoral votes to win an extremely close election.

Three weeks ago, however, two apparently unrelated stories came to light which forced Quarters, a self-styled champion of conservative morals, to resign.

First, copies of internal memos from Quarters's campaign surfaced, indicating that Quarters knew that the report he had used to discredit Graham's opponent was false at the time he made the damaging charges. And at about the same time, evidence was uncovered indicating that Quarters, while a member of the House of Representatives, owned stock in a conglomerate which owned a production company which itself made pornographic videos.

A criminal investigation against Quarters is ongoing.

(*Boston Post*, September 10, page 1)

March 3—Washington, D.C.

MATT'S MEETING WITH HIS CHIEF OF STAFF WAS winding down. That was good news, because he had promised Sammy that he would watch the latest Brad Pitt movie with her tonight. The First Lady had a thing about Brad Pitt.

"Have you come to a decision regarding the situation in the Philippines, Mr. President?"

Vernon Browning was following up on a meeting that had been held last week regarding counterterrorism options. There had been increasing signs that key terrorists had been active in the island country, and although Matt was eager to do something, he was struggling to find the right course.

"I'd like to get more details on the two scenarios for increased use of Special Operations," he replied. "We don't have anywhere near enough intelligence to make any significant or overt move."

"Very good, sir," Browning said, gathering his notes and standing to go. "If there's nothing else . . ."

"Actually, Vernon, there is one more thing," Matt said, walking over to his desk and picking up the laptop computer lying there.

How Matt had come into possession of the computer was the latest in the almost countless bizarre and tragic events surrounding his improbable route to the Oval Office.

President Graham had been blunt when he asked Matt to be Vice President. The President was in a terribly weak political position. The manner in which Graham had won the presidential election had completely polarized an already historically acrimonious Congress. Worse still, two years after Graham's election, his party lost its majority in both the Senate and the House.

Graham had to announce his choice for the new Vice President quickly if he was to have any chance of weathering the political firestorm that had been generated by the Quarters scandal. By acting fast, Graham hoped to deflect attention away from Quarters's past and toward the country's future, including the congressional confirmation hearings.

The problem was, of course, that Congress was so furious with the President that it was almost sure to reject whatever replacement Graham chose from his own party, if for no other reason than to humiliate him and prolong the political scandal.

Which made Matt the perfect choice—a recently retired war hero who not only boasted an outstanding career in the army but who had publicly eschewed professional politics, and who hadn't even claimed membership in Graham's party.

If the opposition failed to confirm Matt, suddenly they'd look like the bad guys—bureaucratic hacks who were more interested in playing politics than looking out for the good of the country.

As crazy as the whole thing seemed to Matt, he took comfort in the fact that despite the high-profile nature of the office, the Vice President had, literally, only two constitutional responsibilities: breaking tie votes in the Senate and becoming President if the sitting President died in office. Given the political landscape at the time, it was very unlikely that Matt would be called on to perform the first task, and given who the sitting President was, it was virtually certain that Matt would not be called on to perform the second.

James Graham had been a wrestling champion in college, and he was in the same shape when he was elected President at the age of forty-eight as he had been at the age of twenty-one. He ran three to four miles, five days a week, and he played an hour of full-court basketball on days he didn't run. In his first month in office, he announced that it was his goal to be the strongest President in history, and there was little doubt he had achieved it.

Until he collapsed, five minutes into his final basketball game, merely three months after Matt had become his Vice President.

Preliminary reports were that Graham had suffered a stroke. But it turned out that there was nothing wrong with the President's brain. Or just about any other part of him. He was a marvelous physical specimen—tall, strong, athletic—except for the undetectable defect in his heart, which had led to a massive, fatal aneurysm in a cardiac artery.

Among the seemingly millions of things that had been put into Matt's hands, either literally or figuratively, when President Graham had died, this laptop was probably the strangest. Two days after Graham's funeral, the former President's widow, Veronica, had made a special trip to hand Matt the computer in person, explaining that she had found it among her late husband's private effects. Veronica Graham thought that it might have had politically sensitive material on it, and decided that Matt should see it before she did anything with it.

Even though he had already felt completely overwhelmed by everything he had to assimilate to take on his new role, Matt felt a duty to attend to the request of the former President's widow. Several days ago he had begun reading the entire contents of the files stored on the computer.

About six hours into the ordeal, Matt was ready to resign the presidency.

It was that, or continue to endure the most boring series of reports he'd ever seen in his life. How could so many people have written so much about the five- to ten-year economic outlook for citrus growers? Five to ten *years*? The local weatherman could barely figure out whether it was going to rain the day after tomorrow.

He handed the computer to Browning and said, "Veronica Graham gave this to me." A strange look passed over Browning's face. He probably thought Matt was going to give him another dozen things to do before tomorrow morning. "She said it was President Graham's personal property, and thought I should check to see if there was anything sensitive stored on it."

Two dozen, said Browning's face.

"But I didn't see anything except in one report on judicial nominations. There were a bunch of references to some memos that someone named Cullhane wrote that I wanted to read. I didn't even know who Cullhane was, but when I asked around, I found out he quit just days after the funeral."

Browning swallowed in what might have been relief,

took the laptop, and said, "Yes, Charley was on the speechwriting staff. I couldn't convince him to stay after President Graham died. He had some family problems . . ." His voice trailed off. "But I wasn't aware of any memos on federal judges. And he certainly wouldn't have been the person to write them." The thin man shook his head. He was obviously puzzled. "Are you sure about this?"

"I'm not sure about anything," Matt said, as Carlos entered the room with a knock and handed him a note that Sammy had called. "When you get a chance, take a look for yourself at the report and see what you think. Maybe you can figure it out. It's probably nothing," he said, picking up the phone to call his wife back.

"Probably," Browning agreed, smiling and heading for the door. But then he turned back. "Oh, Mr. President—speaking of judges. The judge in Michigan you were asking about. Evidently he had been suffering from depression. He was being treated, but apparently one night he just took an overdose of sleeping pills."

Matt nodded. He had had his share of low moments, but it was hard to imagine things ever getting that bad. "Okay. Thanks, Vernon. See you tomorrow."

"Good night, Mr. President."

Detroit, Michigan

"I'M REALLY NOT SUPPOSED TO BE DOING THIS," Becca said, as she pulled a thin file folder out of her oversize bag and put it on Lena's kitchen table where they were sharing take-out dinner from Babe's Deli. Then she laughed loudly. "I guess that's why I like doing it so much."

Becca's energy level was somewhat legendary with Lena's family. Lena's grandfather, Yoki, who had met Becca when he was visiting from Kyoto last summer, said she was like a monkey in a hurricane. To Lena, she was just eccentric. But however you labeled her, Becca was funny, and loud, and her personal code of ethics—carefully follow the rules that make sense to you and completely ignore the rest—worked very well for Lena. Because it made no sense to Becca that low-level police reports were supposed to be super-secret. So for a Reuben sandwich on rye and unlimited Diet Coke, she was perfectly happy to show them to Lena.

Like the case file on the LeClerq break-in. Or non–break-in.

Sure enough, Officer Halsey's report, at least the part about the 911 call, was totally inconsistent with young Giselle's memory of their interview. In language which all cops must have learned in the academy, Halsey wrote: "Subject reported that at aproximately 0220 she came downstairs, where she found her grandfather, Philip Laclerk, on kitchen floor. She observed that he was in cardiac distress, and called 911. She performed CPR on Mr. Laclerk until an ambulince arrived and transported him to Sini Grace Hospital."

Plenty of misspellings, but not a word about a reported break-in.

The only other things in the file were a hospital record, which included a bland and useless report from the paramedics about taking Mr. LeClerq to the hospital.

"This is it?" asked Lena, flipping through the few pages, as if she might have missed something. "The whole thing?"

Becca couldn't answer for a second because her

mouth was full. "What's the matter? Isn't it the right one?"

"I guess so," said Lena. "It's the right names and address. But just about everything else doesn't fit."

"What do you mean?" Becca asked.

"Well, for one thing," Lena said, finishing her drink, "Giselle said she didn't call 911. Her grandfather called about a break-in, and the phone was off the hook when Giselle found him on the kitchen floor."

Becca took the file from Lena and flipped through it. "That's weird," she said. "Was anything taken?"

"That's another thing that doesn't fit," said Lena. "If there was a break-in, and Mr. LeClerq surprised them, they still had enough time to grab all kinds of things from the house. The man had rare coins all over the place. And the living room was full of expensive stuff. They didn't take any of that. According to Giselle's mother, all they took were some computer CDs. And the cops dusted for prints, but there's no report of that, either." Lena took a bite of her salad.

"Oh, shit," Becca suddenly exclaimed. "I forgot to tell you about the 911 tape! I looked for it, but it was gone. That's no big deal—they get reused and relabeled all the time. So I called the transcriber and got her to fax me a copy of the transcript. But then I found the original transcript in an envelope in another file. Here." She dug around in her bag and handed Lena a three-page transcript and a manila envelope.

So Lena read the faxed transcript, and then opened the envelope and read the original of the transcript inside. Then she looked up at Becca. "You didn't tell anybody you were looking for this tape, did you?" Lena asked quietly.

Becca looked at her with disdain. "Really. Like anybody would care."

Lena handed her the two transcripts. "One of these was tampered with," she said. "Somebody would care."

Washington, D.C.

MATT THOUGHT THAT SAMMY WAS ASLEEP, SO he was startled when she sat up in bed abruptly, turned on a search light that had been recently installed on her bedside table, and said firmly, "Okay, Colonel Tough Guy, it's talkin' time."

Matt rolled over onto his back, but threw his arm over his eyes to shield them against the glare of a four-thousand-watt lightbulb. How did she always know? Probably some North Carolina hillbilly voodoo thing her grandmother taught her. *Tahkin' tahme.* God. "It's after one o'clock in the morning," he said. "It can't possibly be talkin' time." There was no reply. "And by the way, it's *President* Tough Guy now." Silence. "I already told you I thought the movie was good." Nothing. He was doomed.

"I'm waiting," she said after a few more moments passed.

"Okay, let's talk," he said, sitting up, squinting at the lamp. "But first, can you please turn that thing off, so we don't both get skin cancer?"

Sammy got out of bed and walked across the room to turn on the bathroom light. No first lady had ever looked hotter in a nightgown. Or out of a nightgown. Which was a topic completely off the table during talkin' time. The next several minutes would be spent engaging his beautiful blond wife's frighteningly sharp intellect and common sense, not her bombshell body and wicked sexual appetite. She left the door ajar, and then came back and turned off the bedside lamp.

"There. That's better." She climbed back into the bed and focused her blue laser beams on him. "Now, then," she said. "What's going on?"

Matt took a deep breath. Normally, this kind of decision didn't cause him such grief. Maybe if he talked about it, it would be easier to sleep tonight. Of course, now that Sammy knew there was something bothering him, if he didn't talk about it, it would be tough to sleep ever again.

"In a day or two, it looks like I'm going to be ordering Navy SEALs into the Philippines," he said. Sammy blinked a couple of times. "It'll be covert. There's been some intel that some pretty bad guys have gotten active. But they've been a little sloppy, and we've been able to identify what looks like a headquarters of some kind in the Philippine jungle, and possibly some weapons or ammunition dumps as well."

Sammy just waited. "It's not like I haven't ordered troops into danger before," Matt continued. "But, well, this time, it's different."

Sammy nodded. Her eyes were a little softer now, but no less blue. "This time, you aren't wearing a helmet in a battlefield," she said. "And it's preemptive. The Philippines are an ally. But you're sending the military in there anyway, without their knowledge or consent. It's not the way you like to do things," she said. "It's sneaky."

Of course, Sammy was right. In fact, they'd spoken of this often, when Matt had been Vice President, when President Graham was dealing with intelligence regarding Al Qaeda's presence around the globe. Matt had been severely torn between his firm belief in the U.N., international law, and the sovereignty of nations, and his impatience with most foreign governments' pathetic efforts at dealing with terrorists harbored within their own borders.

But back then, the discussions between him and his wife had been theoretical.

Now Graham was dead, Matt was President, and suddenly everything had become far too real.

"Every time I get one of these intelligence briefings, I think about my responsibilities, and I feel like all I'm doing is sitting around, waiting for something terrible to happen," Matt told his wife. "The Philippines is still reeling from that pair of hurricanes that blasted Manila. Chasing terrorists around in the jungle is the last thing on their mind. We've got people in the field, telling me that there are specific threats that we can address and a specific window of opportunity. I'm going to trust these guys to get in, do what they need to do, and get out, without a lot of fanfare." He paused. "Even if that means I'm technically invading an ally and committing God knows however many international crimes in the process."

Sammy got up, walked over to the bathroom, turned out the light, and returned to bed. She rested her head on Matt's chest and said, "You realize that you aren't going to come up with the single right thing to do here."

Matt trailed his fingers through her hair and took another deep breath. "Yeah, I know," he replied. "But I still wish I could."

EIGHT

DIST. ATTY. O'NEILL: *And where do you live?*

MS. TENTINO: *I live in Apartment 1D of 214 Main Street, Northampton, Massachusetts.*

Q: *And were you living there on January 14 of this year?*

A: *I've lived there for twenty-two years. Ever since I retired.*

Q: *So you were living there on January 14 of this year?*

A: *Yes.*

Q: *And back in January of this year, Ms. Tentino, were you familiar with the defendant, Calvin Thompkins?*

A: *You mean before he shot all those people?*

MR. TALLACH: *Objection.*

THE COURT: *Sustained.*

Q: *Before, uh, before January 14 of this year, were you familiar with the defendant?*

A: *Well, let's see, I made eggnog for Mrs. Gallagher on Christmas Eve, and she told me that this big black man—*

MR. TALLACH: *Objection.*

THE COURT: *Sustained.*

THE WITNESS: *—This big black man moved in—*

MR. TALLACH: *Your Honor?*

THE COURT: *Ma'am. I sustained the objection. Wait for the district attorney to put another question to you.*

THE WITNESS: *Okay.*

Q: *Before all this happened, did you know the defendant?*

MR. TALLACH: *Objection.*

THE COURT: *Overruled.*

MR. TALLACH: *May I be seen at sidebar, Your Honor?*

THE COURT: *No. Go on, Mr. O'Neill.*

Q: *Back in January, before January 14, how did you know the defendant?*

MR. TALLACH: *Objection.*

THE COURT: *Overruled. You may answer.*

MR. TALLACH: *Your Honor—*

THE COURT: *The objection is overruled, Mr. Tallach. I am instructing the witness to answer.*

THE WITNESS: *I can answer?*

THE COURT: *Yes.*

THE WITNESS: *Can you repeat the question?*

(Trial Volume V, Pages 200–201)

March 10—Northampton, Massachusetts

ZACK KNEW THAT IT WAS PROBABLY IRRATIONAL, but something about the last meeting with Calvin Thompkins had made him much more sanguine about representing the man. Maybe it was because Thompkins was obviously mentally ill, or maybe it was because of the deaths of his wife and child. But now Zack couldn't stop the flood of questions running through his mind as he waited for Terry to emerge from his office. If Thompkins was rich enough to need an accountant, how did he qualify for a court-appointed attorney? Had he really spent all of his money on private investigators? If Thompkins had no other options and still refused to pursue an insanity defense, was *that* evidence that he was mentally ill? Could Zack ethically present an insanity defense even if Thompkins didn't want him to?

"So, I guess this means you're still in the case," Terry said as he pulled open the door of Zack's Honda.

Terry looked like a curly-haired mountain that needed a shave. Would he ever learn to move the seat back *before* getting in?

"And can you remind me why you insist on driving this little tiny tin can, for God's sake," he grumbled, shoehorning his large frame into the car and then struggling to wrestle with the seat.

Guess not.

"For the record, I happen to know that you can afford at least a freakin' Camry, if you're so completely committed to being dull," Terry continued, as they pulled away from the curb. He grunted in triumph as the passenger seat finally slammed back as far as it could go.

There was no point in replying to the car comments. They would never stop. "Yeah," Zack said. "Well. I just know that before Cal told us why he shot those people, I wasn't sure I could stay in it. But now . . ."

"Now we understand why he did what he did, but that doesn't change *what* he did," Terry replied. "We're still stuck with some pretty ugly facts, here, Counselor.

'Mr. Thompkins, didn't you premeditate your actions?' 'Uh, yeah, but my wife and son were blown up five years earlier.' 'Mr. Thompkins, didn't you walk into an apartment and intentionally turn six people into hamburger with an AK-47?' 'Uh, yeah, but I'm a very smart guy. I did graduate work at M.I.T. Really.' 'Thank you. I have no further questions.' "

"I know," Zack said. "I'm just saying that when I first saw what he did, I wasn't even sure that I wanted to bother. So what if he didn't get a fair trial? He deserved to be found guilty." He shook his head. "That never happened to me before. I can't be a lawyer like that. At least now I care enough so that I can do the trial."

"That's swell," Terry said, "but here's a tip. Don't get too attached to this guy. His long-term prospects look a little shaky."

At this point "a little shaky" seemed optimistic. "Yeah," Zack said. "I know. The whole thing is a horror show, but I can make sure he gets a fair trial, at least. He'll tell his story to the jury, and he'll get creamed."

"That's fine," Terry said. "Now you want to tell me why we're going to talk to Cal's 'financial advisor'?"

"By the way, how does somebody with a financial advisor get a court-appointed attorney?"

"Another good point," replied Terry, as they merged onto the interstate. "So what you're telling me is that you don't know much about anything right now."

Zack nodded. "That's pretty much the story."

"And we're on our way to Springfield because . . ."

"I can't think of anything else to do," replied Zack.

"And thus, a plan was forged."

STEVE DOCTOROW'S OFFICE WAS IN A SPECtacular high-rise building in the business district of downtown Springfield. Zack could see his reflection in the huge brass handles on the double glass doors as he and Terry entered the expensively decorated reception area. Dad would have loved this place. It oozed money.

A compact, balding man with a serious demeanor was speaking to the receptionist, and immediately came around the desk to introduce himself.

"You must be Cal's lawyers. I'm Steve Doctorow." They all shook hands. "Why don't we talk in my office?" he said, leading them down a long hall.

They passed several small rooms, each occupied by a different young accountant, obviously very busy with work. The place just reeked of wealth. How much money did Thompkins used to have?

Doctorow's office was much bigger than the ones they'd passed in the hall. Dozens and dozens of files and books were organized neatly in shelves along the walls. At one end of the room was an enormous, tidy desk, and at the other was a couch and a couple of easy chairs surrounding a coffee table, on which had been placed a fairly thick file folder. They sat down.

Doctorow spoke first. "Cal wrote me a long letter, explaining his, uh, situation, and asking me to speak to you." He pointed at the file on the table. "I pulled his file and made a copy for you. And I just want you to know that whatever I can do to help . . ." He stared off into space. "Given what he told me, I realize that sounds ridiculous," he said, shaking his head.

"What did he say in the letter?" Zack asked.

"That he shot six people in an apartment," Doctorow replied.

"Good to be consistent," Terry muttered, reaching for the file.

"Can you tell us a little about Cal?" Zack asked. "Did

he have any history of mental illness, anything that would explain how he could do something like this?"

"They killed his wife and kid," Doctorow replied. "That's why he did it."

"So you believe that story." Terry glanced up from the file. "That they were terrorists. Or at least that Cal thought they were terrorists."

"If Cal said they were terrorists, they were terrorists," Doctorow said simply.

"How can you be so sure?" Zack asked.

"Because Cal Thompkins is one of the smartest people I ever met," Doctorow answered. "And one of the nicest. There's no way he'd ever lift a finger against someone, or even so much as accuse them of something, without being a hundred percent certain before he did so. He is a very careful person. He'd never just walk into a place and kill a half dozen people."

"And yet . . ." Terry murmured softly, turning back to the file.

"This is a man I've known for over ten years," Doctorow insisted. "From before he needed an accountant. We met doing volunteer work at a homeless shelter when he was still in college." The phone rang, but he ignored it. "Did you know that ever since Cal sold that technology to Cellcom, he has been intentionally overpaying his taxes by tens of thousands of dollars every year, because he was physically unable to serve in the armed forces? And not only has he given hundreds of thousands of dollars, literally, to charity, but since he was twenty-one years old, he has gotten up at six A.M. every Thanksgiving morning to cook a full turkey dinner, just so he could bring it to some needy family that afternoon, pretending to be delivering the first prize in some bogus grocery store contest. This is a good man. He didn't lie about those people he killed."

"I'm not talking about lying," Zack said. As a matter of fact, he didn't know what he was talking about. "I'm talking about stress caused by the death of his family that might have caused him to lose touch with reality."

"Cal sank into a terrible depression after Cheryl and Kevin were killed," Doctorow replied. "But he never lost touch with reality. When he finally started to function again, and he contacted me about what he was doing, he was completely lucid. I spoke to him many times about the money he was spending on investigators, research, training. I told him I thought it was crazy for any number of reasons. My God, this guy was a software designer, and he was hunting terrorists. It was ridiculous. But he had made his choice. He knew there was a chance he'd be killed, but he had decided to devote his life to the fight against terrorism." He pointed to the file Terry was looking through. "That file has the contact information for all the people he paid to help him."

"We'll probably go talk to them next," Zack said.

"Wait a minute," Terry said, closing the file. "Did you just say you knew what he was going to do?"

"I only knew he was trying to track terrorists down," Doctorow said. "I had no idea he was going to get a gun and try to kill them."

"What did you think he was going to do?" Terry snapped. "Invite them over to his house for brunch?"

Doctorow was unmoved. "I know it might seem stupid now, but at the time, I just thought he was going to do what he always did. Immerse himself in the subject. Learn everything there was to learn about it." Doctorow rubbed his temples as if he had a headache. "I actually thought that he wasn't going to find anything new. But if he did, I assumed that he was going to go to the police and let them take care of it." He shook his head and added sadly, "You have no idea how sorry I am that I was wrong."

"Well, now that you know what he was doing, don't you think it was a little insane?" Terry said.

Doctorow looked off into the distance again and was silent for a minute. Then he said, "After what he went through, I'm not sure I can answer that question."

NINE

DIST. ATTY. O'NEILL: *In the afternoon and early evening of January 14, were you home at your apartment at 214 Main Street? Apartment 2C?*

MS. QUALLS: *Yes. I wasn't supposed to go in to work until eight that night.*

Q: *And what apartment is directly above yours in that building?*

A: *Apartment 3C.*

Q: *And did you make any observations on January 14, in the afternoon, about the apartment above you, apartment 3C?*

A: *Observations?*

Q: *Yeah. For example, did you see or hear anything from upstairs that day?*

A: *Oh. Yes. I heard the shooting.*

Q: *Well, can you tell us exactly, to the best of your recollection, what you heard?*

A: *Well, the first thing I heard wasn't shooting. It was more like a screaming, or like a roaring. It was pretty scary. I didn't know what it was. Then, right after that, I heard the shooting, and windows* *breaking, and it sounded like, I don't know. It was, it was like suddenly there was a herd of elephants upstairs. There was a lot of screaming and shouting. And things falling and crashing.*

Q: *Do you remember how long the shooting lasted?*

A: *A couple of minutes. I don't know. A minute?*

Q: *Did you hear anything else after that?*

A: *Well, after the shooting stopped, I heard more of the screaming or roaring, or whatever it was, and then there was a little more shooting. But the roaring just kept going, even after the shooting was definitely over. And then even that stopped. Then I didn't hear anything else. And that's when I called the police.*

(Trial Volume V, Pages 240–241)

March 13—Northampton, Massachusetts

TERRY LOVED EATING DINNER EARLY.

Actually, Terry loved eating dinner at any time, but when he was meeting Zack at The Sunspot, he loved eating early because that's when the grad students and the secretaries showed up for happy hour. And since the waitress population at The Sunspot was well known to be far above average, early dinner there was generally a pretty outstanding experience. Make it a Friday night, and there was nothing better.

Speaking of nothing better, Terry was fairly sure that the tall redhead standing at the corner of the bar wasn't wearing a bra. He squinted a little, and sure enough—

"Or maybe later," Zack said, looking over at him.

The redhead turned away, heading for the restroom. Damn.

"Yeah," Terry said, looking back at Zack. Then he realized he had no idea what he just agreed with. "What?"

"I said that maybe we should go through this list later," Zack said, holding one of the printouts they had gotten from Doctorow. He looked back over his shoulder at the bar and then back to Terry. "Everything all right?"

Terry swallowed. "Yeah," he said. "No, we can do this now. I was just, uh, you know, celebrating a young woman over by the bar."

Zack nodded. "Right. So, why don't we get this over with—"

"Good evening, gentlemen, my name is Sandy, and I'll be your server tonight. Can I start you off with something to drink?"

Whoever was in charge of making Terry's day, they were doing a killer job. Their waitress was young, blond, pretty, smiling, and wearing a low-cut, tight white top that showed the exact right amount of cleavage. Actually, there probably was no wrong amount of cleavage. Terry wasn't keeping close count, but he thought that this might be the fifth time he'd fallen in love that night.

"I'll have a Sam Adams, please," he said.

"Me, too," Zack added.

"Awesome," Sandy said, with another smile. "I'll be right back with your drinks, and to take your order." She turned to head for the bar, and, oh my God, the person who made those pants needed to receive some kind of award. Life was perfect, perfect, perfect.

"You okay there, Big Time?" Zack said.

"I'm good," Terry responded.

"Celebrating Sandy?" Zack asked.

"Yeah. Give me a minute," Terry responded, tilting his head slightly to the left. "I'm just going to make absolutely sure she gets back to the bar without any problems." Damn. She even walked great. "Okay." He pulled himself back to Zack. "Where were we? Doing something very important, right?"

"Right. Deciding which of these private investigators to see first." Zack handed some papers to Terry.

Part of the file that Cal's accountant had given them was a fat printout of names and addresses and dates and amounts of money spent on various private investigators between the time that Cal's wife and son were killed and the time he shot the people in that apartment. He had hired literally dozens of investigators. And the amount of money he had spent was in the hundreds of thousands of dollars. The guy really was nuts. Terry gave the papers back to Zack.

"I don't know," Terry said. "What do you think? Talk to the one he spent the most money on?"

"I was thinking about talking to the one he used last," Zack said, just as Sandy returned with the beers.

As Zack ordered some pasta and chicken thing, Terry carefully and subtly made sure that while Sandy had been away, nothing had happened to her shirt or pants. Or anything else. When she turned to him, he ordered a steak.

As she left to put in the order, Zack continued. "I'm still not exactly sure what we're doing here, but I really want to understand what was going on in Cal's mind when he decided to go into that apartment."

Terry said, "Yeah. I'm still not so sure about what we're doing, either. I mean, who cares what he thought? If he's not going to say he was insane, what difference does it make? So what if he thought they were terrorists?

He meant to kill them, and he killed them. I don't see how that helps us."

"I just can't let go of the fact that he did all this research," Zack said. "I mean, what did he find? What made him think that killing six people was the right thing to do? I just have this instinct that the jury needs to hear the whole story."

"Are you thinking jury nullification?" Terry asked. Talk about Hail Marys. In technical terms, jury nullification was when a jury acquitted a defendant regardless of the facts proven at the trial. In reality, it was the defendant saying to the jury, "We all know I did it, but I think you should vote not guilty because, let's face it, I really look good in this tie." O.J. pulled it off. And in about half the TV lawyer shows, the defendant pulled it off.

But in real life, approximately nobody pulled it off.

"I don't know," Zack said. "I'm starting to think that might be all we have."

"Oh, God," Terry said. "Cottonwood is going to love this. I'm looking forward to our conversation with him about how the lifestyles of the victims are relevant to whether they were murdered."

"It's not like we've got a lot of options here," Zack said. "And if we're going to have any chance of convincing Cottonwood to let this stuff in, we're going to have to have something more than Cal's testimony. He's never going to let him just get up there and say 'I shot them because they were terrorists.' " He handed the printout back to Terry. "Why don't we do this? You start calling the investigators. In whatever order you think is best. I just want to see if we can meet with the ones that were working on the six people that Cal shot."

"Okay," Terry said. "And while I do that, you get in a few extra sessions at the tanning booth."

"Sure," Zack said. "And maybe I'll also be working

on some pretrial motions. I'm getting a little tired of our guy getting bashed so regularly in the media, but I've got to be careful how I play this." It seemed like every day another newspaper article came out, reminding everyone about the bloodbath. And making Cal look about as sympathetic as, well, as a mass murderer. Every Monday, in the left-hand column of the front page, under Cal's mug shot and a picture of an electric chair, with the title "The Hangman's News"—what a class act—the *Post* published the results of their latest poll about the Thompkins case: Guilty, Not Guilty, or Undecided. So far, the returns were not encouraging. "I've got to do some research."

Sandy returned with their salads, another round of beer, and another smile. As she left, Terry said to Zack, "I just wanted to let you know that I am fully aware you brought me to dinner here so I'd say yes to whatever you suggested." He watched as Sandy disappeared into the kitchen. "And I also wanted to let you know that it is working perfectly."

Worcester, Massachusetts

FOR A TINY LITTLE GIRL, NATALIE REGGIO WAS turning out to be a pretty big pain in Sergeant Pete Vanderwall's butt.

Pete was looking over the reports that his officers had written up about the bar fight last week. Natalie was the only material witness that had yet to give a statement.

And according to Patrolman Freddy Kramer, she absolutely refused to talk to anybody about anything that happened that night until she talked to the officer who had taken her to the hospital.

Pete had no problem with interviewing witnesses and writing up reports. But he didn't like the idea of witnesses, victims, drunken brawlers, and/or subjects of criminal investigations controlling police procedures, so he intended to take his time before going to see her. There really was no rush in getting her statement. Most of the other witnesses had already filled in all of the blanks. It was a run-of-the-mill barroom brawl, starring Natalie and her drunken boyfriend.

But Pete liked to run a tight ship, and that included putting a statement in the case file from every material witness in an investigation. Natalie Reggio's stubborn refusal to talk was an irritant that he didn't need. She had a lot of nerve acting like this after almost getting herself killed that night. Talk about ungrateful.

Whenever Pete finally got to the hospital, he was going to give Natalie Reggio something very serious to think about.

Wakefield, Massachusetts

BY THE TIME CAL RECEIVED THE ENVELOPE, HE had already forgotten that he had asked for it.

A few days after the shooting, a minister had come to see Cal and ask if there was anything he needed. He told Cal that soon after the shooting and the arrest, he had been asked by Steve Doctorow to go to the hospital and visit him.

The only thing Cal could think of was to ask for information about his court-appointed lawyer. Except for the time he had been unjustifiably hassled by police in college when he had been out for a late-night run, Cal had absolutely no experience with the criminal justice system. From movies and TV, he believed that all court-appointed lawyers were well intentioned but inexperienced, and barely better than having no lawyer at all. So Cal had hoped to find out what he could about Zachary Wilson, to prepare himself in advance for the worst.

The small manila envelope had already been opened by the guards. It contained a short, handwritten note from Steve and a newspaper article. Cal read the note first.

Dear Cal,

I can't imagine what you're going through. I tried to come see you at the hospital as soon as I heard you were arrested, but the police wouldn't let me in.

Anyway, this is the only thing I could find on Attorney Wilson. He seems like a good lawyer, and a good guy, too. Not exactly what I expected, but better than I hoped.

If you need anything, please write to me, or call me, if they let you.

—Steve

The article was in a newspaper called *The Lawyer's Weekly,* and it was titled "Adopting a New Set of Priorities." It was a full-page article, on the front page of the second section of the paper. But Cal never even read the first line. There was a big picture of Zack, holding what looked like a three- or four-year-old little boy on his hip with one arm. Zack's mouth was open, as if he were making a face, or singing, and the boy was laughing.

Cal felt a strange, sudden congestion between his eyes, as if his sinuses were flooding. His gaze lowered to the caption of the picture.

Attorney Zachary Wilson and his son Justin share a joke on their way to Justin's preschool.

Cal's eyes involuntarily drifted back up to the picture. The little boy didn't look a lot like Zack. He had dark hair and a round face. It was possible that he had some Native American blood.

His name was Justin. And when he laughed, he hugged himself.

Cal felt a spasm shake him and heard himself sob. It surprised him. His eyes were watering. He swiped at them, but he couldn't bring himself to look away from the picture. His head ached. The picture blurred. He wiped the tears away again. The little boy's face was gleeful. And when he laughed, he wrapped his little arms around himself, as if he were so happy that he might burst.

And this time when the sobbing started, Cal wasn't able to stop it. He just started to cry. Loud and hard. Tears ran down his face like rivers. Giant, sloppy sobbing noises came from him. He gasped for breath. His nose was running. A guard came over to his cell door to ask what was wrong. Cal ignored him. His gaze remained fixed on the now very blurry little boy, hugging himself while he laughed.

But all he could see was an image of Kevin. Because that was exactly what Kev used to do when he laughed.

Detroit, Michigan

"DETROIT POLICE. THIS CALL IS BEING RE-corded," the voice on the phone said. Why was it that the people who answered phones at police stations had such nasty voices?

"May I speak to Officer Halsey, please?" said Lena.

"Your name?"

"Lena Takamura."

"Please hold."

After over a week of chasing him on the phone, Lena was finally going to get to speak to the elusive Officer Halsey.

To be fair, her trouble connecting with him hadn't been all his fault. Lena's hours at the restaurant and at the convenience store were totally random and way confusing. She was so afraid that she'd forget when to go to work that she had to write her schedule on a piece of paper and tape it to the kitchen counter.

But even with her crazy schedule, Lena had managed to leave Officer Halsey several messages since she'd discovered that the 911 transcript had been altered, letting him know that she just wanted to ask him a few questions about the LeClerq case. For a uniformed patrolman, he sure was busy. He'd only left her one message in return, saying that he would be sure to be available today, at five P.M.

The problem was that as soon as he picked up the phone, Lena knew how the conversation was going to turn out. He'd say that all he did was write in his report what Giselle said to him, and that if Giselle said something different now, well, there was nothing he could do about it except write up another report saying that she'd changed her story. Then Lena would say that one of the reasons she asked was because of the altered 911 transcripts. He'd say that he had nothing to do with that and had no idea what she was talking about.

And Lena's world-record streak of finding non-stories would be intact.

Then Becca's voice came over the phone. "Lena?"

"Hey, Becca. What's up?"

"Nothing much. I heard them call your name over the intercom—"

"Yeah, I'm holding for Halsey. I finally got him to say that he would speak to me—"

"That's why I picked up," Becca interrupted. "I just found out that Halsey quit."

"What?" That couldn't be right. Lena had gotten the message he'd left for her about three days ago. "What happened? Where'd he go?"

"I don't know," Becca replied. "I heard somebody say his father got sick and he needed to go back to Los Angeles, or Las Vegas, or something. I mean, these guys have emergency leave, if they want it. I have no idea why he quit."

"Was he in trouble or something?" Lena asked.

"No idea," Becca answered. "Listen, I gotta go. I'll call you when I get home, okay?"

"Okay, bye," said Lena, hanging up.

A cop goes to a crime scene, lies on his report about a break-in, then tries to cover up the lie by altering the transcript of the 911 tape. Then he dodges phone calls for as long as he can, and finally quits?

It didn't make sense. But Lena's world-record streak was definitely in jeopardy.

Harvard, Massachusetts

AS EL AMIN BANKED THE SMALL AIRPLANE TO the left for another pass over the field, he recognized that he was going to have to make an adjustment for the weight of the cargo, but otherwise, everything seemed to be working well.

Last week, he had measured the length and width of the park that the fools would all crowd into on their pretentious holiday. He walked each way twice, carefully making sure that his strides were consistent. Then he found an empty field near the small airport that housed his low-speed Cessna and marked off the dimensions of the park so that he could see them from the air.

He made several passes back and forth over the field, until he knew exactly how long it would take for him to fly from one end to the other and then turn around and make another pass. Given the size of the crowd and the chaos that was sure to follow, he expected that he'd be able to drop six and maybe even twelve grenades before he delivered his final blow.

He checked the altimeter, reached into the crate, and dropped the first rock out of the small window to his left, just as he started the stopwatch with his other hand. Then he dropped another, and then a third. Later he would check to see where they landed to be sure they hit within the boundaries of the park. The calculations were precise. Dropped from approximately three hundred feet, the kill zone would be at its maximum. Depending on how many he was able to successfully drop, and how close people were standing together, he could kill hundreds before the spectacular finale.

With God's help, even when they closed their eyes, they would still see the carnage.

TEN

Dear Kevin,

The doctor says I've got to write you a letter, but [illegible] anything

(Letter #1 from Calvin Thompkins to deceased son, Kevin)

DIST. ATTY. O'NEILL: *Do you recall where you were at approximately 3:15 on the afternoon of January 14?*

MR. HICKSON: *Yeah. I was walkin' home with some friends of mine down by McDonald's.*

Q: *Were you coming from McDonald's?*

A: *Yeah.*

Q: *And where was this, exactly? What street were you on?*

A: *Oak Street.*

Q: *In Northampton?*

A: *[The witness nods.]*

Q: *You have to answer yes or no.*

A: *Yes. Northampton.*

Q: *Where is Oak Street relative to Main Street in Northampton? If you know.*

A: *It's right behind it.*

Q: *And while you were walking with your friends, did you notice anything unusual?*

A: *Well, there was gunshots, and these windows were breaking. And then this dude in a bathrobe comes crashing out the third-floor window and falls into the courtyard right in front of us. Smack on his face.*

Q: *Where was this?*

A: *At this building on Main Street.*

Q: *214 Main Street?*

A: *I don't know the address.*

Q: *Okay. Did you see the condition of the individual that fell?*

A: *His condition? He just fell three stories out a window. His condition was dead.*

Q: *Okay. What did you do then?*

A: *Everybody else started running, but I just stood there. I ain't seen nothin' like that before. Then I hear this screaming, and I look up, and this other dude is screaming his head off, looking out the window the first dude fell out, down into the courtyard. Then he turns around, and then I heard more shooting. And that's it. I left.*

Q: *Could you describe the expression on the face of the individual that was screaming? The one that came to the window?*

A: *It was crazy. He looked real mad. His mouth was wide open from the screaming. I don't know. He looked real mad.*

Q: *And had you ever seen this individual before?*

A: *Naw. I never seen the dude before in my life. He*

was some old dude. Probably about thirty or forty years old.

Q: *Do you see him in the courtroom today?*

A: *[No response.]*

Q: *Mr. Hickson.*

THE COURT: *Mr. Hickson. Do you see the individual that Mr. O'Neill just asked you about in the courtroom today?*

THE WITNESS: *I gotta answer?*

THE COURT: *Yes.*

THE WITNESS: *Will I go to jail if I don't answer?*

THE COURT: *Yes. I order you to answer the question. If you don't answer, I'll hold you in contempt of court.*

A: *Yeah. I see him.*

Q: *Can you point him out for the jury, please?*

A: *He's sitting right over there. The black dude at that table, sitting next to the two white dudes.*

Q: *May the record reflect that the witness has identified the defendant?*

THE COURT: *Yes.*

(Trial Volume VI, Pages 111–112)

March 14—Northampton, Massachusetts

DISTRICT ATTORNEY FRANCIS X. O'NEILL HAD just finished checking his calendar to make sure that next week's lunch appointments were all with sufficiently important people when Frieda's voice came over the intercom and rained on his parade.

"Mr. O'Neill? Superintendent Mekita is on line one."

F.X. slammed shut his appointment book and gritted his teeth. Mekita ran the prison where Thompkins was being held. There was no reason for a call unless there was bad news. He hated bad news. And he hated even more not knowing what the bad news was going to be. He relaxed his jaw just enough to say "Did he say what he wanted?"

"Not exactly, sir," Frieda replied. "He just said he wanted to give you a heads-up about something. Would you like me to find out—"

"Never mind," said F.X., punching the button for line one. He grabbed the phone. "O'Neill."

"Uh, yes, Mr. O'Neill, this is Superintendent Robert Mekita at MCI-Wakefield," the voice said. "How are you today?"

F.X. didn't normally deal with superintendents, because aside from running the prisons, they weren't of any particular use to him. The very fact that Mekita would call him directly was goddamn irritating. There was no reason for it, other than to try to appear important.

But you never know when someone might need to do you a favor, so F.X. decided to make nice, even though he was having a hard time containing himself. He needed to know what had happened to Thompkins. You couldn't very well prosecute and execute somebody who got killed in a prison fight.

Get on with it. "Fine, Bobby, fine. How are things up in Wakefield? Is Kathy Gates still working in records? Her husband, Walt, is working out of the Middlesex D.A.'s office, you know."

"Is that right? You know, I'm not even sure if Ms. Gates is still in our records department," Mekita answered. "I should make a note to check on that."

There was a pause. For the love of God, was he ever

going to get around to what happened to Thompkins? F.X. couldn't stand it.

"So how can I help the good people at MCI-Wakefield, Robert?" he asked finally.

"Well," Mekita started, "I really just called out of professional courtesy. As you know, Inmate Calvin Thompkins has been in our custody since he was released from the hospital, and I wanted to inform you that he apparently has had some kind of nervous breakdown and has been transferred to Bridgewater for an evaluation."

F.X. knew he wasn't the world's greatest lawyer, but he sure as hell knew when the press was gonna come knocking. At least Thompkins wasn't dead. But it made no sense to sit around and wait to see if the press was going to try to find a way to make this clown sympathetic. They'd already gone public with the deaths of his wife and kid. "When was this, now?" F.X. asked.

"Transportation took him over this morning," Mekita replied. "I guess he started acting up yesterday—"

"Listen, Bobby," F.X. interrupted, placing his finger on the disconnect button. "I'm sure you can understand—" and right in the middle of speaking, he hit the button, killing the connection. It was a trick he'd seen a defense attorney use once, and he loved it. He imagined that very important people used it often. It ended unnecessary conversations without any embarrassment. Who would ever think that people would hang up on themselves? Mekita would have gone on and on, and the district attorney had important things to do.

"Frieda," he called out, flipping his appointment book open again. "Please call Mr. Mekita back, and tell him I'm sorry we got cut off, and that I told you to reconnect us, but that in the meantime, I got pulled away to an important meeting. And then get me Denny Garrity over at the *Post.* Oh, and have Stacey bring the Thompkins case autopsy reports in here right away."

He was going to have to get that pregnancy thing going sooner than he'd thought.

March 24—Natick, Massachusetts

AS TERRY BLASTED CLASSIC AEROSMITH THROUGH his Lexus's stereo, Zack's mind drifted to Cal's case. One of the ways to establish an insanity defense would be to show that Cal had a mental defect that caused him to be unable to control his actions. Could the sudden, violent death of his family create that kind of a mental defect? Was blind vengeance the result of a mental defect? Had Cal truly lost the ability to control his actions?

Suddenly, the music stopped, and Terry spoke. "Are you loving the ride in this baby, or what?"

Terry was all about cars. Actually, Terry was all about a lot of stuff.

"Isn't this the same car you've had for, like, three years?" Zack asked.

"A year and a half," replied Terry. "But I just got new tires. There's a whole new feel to it now."

"Well, it still smells good," Zack said.

"Probably something about my no-four-year-olds-eating-French-fries-in-the-backseat rule."

As they pulled off the Mass Pike onto the exit for Framingham, Zack's cell phone rang.

"Zack Wilson," he answered.

"Hi, Attorney Wilson, this is Adrianna Pino, from News Six." On his cell phone? "I was wondering if you had any comment on the transfer of your client to Bridgewater State Hospital."

According to the doctors, when Cal started hunting terrorists, he was merely postponing the time when he really let himself feel the loss of his family. And after he was arrested for the shootings in the apartment, his grief finally caught up with him and completely overwhelmed him. He was going to be in pretty bad emotional shape for a while.

"Excuse me, how did you get this number?" Zack asked.

The persistent Ms. Pino ignored the question. "Can you confirm reports that he's suffered a nervous breakdown?"

Zack had a policy of being available by phone from four to five in his office every weekday afternoon. Normally, that meant available to his clients, but ever since he'd taken Cal's case, he'd pretty much spent that hour of the day fielding phone calls from the press. His cell phone number was kept private for emergencies. The four thousandth attempt by the media to obtain a quote on Cal's case did not exactly constitute an emergency.

"I'm sorry, ma'am, but we're not interested in making public statements about this case," Zack said. "And please don't use this phone number again, or tell anyone else about it." He turned off the phone's ringer and flipped it closed.

"That'll show 'em," Terry said dryly, fiddling with some new device he had recently bought that supposedly helped navigate routes to unfamiliar destinations. Just what Terry needed. Something else to yell at when he got hopelessly lost. "Those vultures really piss me off." He stopped at a red light, pressed another button on the device, and the display on the automatic navigator screen changed. "Aha!" he exclaimed. "Here we go. I make a left onto Route 135, and then a right into Natick Center. This is going to be easy."

"Strikingly similar to the directions you got over the phone," Zack said.

"Don't mock the technology," Terry replied, as he made the left turn. "One day you may be lost in the middle of a strange city, and this thing will save your life."

"Yeah, if I suddenly and inexplicably lose the ability to use a map or a telephone, or forget how to stop and ask for directions from someone else," Zack countered.

"I can't hear you," Terry said. "I'm too busy concentrating on how much better my life is now that I have an advanced navigational system in my car." He signaled to make a right turn and pulled onto a one-way street.

"I'd still like to know how that reporter got my cell phone number," Zack said. "That's just great."

Terry came to another red light and looked over at Zack. "By the way, it's also great that every week I get to read 'The Hangman's News,' or listen to that jackass O'Neill give another press conference, or watch another paper reprint that stunning mug shot of Cal on the front page. One of these days, I'd like to say something other than 'No comment' to these idiot papers about their idiot polls about how guilty our idiot client is."

Terry was right. The media and Fran O'Neill were proving to be absolutely shameless. But Zack never tried his cases in the press. And even if he had wanted to, everything he or Terry might say would be printed under another full-page picture of Cal's horror movie head shot.

"This whole thing sucks," Terry said, checking his new gizmo.

They turned right again, and passed a couple of good-looking women. The one with the long dark hair was walking a puppy. Justin asked for a puppy about once a week. It was a tempting idea.

Then they made another turn onto a one-way street that looked very similar to the one they had been on a few minutes ago. "By the way, are we lost yet?" Zack asked.

"Shut up," Terry said, slowing down as he approached the next intersection and turning left. They were heading into a rundown part of town. "I know exactly where we are." He checked his navigational device. "According to my calculations, we should be just about at the corner of Holbrook Lane." He looked up at the passing street sign and read out loud, "Iris Street." He pulled over to the side of the road, punched a few buttons on the screen, and then said, to no one in particular, "Fuck me naked."

As soon as Terry figured out how to get there, they'd be visiting Johnny Rychek, a private eye that Terry had said actually sounded promising. Most of the others he'd spoken to were dead ends. One investigator had spent nearly a hundred thousand dollars flying all over Europe and Africa, chasing down some bogus leads Cal had gotten from the Internet. Another had taken weeks to research and then shadow a supposedly suspicious man through California and Arizona only to find that he was nothing more than a harmless tourist from the Middle East.

When it was all said and done, the accountant's printout of Cal's expenditures on investigators turned out to be little more than a blueprint for spending an astonishing amount of money in a relatively short amount of time.

Finally, Terry pulled into the driveway of a small, worn-down white house with a sign on the front door that read "Rychek Investigations." A tall chain-link fence separated it on one side from a lumberyard's storage area. On the other side was another small house where a tired-looking, mud-spattered dog was patrolling the front yard, which was littered with spare tires, a rusted shopping cart, and what looked to be two to three weeks' worth of garbage.

Suddenly the notion of getting a puppy for Justin didn't seem so appealing.

"You sure you don't want me to go to Florida with Justin instead?" Terry asked, as they emerged from the car, watching the dog walk over to Rychek's front yard and pee on the remains of a dead shrub. "I know you're going to miss it here in the glamorous world of criminal defense."

Long before he had taken Cal's case, Zack had set up a one-week vacation for himself and Justin at Disney World. The next pretrial court appearance before Judge Baumgartner was scheduled for the week after they returned. So Zack would go to Orlando for a week and do nothing but take it easy and have fun with his son.

Terry knocked on the front door and a thin man with a portable phone pinned between his ear and his shoulder let them in and gestured for them to follow him. The place smelled disgusting—like a mix of moldy food and stale smoke—and looked worse than it smelled.

The man was on the phone listening to someone named Eduardo explain why some job hadn't yet been done. He led them down a dim hallway leading to the back of the house, and just before they turned into his office he lit the cigarette that was hanging from his lips. He blew out the match and tossed it onto the floor of the hallway. Mr. Hospitality.

"That's bullshit and you know it," Rychek said into the phone. He cleared some papers from the two chairs that were in front of his desk and motioned for them to sit. Zack sat down. Terry started to pace. "Why not?" he said into the phone again. The smoke from the lit cigarette curled around his head. "Okay. Relax, Eduardo, relax. Take it easy, for Chrissakes. Just take the picture." Another pause. "No. Listen to me. Take the picture. I'm hemorrhaging money here. Use your head, find the guy, and take the picture, okay? Call me later."

He hung up, put the phone down on top of the nearest pile on the desk, and smiled apologetically. "Sorry, guys. My wife's younger brother. Good kid, but I swear to God he's a fuckin' moron, you know what I mean?" He reached over the desk and held out his hand. "Johnny Rychek," he said. "You must be the lawyers. Terry, right? And Zack?" They shook hands. "How's my man Cal? I heard from his accountant, Steve Moldock—"

"Doctorow," Zack interjected.

"Right." He put out his cigarette butt in one of the ashtrays on his desk. "That you'd probably be out to see me. I read in the papers that Cal's in a jackpot. I'm real sorry to hear that. Cal's a class guy. A real gentleman, you know? Scary picture, though, huh?"

"Yeah," Terry said. "Well, we're looking to find out what you were working on for Cal. He's told us some pretty amazing things about these people he shot in that apartment."

Rychek lit another cigarette, squinting through the smoke. "I got just what you're looking for."

He went over to a bookcase that stood against the wall to the left of his desk and started picking through the stacks and stacks of videos and audiotapes that cluttered the shelves. "I know I got 'em here somewhere," Rychek continued. "Cal told me I gotta destroy all my paper files, but I saved the tapes."

Zack looked over at Terry. *What?*

"Wait a minute," Terry said. "Did you just say that Cal told you to destroy your files?"

Rychek kept digging through the tapes. "Yeah. He said these people were terrorists and that I needed to protect myself. He said that if they found out I was spying on them, they might come after me. So he said I had to destroy all my files."

Worcester, Massachusetts

POLICE SERGEANT PETE VANDERWALL WASN'T surprised when he found Natalie Reggio awake in her bed at one-thirty in the morning. They had spoken on the phone, and he had told her that he was pulling an overnight shift and only would be able to stop by after midnight to take her statement. She had left her door ajar, and he knocked before he went in.

If anything, she looked smaller in the hospital bed than when he'd brought her here after the bar fight. Her head was bandaged, and there was some bruising around one of her eyes and on the left side of her forehead, but otherwise, she just looked tired and little.

According to the nurse on duty that night, her full name was Natalie Jean Reggio. She was seventeen years old, and had suffered a fractured skull as a result of the fight at Rockets. By the time Pete had brought her in, her blood alcohol level was above .20, and she had slipped into a coma from the blow to her head. Fortunately, she emerged from the coma the next day, but there had been brain swelling, so she had to remain in the hospital for some time. She was lucky to be alive.

From the other officers' reports, Pete had learned that Natalie had gone to Rockets with her boyfriend, a kid named Nick, and everybody was drinking. Another girl, named Robin, was dancing a little closer to Nick than Natalie liked, so she threw a drink in Robin's face. Robin and Natalie started to fight, which would have been bad enough if Robin's boyfriend hadn't come over to help. Nick got in his way, a bouncer came over to break up Robin and Natalie, one thing led to another, and suddenly people were on the floor, and chairs and tables were flying all over the place.

Exactly how Natalie got the injury to her head remained a mystery. There were two leading theories: she had gotten hit with a beer bottle, or she had slipped and fallen off a table, but that was something for the D.A. or a jury to figure out. All Pete wanted to do was to get a statement and get back to the station.

There was an older woman asleep in the other bed in the room, so Natalie was watching the TV muted. She turned it off when she saw Pete. He left the door open as he entered the room, got his pad and a pen out of his pocket, and took a seat beside her bed. "I'm Sergeant Pete Vanderwall—" he began to say, but she cut him off.

"I know who you are," she said softly. "You're the one that saved my life. I—I wanted to get a chance to apologize to you for my behavior." She met his gaze head-on. This was something new—a kid who was willing to take responsibility. "And to say thank you for what you did that night." Her eyes welled up with tears, but she pushed ahead. "I don't remember everything that happened, but I do remember calling you"—she took a deep breath and kept going—"calling you an asshole, and trying to kick you. I can't tell you how embarrassed . . ." was as far as she got. Her voice broke, and her gaze fell. The tears rolled down her cheeks.

Pete reached for some tissues that were on the wheeled bed tray and handed them to the kid. She wiped her face and gently blew her nose. She was obviously still in a lot of pain. She was tiny, but she had guts. He couldn't remember the last teenager in her kind of trouble that had the balls to face up to what they'd done and apologize like that.

If this had happened when he was a rookie, Pete would have assumed that such a traumatic event would scare Natalie into completely and immediately turning her life around. But after years of watching kids self-destruct, he had moved squarely into the "I'll believe it when I see it" camp. Maybe Natalie was going to surprise him and actually do something with her life. But it was going to take a whole lot more than a tearful apology, no matter how gutsy, before he would start to feel hopeful for her. She was probably well on her way to being a full-time drunk. Would she go to AA meetings? Would she dump all the friends that she hung out with, the ones that drank every weekend, maybe every night? Would she spend her day working or going to school, instead of hanging around malls, convenience store parking lots, and bars? Natalie had a lot of issues to face, a lot of questions to answer.

"All right, Natalie, I appreciate that," Pete said. "But right now, I need you to calm down and tell me what happened that night. You can start by telling me how you got into that bar, and what you were doing drinking at your age."

Framingham, Massachusetts

"I'M GOING TO KILL HIM MYSELF," TERRY ANnounced. "Never mind the trial. I'm just going to kill him myself."

Terry had a point, but he was already doing over

eighty-five on the Mass Pike. He didn't need any more encouragement. "At least we got the tapes," Zack replied.

Terry switched lanes to pass an eighteen-wheeler. "Yeah. A completely inadmissible audiotape of phone conversations in Arabic, which, if we're lucky, are half audible," he said. "And a videotape of unrecognizable people coming in and out of an apartment building. If I were the D.A., I'd set him free right now."

"It's more than we had when we started," Zack countered. "Maybe while I'm out of town, you can find somebody to translate the tape for you."

Terry made a sound of disgust. "It's like he set out to commit the perfect crime. Kill a bunch of people, stay there until the cops come, admit it, and then make sure that whatever evidence might possibly help you is destroyed. The guy's a freakin' criminal genius."

Terry definitely had a point.

ELEVEN

DIST. ATTY. O'NEILL: *Can you describe what you saw when you arrived?*

MR. WALLACE: *Yes. Well, my partner and me went into the apartment, because another unit was responding to a victim in the hallway.*

Q: *You mean the defendant?*

A: *Yeah. I guess so. I didn't really see because I went right into the apartment.*

Q: *And what did you see when you went into the apartment?*

A: *It was incredible. I never seen anything like it in ten years working as a paramedic.*

Q: *Well, can you describe what you saw?*

A: *There was bodies laying all over the place, and blood everywhere. It was like a war zone.*

(Trial Volume VI, Page 180)

Dear Kev,

It's hard for me to write these letters, because I miss you so much. And I feel so bad.

I can't stop thinking about everything that happened that day, and I'm afraid you might have been scared, or you might have suffered

I can't do this.

(Letter #6 from Calvin Thompkins to deceased son, Kevin)

SENATOR WILBRAHAM: *Mr. Curko, what was your position in the Graham administration?*

MR. CURKO: *My official title was Special Assistant to the President, Director of Communications. But my role in President Graham's administration was speechwriter. I was President Graham's head speechwriter.*

Q: *And did you stay on in that capacity after President Graham's death?*

A: *Yes, at first I did. When President Ferguson took office, he asked—I think he asked the entire senior staff to stay on, to assist him in his transition.*

Q: *Why did you ultimately resign?*

A: *Well, I didn't feel that I was the right person for what President Ferguson needed in that position. When I served in President Graham's administration, speeches were prepared for him well in advance, leaving ample time for his review, staff meetings if necessary, revisions, et cetera. From the first day that President Ferguson took office, it was clear that he had a very different style of communicating with the public.*

Q: *Are you talking about his first speech as President?*

A: *Exactly. Apparently, he wrote that entirely by himself, hours before he made the speech. I didn't have anything to do with it.*

Q: *You weren't consulted at all?*

A: *No. I thought some of the speech was remarkable,*

but I would have suggested alternatives to certain passages had I been given the opportunity.

Q: *Mr. Curko, in your capacity as head speechwriter, were you familiar with an individual named Charles Cullhane?*

A: *Yes. Charley Cullhane was one of the junior staff members in the Communications Office. He resigned for personal reasons shortly after President Ferguson took office.*

Q: *But he worked for some time in the Graham administration?*

A: *Yes. He came on board during the first year of President Graham's term.*

Q: *Were you Mr. Cullhane's supervisor?*

A: *I guess you could call it that, yes. Charley reported directly to me.*

Q: *At any time, did you order Mr. Cullhane to prepare memoranda compiling certain information regarding federal judges or potential nominees for appointment to federal judgeships?*

[Witness consulting with counsel.]

A: *At no time did I ever order Mr. Cullhane to prepare any such memos.*

Q: *Were you aware that Mr. Cullhane prepared such memos?*

A: *No, I was not.*

Q: *Were you aware of anyone in the administration ordering Mr. Cullhane to prepare such memos?*

A: *No, I was not.*

Q: *When did you become aware of the existence of memoranda which compiled such information?*

[Witness consulting with counsel.]

A: *I believe that it was in May, about a month after I resigned. I was contacted by a member of Vernon Browning's office, who informed me about the existence of the memos.*

(Transcripts of the Special Senate Subcommittee Hearing on the Cullhane Memos, Volume XV, Pages 85–87)

April 6—Washington, D.C.

MATT AND SAMMY HAD JUST FINISHED A LATE dinner at the residence—some kind of salmon thing that Sammy loved and that Matt tolerated. But the blueberry pie à la mode was really working for him. Sammy wasn't a big dessert person unless chocolate was involved.

"I ran into Veronica Graham at a luncheon today," Matt said. "She asked me if I had a chance to look at that laptop she dropped off after Jim's funeral."

"Did you tell her about those memos you were wondering about?"

Matt had spoken to Sammy about that mystery some time ago. "No," he said. "I didn't see the point."

"Mmm-hmm. Did you tell her that you gave the computer to creepy Vernon Browning?"

From the first moment that she met him, Sammy had distrusted Browning. But for Matt, especially on the day the world turned upside down, the man had been a godsend.

It had all happened so suddenly. At 9:05 that morning, Matt was sitting at his desk, reading through an endless pile of political aides' résumés. He had no experience in putting together the kind of staff that he needed, and no political connections, so he was starting at absolute zero. Add to that Matt's natural reluctance to delegate, and the frequent interruptions for actual vice-presidential duties—a weeklong trip to attend the NATO conference in Iceland, an even longer visit to Poland, Hungary, and then Russia for economic meetings, an endless number of important funerals and political fund-raisers—and Matt's progress in assembling his staff was embarrassingly slow. For a man who was first in the line of succession to the most important job in the world, Matt's offices were startlingly underpopulated. A secretary, a few temporary assistants on loan from the White House, a handful of interns.

Until 9:06, when a dozen Secret Service agents burst into Matt's office and carried him, just about literally, to an underground bunker, where he was soon joined by the National Security Advisor and the Speaker of the House.

And at 9:25 A.M., the three of them sat staring at a speakerphone in the middle of a conference table, as the Chief of Medicine at Walter Reed Army Hospital explained to them that at 9:17 that morning, President Graham had been pronounced dead of an aneurysm.

In the hours that followed, Browning was everywhere. He worked tirelessly with the Press Secretary, the Director of Communications, and the rest of his staff to manage the tremendous flow of information that was surging through the media. He seemed to be continually on the phone with senior members of Congress. And knowing that Matt had not had an opportunity to put together any kind of staff to support him in the White House, Browning offered to stay on as Chief of Staff for as long as Matt needed him. Then, at Matt's request, he organized and attended emergency meetings with the Cabinet and then with senior staff, so Matt could ask each and every one of them, as a personal favor to him and, more important, as a favor to the country, if they would stay on in their capacities while Matt finished out the final year of President Graham's term of office.

"I told her that I skimmed through what was stored on the computer and then I gave it to *Chief of Staff* Browning, who stayed on at his post at my request, by the way, and who continues to be an invaluable assistant in my transition." He held out a forkful of the pie to Sammy. "Are you sure you don't want any of this?"

Sammy made a face. "That doesn't keep him from being creepy," she retorted. "And Veronica Graham knows he's creepy, too. So what did she say when you told her?"

Matt redirected the fork to his own mouth. Oh, boy. Sammy had no idea what she was missing. "She said that she was sorry about adding something else to my busy schedule, but she was afraid there might have been something important on the computer, and then she said that she was sure that Vernon would be able to answer any questions I had."

"Mmm-hmm," Sammy said. "I bet she did."

"What is that supposed to mean?"

"Nothing," she said. Which, in the language of Sammy, really meant *something, but you aren't ready to believe it yet.* They'd come back to it. "Then what happened?"

"Then she handed me a small case of CDs," Matt said, "and told me that she'd found them as she was unpacking after the move. She thought Jim might have used them on the laptop, and so she decided, just to be safe, that she'd give them to me to look into in case there was something sensitive on them."

"So, did you check to see if they had those memos on them?"

"Yeah. They aren't there." Dessert was finished. Damn.

"So what's the problem?" Sammy asked.

"I don't get it. Veronica Graham's a very bright woman. First she goes out of her way to hand me a computer which she's afraid has sensitive things on it, which it doesn't, and then she gives me a bunch of CDs because she's afraid that they might have sensitive things on them, which they don't. Why is she giving this stuff to me? She knows how much time all this takes. She knows how valuable a President's time is. I had to blow off two important meetings to go through those useless CDs. She's acting like this is some giant priority . . ."

"Maybe it is. Maybe you just haven't seen what she wants you to see."

"But if she wanted me to see something, why doesn't she just come out and show me?" Matt argued.

"What if she can't?" Sammy replied. "What if whatever she wants you to see is too controversial or painful for her to be direct? Whatever it is, though, you can be sure that she didn't give the computer to Vernon Browning for a reason."

"Oh, please," Matt said.

"Oh, please yourself," Sammy responded. "I've seen her look at that man, and she doesn't trust him any more than I do." She paused for a moment. "I have no idea what's on that computer, or on those CDs, but I'm absolutely sure Veronica didn't show them to Vernon Browning because she didn't want Vernon Browning to see them."

"Which, as unreasonable as that is, still doesn't explain why, if there's something I need to know, she doesn't just tell me. I mean, all she'd have to do is point something out to me . . ." His voice trailed off.

"What is it, Matt?" Sammy asked.

"She *did* point something out to me," he said, pushing back from the table and heading for the door. "I know where the Cullhane memos are. They're in my briefcase in the library."

"Hey, wait for me," Sammy said, jumping up and following him. "I want to see, too."

Matt walked down the hall with Sammy until they reached the library. They entered the large room, and Matt walked over to his briefcase. "You know those CDs that Veronica gave me?" he said.

"I thought you looked at them already," Sammy replied.

"Not all of them. Two of the CDs in the case were music CDs." Matt took a couple of disks out of the briefcase and held them up. "*Sinatra Classics from the Fifties* and *Mozart's Clarinet Concerto.* I just figured Jim liked to listen to these while he was working, or maybe that they were stuck in there by mistake."

"Or maybe they were the only ones Veronica wanted you to pay attention to," Sammy said, as Matt sat down and started up the laptop he kept on the desk in the library. Sammy pulled over a chair and sat beside him.

"Just because they're labeled one thing doesn't mean . . ." His voice faded as he inserted the Sinatra CD into the computer. And sure enough, the disk contained text files, not music. Each file name was merely a number. Matt opened the file labeled number 1. A memo titled only *Judge John Swain, U.S. District Court, Arizona* was displayed on the screen. Matt read it silently, while Sammy looked over his shoulder. When they finished, Matt closed the file and opened number 2. That memo was titled *Judge Risa Abramson, U.S. District Court, New York.* Again Matt and Sammy read the memo. "You want to keep going?" Matt asked, looking back at Sammy. She nodded, very serious. Number 3 was titled *Judge Mitchell Stanton, U.S. District Court, Michigan.*

"That's the guy who killed himself," Matt said, as they began to read. When they were finished with that one, Matt closed the file, turned off the computer, and turned to his wife. He had never seen anything like this in his entire career. He didn't even know where to begin.

Sammy held out her hand, and he took it. "This is worse than I thought," she said quietly. "What are you going to do?"

Matt took a deep breath. "Well, it looks like the first thing I need to do is to talk to the former first lady," he told his wife. "I owe her at least that much."

Detroit, Michigan

LENA'S HOURS AT THE CONVENIENCE STORE ON Sunday were hideously early. She had to be there at five A.M. to open up with pompous Gary, receive all the papers, and get them ready for the day's rush.

So when she got home at two that afternoon, Lena was already dead tired, and definitely not up for another discouraging few hours futilely searching for Officer Halsey. Her plan was to spend the rest of the day on the couch, going through last week's obits and police blotters while she watched the Pistons. It wasn't that she really liked basketball—she just felt vaguely disloyal when she didn't watch. Everybody else in Detroit did. It was like some kind of Midwestern requirement.

When Lena went into the kitchen to get the stack of newspapers, though, they weren't on the counter by the phone, next to the refrigerator. That was weird. Well, okay, *maybe* that was weird.

That was the problem with being a messy person.

Lena never knew when she really lost something, or when she was just looking in the wrong place for it.

Like her DVD of *Dead Again*. Now, *that* was lost. Lena loved that movie—Kenneth Branagh and Emma Thompson were just perfect—and had spent hours one night looking all over her apartment for it when she just didn't want to watch anything else. In the end, she'd exhausted herself searching, spent a few minutes rereading an old letter she'd uncovered, and then fell asleep. She never did figure out where that DVD went. It was possible that she'd loaned it to somebody at school . . .

Anyway, she *knew* last week's newspapers were around here somewhere. She saw them just yesterday—or was it the day before?—when she'd been late to work and had spilled some coffee on the counter, next to where she'd taped her work schedule so at least she'd never lose that. Where could they be?

In the living room, she looked under the pile of junk mail that she'd left on the couch, and then under the magazines that she'd stacked up on the coffee table the other day in a totally unsuccessful effort at reorganizing her apartment that had lasted until she got distracted by a story in last month's *Rolling Stone*. Then she went into the bathroom and checked the magazine rack, which was overflowing with reading material dating back to her sophomore year. No luck.

Her last chance was the bedroom, and sure enough, there they were, sitting right on top of all of the other papers that she'd been keeping for the past however many years. Jeez. She really must be losing it. She couldn't believe that she'd stacked last week's newspapers on top of the already-read pile. She had absolutely no memory of doing that. It really was weird, because usually it took her forever to move papers onto the already-read pile.

Wait a minute. Not only did it take her forever to move papers into the already-read pile. She *never* moved them into that pile unless she actually had already read them. Lena may have been messy, but she was organized.

Okay. Maybe not exactly organized. The first time Becca saw Lena's apartment, she laughed for ten minutes and then said it looked like a recycling center that had been hit by a tornado. But despite the clutter, Lena knew where a lot of her stuff was. And she knew that she never moved unread stuff into the already-read pile.

In fact, if she were inclined to be paranoid, Lena would have suspected that somebody else moved those papers.

But that would have been stupid. Break into a messy person's place and move a few things around. What? To make them think somebody broke into her apartment? Sure. That was likely.

Oh, well. Lena grabbed the papers and headed out to the living room and turned on the TV.

After she spent five minutes looking for the remote.

TWELVE

Dear Kev—

I really wish I could send this letter to you. I miss you so much I can barely breathe sometimes. It's hard for me to get out of bed. All I want to do is cry.

All I do is cry.

I think about you and Mommy all the time. I miss you so much. I will see you again one day.

Love, Daddy

(Letter #14 from Calvin Thompkins to deceased son, Kevin)

Accused Mass Murderer to Be Reevaluated for Mental Impairment

Calvin Thompkins, the man authorities believe was responsible for the brutal murders of six U. Mass students this past January, is expected to soon be reevaluated by psychiatrists to determine whether he is sufficiently healthy to be transferred back to the prison where he had originally been awaiting trial. Attorneys for Thompkins have not been available for comment on Thompkins's recent transfer to the mental hospital and whether it would result in an attempt to raise an insanity defense at trial . . .

Boston Post polls show that public sentiment did not change significantly after Thompkins was transferred to the hospital and after it was learned that his wife and five-year-old son were killed in a terrorist bombing in 1998. The latest polls show that if put to a vote now, area citizens favor a guilty verdict by a margin of approximately eight to one, with about ten percent of those polled claiming to be undecided . . .

(*Boston Post*, April 14, page 1)

POSTMORTEM EXAMINATION: HELENE GHAZI

External: *The body is that of a well-developed, well-nourished twenty-year-old female approximately 64 inches long and weighing approximately 120 pounds . . .*

Injuries: *Gunshot wound to the neck, entering 1.5 cm to the left of midline at the posterior cervical vertebral column, traversing the trachea from left to right, perforating the common carotid arteries, and exiting at the midline . . .*

Multiple gunshot wounds to the chest . . .

Internal: *The gastrointestinal system, hepatobiliary system, and hemolymphatic system are free of anomaly. The urinary bladder contains 6 ml. of clear urine. The female genitals and reproductive organs and system are unremarkable and show no signs of lesions or injuries.*

Opinion: *Death is attributed to gunshot wound of the neck and multiple gunshot wounds to the chest . . .*

POSTMORTEM EXAMINATION: MARIANNE DUHAMEL

External: *The body is that of a well-developed, well-nourished twenty-one-year-old female approximately 68 inches long and weighing approximately 145 pounds . . .*

Injuries: *Gunshot wound to the head, entering the right temporal lobe . . . resulting in extensive cerebrocranial injury . . .*

Multiple gunshot wounds to the chest . . .

Internal: *The gastrointestinal system, hepatobiliary system, and hemolymphatic system are free of anomaly. The urinary bladder contains 11 ml. of clear urine.*

Opinion: *Death is attributed to gunshot wound of the head and multiple gunshot wounds to the chest . . .*

(Excerpts of the Autopsy Reports of Helene Ghazi and Marianne Duhamel, Trial Exhibits 45 and 46)

April 15—Holyoke, Massachusetts

SOMEWHERE, A DUCK WAS LYING BACK IN BED, smoking a cigarette.

Zack was in Florida, probably on some sandy white beach, drinking daiquiris with dozens of gorgeous women in bikinis. Cal was in the nuthouse, not nutty enough for them to get an insanity verdict, but just nutty enough not to be of any help at all. Last night, a reporter had called asking for Terry's comment on a rumor that the Commonwealth was going to try to exhume one of the victims' bodies because there was speculation that she was pregnant when Cal shot her.

And if that wasn't bad enough, it was now already ten minutes past the headache that Terry had gotten when he found out that Dr. Deborah Lanouche had been delayed by traffic.

Dr. Lanouche was the woman who was supposed to translate the audiotape that the investigator had given to them. She had been referred to Terry by the head of the Department of Arabic Studies at Northeastern University. Her credentials made her a perfect candidate for translating the tape and for testifying as an expert witness, if that was necessary. Terry hadn't even laid eyes on the woman, and she was already pissing him off.

It had nothing to do with the fact that she spoke Arabic fluently, or that she was late. It had to do with the fact that all expert witnesses had signed a secret pledge at some point in their lives, guaranteeing first that they would act like the most arrogant people on earth, and second, that when testifying at trials, they would work their asses off to try to prove to juries that they were smarter than the lawyers, instead of just doing what they were paid to do. Terry took comfort in the fact that she was probably old and ugly.

About fifteen minutes after she was supposed to, Dr. Lanouche came into the Arabic Studies office. She was neither old nor ugly. Terry didn't exactly know what she was. But she still pissed him off.

She was wearing some long, shapeless, dresslike thing that completely hid her body from him, which was somewhat annoying, although the embroidery on it was nice, if you went for that kind of thing. The laugh lines around her eyes and mouth and her tanned skin and jet-black hair might have been attractive to someone who was into older women, but then again, it was hard to know exactly how old she was, which was also annoying. And her nose was a little thin. She introduced herself to him, speaking in perfect English with the slightest of accents. She apologized for being late and brought him into her office. It was a small room with a smallish desk covered with a computer and several stacks of papers, a large bookcase overflowing with books about the Middle East, and photographs all over the walls of smiling young children from third-world countries.

After being in her presence for all of about forty-five seconds, Terry was getting the sense that this was a good and intelligent person, someone that he might enjoy getting to know.

Of course, that, too, was kind of annoying.

"So, Mr. Tallach," she said, as they sat down across the desk from each other, "I am intrigued by the idea of translating your tape for you, but I have to confess a small concern on my part." Oh, brother. Here we go. *I am very important, and you are not very important, so I don't think I will be able to spend my invaluable time on your not very invaluable problem.* "As I'm sure you must know, especially since the tragedy of September 11, people of Arabic descent and people of the Islamic faith have suffered terrible persecution, especially in this country. I don't think it is overstating it to say that so much suspicion has arisen that in certain parts of the country, there is a witch-hunt mentality running in the streets."

"Are you talking about racial profiling?" Terry asked. He had a hard time quarreling with anyone who gave extra security attention to Arabs since 9/11. The hijackers weren't exactly the most racially diverse group of psychos he'd ever seen. Last time he checked, he hadn't seen many Eskimos on the list.

"I'm talking about people losing friends, and sometimes even losing jobs because other people start rumors that are unfounded. And about children getting picked on and beaten up by other children just because they have Arabic-sounding names. That kind of thing." She paused for a moment. "That's why I need to know a little background about the tape you'd like me to translate before I can feel comfortable getting involved."

So that was different. Still kind of annoying, but at least different.

"Okay. This is going to be interesting," Terry said. "As I mentioned on the phone, I'm representing the guy who's been accused of murdering those six UMass students. The reason I've come to you is because he says he killed some of the people who are speaking on this tape because they were terrorists. So that might make you not want to do this." And that would be the ball game. *Thanks for coming, now kindly take your whack-job tape to someone else.*

But no. The doctor merely sat quietly and waited for him to continue. Good for her. "But right now," he continued, "what I know about these people is pretty pathetic. They went to UMass. They lived in Northampton. At least some of them spoke Arabic. Big deal."

Terry stood and took a closer look at the picture of identical twin sisters with the darkest eyes he'd ever seen. They were about Justin's age, and were smiling like crazy. One of them was missing a tooth. "So I'm hoping to get a translation of this tape, because it contains phone conversations between the people who were killed and whoever they were talking to on the phone. All of the conversations are in Arabic—at least I think it's Arabic."

Lanouche smiled but said nothing. This was odd. What was going to happen if he had actually found an expert who wasn't an asshole? It was probably one of the signs that the world was ending. "I guess what I'm saying is that for all I know, this tape isn't going to prove jack about terrorism. So that might make you *want* to do this. It might show that my client was nuts for thinking that they were terrorists. They might have been on the phone with crazy Uncle Louie, talking about last year's Super Bowl. Who knows?" He sat down again. She was still smiling at him. She had a nice smile.

"And does it make any difference to you whether these tapes prove jack about anything at all?" He could tell that she loved saying "jack." Hearing her say the word with her perfect English and her slight accent was kind of nice, too. She wasn't mocking him. It seemed like she was just happy to take a new English phrase out for a spin.

"Actually, no," Terry said. "All I want to do is find out as much as I can about the people who were killed. We kind of know what happened, and we know why my client says he killed them. But we don't have any idea whether he knew what he was doing when he killed these people."

"I see," she said. "I don't completely understand why it matters, though. Is it legally acceptable to kill another person even if you are correct in your belief that the person is a terrorist?"

Damn good question. "That's, uh, that's something we're working on right now," Terry said.

Dr. Lanouche nodded. "I think that if I were to make a guess, I would say that your client's situation is desperate, perhaps even hopeless. Right now, you are focusing on a tape which might not be audible, and which probably contains nothing useful for your client." Terry didn't respond. This woman was smart. She knew Cal was screwed. "Yet you have come to ask me to translate this tape. You work hard for your clients," she said. It wasn't a question. Then she took a deep breath and let it out. "Is it possible that if I translate this tape, I might be called as a witness in the case?" This wasn't good. She didn't seem like a chicken. What was she afraid of?

"Actually, it's very unlikely," Terry said. "I don't think this tape would be admissible evidence. But I can't say it's impossible."

She smiled again, this time a little sadly, leaned her elbows on the desk, folded her hands together, and rested her chin on them. "I need to tell you a few things, then," she said, "before we go any further. May I?"

"Of course," Terry said.

"I am fluent in both Arabic and English, as well as French and German," she said. "I am a very good translator, and I think that I would be a very good witness." She shrugged. When had she stopped being annoying? "And yet, I think that if I were to testify on your client's behalf, I might be questioned about other things. Such as the fact that I am a politically active lesbian. Or the fact that I spent a night in jail after being arrested for civil disobedience in connection with an effort to make a very well-known local university divest itself of holdings in apartheid South Africa." It would have been more fun if they were having this conversation at a party, because this was a pretty damn interesting woman. A strange woman, but interesting. "I am also what many would call a bleeding-heart liberal. I care a great deal about things in the world, and I have a great many opinions about them. I am not afraid to speak my mind, and I have, on many occasions. I thought you should know this so that if it were a problem for you and your client, you could get someone else to translate the tape."

"I appreciate your telling me this," Terry said, "but believe me—this case has so many problems that if all we had to worry about was your sex life, we'd be thrilled." She raised an eyebrow. "Sorry. Not that way," he continued. "Somehow I get the feeling that if you ever did get to testify, the D.A. would be the one who'd be sorry, not me."

The smile again. "That's very kind of you," Dr. Lanouche said, standing up and extending her hand. "In that case, I would be very pleased to translate the tape for you. I admire people who work hard in the face of difficult circumstances."

"Thank you," Terry said, shaking her hand and then handing her the tape. "That's very kind of *you*."

As he turned to go, she said, "Mr. Tallach, was I right about my guess? That right now, your client"—she spoke gently—"doesn't have jack?" She was serious. And not annoying at all.

"That would be a very good guess," he said.

Washington, D.C.

VERONICA GRAHAM WAS LYING.

"Naturally, I'm extremely upset about this," she said, taking another sip of her coffee. Every single strand of her thick white hair was in place. Her tanned face was smooth and perfectly made up. Her gray suit was immaculate. She looked Matt square in the eye and never seemed to blink. Her voice didn't waver in the least. She was about as extremely upset as a bowl of oatmeal.

"I understand," said Sammy quietly. The three of them were having a private lunch at the White House residence. The press had been told that it was a chance for the new President and his wife to reach out to the former President's widow. Matt had decided to leave out the fact that they would be talking with her about the unethical, and possibly criminal, activities of her deceased husband.

"And I'm sure you realize how upsetting it is for me, too," he said. Unlike Veronica, Matt wasn't lying. He wished he could be as unaffected by this mess as the former first lady. But he was climbing the walls. Every day for the past two weeks, he had continued to perform the duties of the Office of the President as if nothing had changed. But during the night, he could do nothing but talk to Sammy about the Cullhane memos. Who ordered them? Were they ever used? If so, what for? Who could they trust to find out?

It was obvious that each and every one of the memos was a compilation of blackmail material. All read like government-issue supermarket tabloids. Five judges on the list were closeted gay men, two were closeted lesbians. An even dozen were recovering alcoholics. Five were cheating on their spouses. One judge had gotten a mistress pregnant and had secretly paid for an abortion. Another had an abusive husband. The wives of two nominees had attempted suicide. The brother of one judge was suspected of being involved in Internet child porn. Over a dozen children of the judges were victims and/or perpetrators of alcohol and drug abuse and violent crimes.

And the list went on and on. It was appalling.

"You know that there was a memo in here on Judge Stanton? The one who committed suicide?"

"I had no idea," Veronica said, again without a flicker of emotion. "Of course, I didn't expect anything like these memos were on the computer or CDs that I gave you, but that is simply water over the dam." Unlike Veronica, Sammy looked like she might burst into tears at the drop of a hat. "I knew when Jim entered public life that our lives might get difficult, so if this leads to some kind of an investigation, I'll be prepared. As for myself, naturally all I can do is deny any knowledge of wrong-doing. When Jim was President, he always kept his work separate from his family life." She stood up to go, and Matt and Sammy stood as well. "I can only hope that whatever happens, the truth about this comes out. I think that's always best, don't you?" She fixed him with another stare as she extended her hand.

She made it sound so simple.

But of course, she was right.

Orlando, Florida

"DADDY, ARE YOU READY FOR SOME FIREWORKS?"

Zack looked down at his son and smiled. He had probably spent more time smiling these past few days than any time he could remember, with the possible exception of that week in Germany when he first met Wendy. She would have loved that Justin was teasing Zack. Father and son had seen fireworks every night of their vacation, but Justin knew very well that after they got some ice cream they were leaving Disney World right away, heading to their hotel to pack, and then going directly to the airport. Zack already loved Justin more than he thought was possible, and now here the kid was, not even in kindergarten, and already developing a sense of humor. Zack knew several people who had managed to graduate from law school without one.

He scooped Justin up into his arms and spoke into the little boy's neck, tickling him. "You are kidding me, right?" he said as Justin giggled and squirmed. "I think you love fireworks just a little bit too much!" He pulled back and rested his forehead on Justin's forehead as

Justin hugged him around the neck. "Are you ready for some ice cream?" Zack whispered, barely audible above the din of the crowded street.

"Yes, I am," Justin whispered back.

Zack put him down and held his hand as they walked toward the ice-cream vendor. Angry Dad had never taken vacations with his children. Every winter after Christmas, he and Mom would go away for a couple of weeks and hire someone to stay at home with Zack and his brother and sister. Then, during the summer, he and Mom would go away again, while the kids were at summer camp.

It was all part of the spectacular parental training that Zack made a daily effort to forget.

A few minutes later, he and Justin reached the child who was working as a vendor—when had the world gotten so young?—and ordered a couple of cones. The song coming over the loudspeaker was "When You Wish Upon a Star." Justin loved that song. Zack forked over enough money to buy about a week's worth of groceries, took the cones, and then turned to hand one to Justin.

But Justin was gone.

Right in the middle of Disney World. One moment, he and Zack were hand in hand, standing in line, and the next moment, he was gone.

Zack looked out into the crowd of vacationers surging down the biggest street in the park. Justin was nowhere. The loudspeakers began to blare "It's a Small World." A wave of nausea passed through Zack. He had to be here. To Zack's right, a very tall man with a backpack was bouncing a crying little girl on his shoulders. Justin was standing right here five seconds ago. To Zack's left, a swarm of people surrounded Cinderella, who was looking down the street and exchanging a wave with Goofy. Across the street, a little dark-haired boy was on the opposite sidewalk. He turned and looked right toward Zack. It wasn't Justin.

Every inch of Zack was covered in a damp layer of sweat. His right hand was sticky. He looked down and saw that he had crushed the cone he was holding in that hand, and the ice cream was all over his fingers. He dropped it into the garbage pail. How did this happen? How did this happen? What was he going to do? "Justin!" he called out, terrified. "Justin!" How did this happen?

"Daddy! Daddy! Look! I'm holding Cinderella's hand! Come here!" Zack whipped around to see Justin's beaming face next to Cinderella. The beautiful young woman in the beautiful blue gown and the long white gloves looked down to see where Justin was pointing, and then looked up at Zack with her beautiful smile and waved.

And Zack nearly lost it, right there, smack in the middle of Main Street, U.S.A.

THIRTEEN

Dear Kev—

It seems funny, but this is the first letter that I've ever written to you where I wasn't crying right at the beginning of it. I'm sure I'll start soon, but the doctor says it's important for me to remember the things about you that make me happy and proud, not only the things that make me sad and angry.

I'm sure you know this, but I'm not sad and angry at you. I'm so proud of you. You were such a good person. Here come the tears. I'm going to stop now. I'll write again soon.

Love, Daddy

(Letter #20 from Calvin Thompkins to deceased son, Kevin)

Baby Killer, Too????

Accused mass murderer Calvin Thompkins will appear in Hampshire County Superior Court tomorrow morning for a pretrial hearing before Judge Harold Baumgartner. Although the reported purpose for the hearing is to set a date for trial, reports in other news media have fueled speculation that District Attorney Francis X. O'Neill intends to use the hearing to present a motion seeking permission to exhume the body of one of the alleged victims in the case to determine if she was pregnant at the time of her death. The speculation apparently arose when it was learned that the autopsy of one of the female victims of the shooting, Marianne Duhamel, did not make mention of the victim's reproductive organs or system. In a typical autopsy, such organs would be examined, and the report would reveal whether the victim was pregnant when she died.

Thompkins, a 39-year-old African American male, is accused of gunning down Duhamel along with brothers Marc and Mitchell Nathenson, Rudolf Lange, John Bercher, and Helene Ghazi, all residents of Northampton. The six were students at the University of Massachusetts at Amherst and were home on January 14 when Thompkins allegedly shot his way into their apartment, taking the lives of all inside.

Legal experts say that if prosecutors can show that there is probable cause to believe that Thompkins's alleged shooting spree also killed a fetus, he could face additional charges.

The latest poll results show that nearly 90% of Boston-area residents believe Thompkins is guilty.

Thompkins could receive the death penalty if convicted.

(*Boston Post*, April 20, page 1)

April 21—Detroit, Michigan

AS LENA WAITED ON HOLD, SHE TUCKED THE phone between her shoulder and ear and used both hands to pick up a pile of magazines that kept her from sitting on the couch the way she liked. When she finally got seated, she decided that it really was time to pick up her apartment. Right after she found something to write with so she could take notes on the phone call that would break the LeClerq case wide open.

Or slam it shut forever.

Lena liked to think that hard work was all it took to be a good investigative reporter. But she was starting to think that luck might have something to do with it.

Becca and Lena had been going crazy trying to find out where in Los Angeles or Las Vegas Officer Halsey's father lived. Lena had been going through every directory of either city she could find, calling every Halsey listed, and Becca had hacked into enough personnel records to get her at least ten years in prison, but neither of them had found what they needed.

And then fate reached out to them through Becca's employee mailbox. Apparently, the City of Detroit had switched insurance carriers, and everyone needed to fill out a new benefits form. On page two, Becca noticed that they asked for the names and addresses of her parents. She figured that if she could find one of Halsey's old benefits forms, she'd be able to give Lena the address.

Two days ago, she did better. Not only did she find Halsey's old forms—she found out that he didn't write down his parents' address, because he listed them as deceased.

So now Lena had evidence that after investigating a crime, Halsey falsified his report and then went into hiding when she'd tried to confront him about it. Add to that the doctored 911 transcript, and Lena felt like it was time to contact someone with some authority in the police department and try to figure out what was behind all of this. A quick check with Becca identified Halsey's former supervisor as Sergeant Theo Kanteros, and Lena immediately put a call in to him.

The good news was that Sergeant Kanteros was a lot

easier to reach than Officer Halsey. The bad news was that he had no idea what Lena was talking about.

So she spent about ten minutes telling him everything she knew—leaving out the part about how she wouldn't know anything if Becca hadn't been feeding her information—and Kanteros told her he'd call back.

The next day came and went with no call, and so Lena decided to call him.

"Yeah, Ms. Takamura?"

Lena was puzzled. Yesterday, by the end of the phone conversation, it was all "Lena" this and "Lena" that. Now the sergeant had a funny tone to his voice.

"Uh, yes, Sergeant, this is Lena Takamura. How are you?"

"Yeah, Ms. Takamura. I checked into that matter we discussed yesterday, and I'm sorry that I have to decline any comment. And I think it would be best for everyone involved if we let it go at that."

"But, Sergeant—"

"I'm sorry, Ms. Takamura," he interrupted firmly. "I'm going to say again that for reasons I can't go into, it would be best for everyone involved—everyone—if we let this entire thing drop, okay?"

"But—"

"Good-bye." And he hung up.

Northampton, Massachusetts

A STRANGE FEELING PASSED THROUGH CAL Thompkins as he sat down at the table next to Terry and Zack. A bad dream had disturbed his sleep last night. He and Zack were standing side by side in a courtroom. Kevin was the judge. Zack was speaking to Cal, but there was so much noise in the room that Cal couldn't hear what he was saying. Then Kevin shot a gun into the air to quiet everyone down, and Zack leaned over and whispered into Cal's ear, "It's over."

But now Cal felt more than just tired. He felt weak, drained, and actually a little bit hungry, but there was something else he couldn't quite put his finger on.

The courtroom was packed, mostly with reporters. Cal hadn't seen so many pads and pens since college. There were microphones everywhere, and three large cameras had been set up in strategic places in the courtroom. One was aimed at the judge's chair, one was set to film the lawyers, and a third was aimed at the witness stand. When they spoke in the holding cell earlier that morning, Zack had told him that there would be no witnesses testifying today. Terry had jumped in to say that the third camera was yet another example of how the people who were reporting on this case had their heads up their asses.

Cal had only recently come to the surface after spending weeks in an emotional collapse. The psychiatrists said that when he finally allowed himself to feel his loss, his grief had been too much for him to handle. And although now his first thoughts in the morning and his last thoughts at night were still of the faces of his wife and little boy, somehow, other thoughts had begun to occupy his mind during the day. Cal still wasn't sure whether he was comfortable with that.

Somebody shouted, "Court! All rise!" and the entire courtroom got quiet all at once. Everybody stood up. For a second, it felt like Sunday service just before the pastor said the final prayer. Then the old, overweight judge sat down in his chair, and everyone else sat down. The judge and the lawyers started talking about the trial date. Cal took the legal pad that Zack had given to him and started to write.

Dear Kev—

I'm in court for another pretrial conference. I felt a little uncomfortable today when I walked into the courtroom. I don't know why. Usually, these pretrial things don't mean anything to me.

Anyway, I wanted to tell you that one of my lawyers, the one named Zack, has a little boy named Justin. I've never met Justin, but I get this feeling that you'd like him. I saw a picture of him once, and he reminded me of you.

Zack stood up. "Yes, Judge Baumgartner, we do have a motion." Then the judge started asking him questions. The white-haired D.A. looked like he was more interested in who was in the audience than what Zack had to say. The young woman sitting next to the D.A., though, was paying real close attention.

The picture also reminded me of some of the fun things that we used to do. I loved the races we had. You were getting faster every day. You almost beat me that time we raced outside the hotel in South Carolina. Remember that? And do you remember the drawing game? I used to love that game. I still don't know where you learned how to draw horses so well. Did Mommy teach you that?

Somebody said something from behind Cal, and a sort of swell of movement and noise drowned out Zack for a second. The judge started banging his gavel. Two men and a woman left the courtroom in a hurry.

"Ladies and gentlemen," the judge started quietly after things had sort of settled down. He looked really friendly. Judge Grandpa. "This is not the first time we have all been together on this case, and I know that it will not be the last time, either. As you know, our American system of justice proudly conducts itself in public, for it is one of the safeguards the people of this country have against the misuse of power. However." He took a sip from a coffee mug on his desk and put it down. "The principal role of the justice system is, of course, to render justice. And in order for that to happen, the lawyers, the defendant, and I all need quiet, so we can hear what is being said, and, should we choose to do so, so we can actually think." He stopped again. This time he stared straight at the spot in the courtroom where the noise had come from. Then he smiled, and looked back at the middle of the room, and said, "I am now ordering the court officers to summarily remove anyone from this courtroom who makes any noise whatsoever which, in their opinion, is disruptive. I doubt that will be necessary. And of course, if that measure does not satisfy me that this proceeding can continue in a proper fashion, I will order that the courtroom be cleared, and no one will be in attendance for this hearing." The place got real quiet real fast. The court reporter's pen made a scratching sound as she wrote something on a pad next to the tape recorder she was using. The judge looked back at Zack, who had remained standing. "I'm sorry, Mr. Wilson," he said. "Please go ahead."

"Thanks, Judge," Zack said. "Your Honor, before I begin, I need to request that the record of this proceeding reflect that I am one of the very many Anglo-American males in this courtroom. My cocounsel, Mr. Tallach, is one of the very few Scottish/Jewish American males." He leaned forward slightly and looked across at the prosecutors' table. The white-haired D.A. was trying to play it cool, but his smile was fake. "The district attorney, Mr. O'Neill, is also an Anglo-American male; his cocounsel, Assistant District Attorney Ruben, is a Jewish American female; and Police Chief Darryl Brooks, who is also seated at opposing counsel's table, is an African American male." Then he looked back at the judge. "And finally, Your Honor is an Anglo-American male."

Terry and Zack had told Cal that they were going to complain to the judge about the fact that in just about every news report of the case, he had been referred to as "a large, African American male." While the district attorney squirmed around in his chair, Zack showed the judge that nobody's else's race or size was ever mentioned in any of the reports. Then Zack showed the judge some other cases where a white guy was charged with murder, and how, in far more than half of the news reports on that case, the defendant's race was never mentioned. The district attorney whispered something to the young woman next to him, who was still reading the papers Zack had given to them.

It was funny how big a deal white people made about stuff like that. Did they really think this was going to change things? He walked into an apartment and shot six people. He was black, he was six foot five inches tall, and he weighed two hundred and fifty pounds. This was America, not someplace in an Ursula Le Guin novel. People were going to notice.

> Remember the joke book we were writing? I'd like to read it again. I wish we had spent more time writing those jokes. I thought you were really getting good at it, Kev. That one about the toaster still makes me laugh when I think about it.

Now Zack was talking about stuff that the district attorney had said to reporters, like "I'm confident that we have a strong case." He said that like ten times. And he said about five times, "We believe that after a full trial of the facts in this case, the jury will return a verdict of guilty." And the one he used the most, like twenty times, was "Race is not a part of this case. The fact that the defendant is a black man has nothing to do with why he is being prosecuted under the death penalty statute. We believe that this crime warrants the death penalty, and if the defendant is convicted, as we fully expect, then we also expect that he will face execution." The D.A. was smirking. He reached over and took the legal pad his assistant was writing on, wrote something himself, underlined it about a hundred times, and then pushed it back to her with a smile. The young woman read it and looked up at him, but he had already turned away, and was now smiling up at the judge.

Zack looked up from the papers he was reading from and spoke right to the judge. He was finishing up. "Your Honor, my cocounsel and I have submitted affidavits attesting to the fact that we have made no statements about the case to the press. Disciplinary Rule 7-107 specifically prohibits any lawyer from making a statement about his or her opinion of the case, as well as several other things we've outlined in the memorandum supporting our motion. I think the prosecutor's office has made a regular practice of flagrantly disregarding these rules, not only injecting their own opinion into the case but also making an issue of the defendant's race, in a not-too-subtle attempt to prejudice and taint the jury pool. The latest example was printed just yesterday, where a very unflattering picture of the defendant appeared on the front page of a newspaper with the headline 'Baby Killer, Too?' under it, followed by some ludicrous suggestion that the Commonwealth might attempt to exhume one of the victims' bodies. These practices should not only subject the district attorney to disciplinary action because they are ethical violations, but they should also be stopped by this court because they threaten to deprive the defendant of any hope of a fair trial. In fact, polls taken by that same newspaper indicate that already ninety percent of the population has made up their mind that the defendant is guilty, and we haven't even started the trial yet.

"In order to address that, the defendant seeks two things from this court. First, an order forbidding the prosecution from making any further statements to the press, and second, sanctions against the Commonwealth to attempt to reestablish an even playing field. Specifically, allowing the defendant to refuse to produce any further discovery to the prosecution before the trial of this case."

There was a slight noise from some people seated in the back of the room who left as soon as Zack was finished, but all it took was a quick look from the judge in that direction, and everyone fell silent again.

The D.A. was whispering something to his assistant, who was trying to listen and, at the same time, pull some book out of her briefcase.

The judge cleared his throat. "Does the Commonwealth wish to be heard at this time?"

The D.A. almost jumped to his feet. "Yes, Your Honor, briefly." He looked down at his assistant, who was flipping the pages of a book open, frantically trying to find something. He reached down and picked up the legal pad she had been writing on, flipped over the first page, skimming her notes. He set the pad down and put on a serious face.

"First of all," he began, "I'd like to object for the record to the ambush tactics that the defense has used today. I received a copy of this motion for the first time about ten minutes ago. However, a few things did come to mind as my brother addressed the court." When the D.A. said the words "my brother," Terry closed his eyes. It didn't look like he really wanted to be in the same family as the D.A. "The Commonwealth's position from the beginning in this case is that there is no racial component to it. The defendant is an African American, and three of the six victims in this case were African Americans. If anyone is playing the race card here, it's the defendant's attorneys, not the Commonwealth."

The D.A. looked pretty pleased with himself. "Furthermore," he said, "the Commonwealth can't possibly control what will or won't be speculated on in the newspapers about possible pregnancies, or anything else, for that matter." His assistant handed him the legal pad again, pointing to some notes she had made. He looked up at the judge again. "As to the other points that were raised in the defendant's motion, the Commonwealth requests a reasonable time to prepare an opposition."

"Very well," said the judge. He opened a large red book, made a note on one of the pages, and looked down at the lawyers. "The Commonwealth will file any opposition to the defendant's motion within two weeks from today." Now the D.A. looked like he was really happy. His assistant didn't, but he didn't seem to notice. The judge continued. "With that understanding in place, I would like to ask the Commonwealth whether it has made statements to the press regarding this case." Terry hit Zack's leg under the table. Zack looked over at Terry, who was staring at the judge, stone-faced. Something good was going to happen.

The D.A. looked a little wary. He touched his tie and said, "Yes, Your Honor. There has been a great deal of media interest in the case, and we have accommodated that interest by organizing press conferences from time to time."

"I see," said the judge. "Do you have personal knowledge of who it was that spoke from your office at these press conferences?"

The D.A.'s face started to change color. This wasn't where he had expected this to go. He was mad. Zack's mouth moved a fraction of an inch. Otherwise, he and Terry looked like mannequins from an ugly clothing store. They were loving this. "As I mentioned, Your Honor, the Commonwealth is not prepared at this time to specifically rebut—"

"Yes, Mr. O'Neill," the judge interrupted. "I understand that. I am merely trying to get some sense of the way the Commonwealth is handling its communication to the media in this case. For example, I am very interested in learning whether the Commonwealth has been offering opinions as to the strength of the case against the defendant or the likely outcome of the trial. Are you personally aware of any comments of that nature coming from your office?"

The Tomato Heads. That's what Cal's son used to call people who got red in the face when they were angry. If Kevin had seen the D.A. right now, he would have thought he'd met the Grand Tomato. But then something shifted, and the D.A. seemed to calm down. The color in his face faded a little and he started to smile like he wasn't mad at all. "Judge, I spoke at those press conferences, and I can assure the court that whatever statements were made, they were completely appropriate. We believe we have a strong case, and I have said exactly what other D.A.s across this country have said for years about cases such as this."

Zack got a puzzled look on his face and leaned forward in his seat to check out the D.A. Terry's eyes widened. He was biting his lip. Whatever the D.A. just said, it wasn't smart.

"Very well," the judge said. He took a minute to write a few things down on a piece of paper. "I've decided to take the defendant's motion under advisement, but pending my decision, I am now issuing a preliminary injunction restraining the defendant, the defendant's attorneys and their staff, and the district attorney's office from making any statements to the press regarding this case. Is that understood?"

Terry stood up. "Yes, Your Honor. The defendant will continue to make no statements to the press."

The judge studied him for a moment, his face flat, and then nodded. "Very good." He turned to the D.A. "Mr. O'Neill?"

The D.A. smiled, but his heart wasn't in it. "Of course, Your Honor." He swallowed and tried to look like he hadn't just lost something.

Then the judge said, "I'd like to see counsel in chambers," and stood up.

One of the court officers shouted, "Court's in recess, all rise!" and everybody stood up. The judge left the courtroom though a door behind his desk. Terry leaned over to Cal, clapped him on the shoulder, and whispered, "Did we rock, or did we fuckin' rock?" Then Zack said, "We'll see you in the lockup before we go." And then they were gone.

I've got to go now, Kevin. I'll write again soon. I think that the lawyers think they did something good here today, but I don't really see it. I still shot those people. Nothing's going to change that, whether the lawyers talk to the reporters or not.

Oh. One more thing. I think I know what it is that I was feeling when I came into the courtroom today. I think I felt afraid. I still do. I'll try to think of you and be strong.

Love, Daddy

FOURTEEN

This is not a time for speeches. It is a time for mourning. Yesterday was a terrible day for Americans. Without any warning, we suffered a deep and painful loss. Our grief will not be short-lived . . .

Approximately one hour after President Graham's death, Chief Justice Kmerski swore me in as President. I don't think of myself as a politician; I think of myself as a soldier. And yet I stand before you in what most would say is the most powerful political position in the world . . .

This will be a difficult job for me. I will need your help as I try to handle the responsibilities of leading our country . . .

As you probably know by now, our Homeland Security director has recommended that I change the terrorism threat status from elevated to high. She based that recommendation on an understandable sense of caution in light of yesterday's tragic events and the unexpected transition that we all will have to make.

I have never liked the idea of a "terrorist threat" level. I think it plays into terrorists' hopes of frightening people. I don't believe that it is necessary to make a big show of predicting whether a terrorist act will take place. We all know that terrorism is possible, and we all know that we must help protect each other from these attacks.

Ever since September 11, we have become painfully aware that our country is at war. Ask anyone who lives in New York, Pennsylvania, or Washington, D.C. Ask anyone who knew any of the victims of that infamous day. Ask anyone who watched the news reports of the destruction and its aftermath.

This is an unusual kind of war, since our adversary aims to kill innocent people rather than to destroy military targets. But the actions of these aggressors constitute warfare, plain and simple.

In that sense, every American citizen is a soldier in this war. Most of us do not wear uniforms, most of us do not have ranks or carry weapons, but we are all at war. So we do not need "terrorist threat" alert levels. We do not need color-coded signs to tell us to be aware, to report unusual activity, to watch out for anything that seems suspicious, to protect ourselves . . .

To those who would say "Too much change has taken place in our government over too short a period of time," I say: Never forget that this is a nation of the people—and the people of this great land have not changed. And never have they been more steadfast in the defense of their liberty and of their country.

And to those who would say "We cannot have a President who has so little experience in government," I say: Never underestimate the will of a soldier who is fighting for his country.

And to those who would say "When will we surrender to the fear and the terror, and give up the freedoms that generations of Americans have died to protect?" I say: Never.

(Excerpts from White House address of President Ferguson, December 10)

April 25—Washington, D.C.

WHEN CARLOS OLIVEIRA SAW THE PRESIDENT come out of the Oval Office and walk toward him, the young assistant was puzzled. According to the official schedule, President Ferguson was supposed to be meeting with various national security advisors and the Chief of Staff for a briefing. Did someone forget a report he needed to track down? Carlos set aside one of the many newspapers that he had been reading for the President and rose from his desk.

"Carlos, I had to move some things around on my calendar today, so I won't be meeting with Mr. Browning or the advisors until later this afternoon. I gave the changes to Mrs. Wittenour." The President glanced down at the stacks of papers covering Carlos's desk and said, "When you get a minute, can you come join me out on the portico? I need to talk to you about something and I want to get a little fresh air."

"Of course, Mr. President. Right away." Carlos could feel the familiar swell of pride inflate his chest and pull back his shoulders as he followed the tall man into the Oval Office. *You will never feel more alive than when you are working for this man,* Poppy had said. *He will do anything for you, and you will want to do anything for him.*

Just as they were about to open the French doors at the back of the office, a woman's voice said, "I'm sorry, Mr. President. Mr. Browning is calling. He says it's important."

The President turned to Carlos. "Why don't you wait outside for me. I'll take this call and I'll be right out." Carlos stepped out of the Oval Office onto the brick and stone porchway that bounded that part of the West Wing of the White House, closed the doors behind him, and watched as two small brown birds swooped down and landed on the back lawn.

He will tell you that I saved his life many times in Vietnam, but I need to tell you what really happened when we were together in that war. We were on a patrol with eight other men. Two of them were new. The army was so stupid. They always sent new men into action too soon. It happened so often the men made up a name for them: FNGs. Fucking New Guys. They always needed more training. They always were getting killed. Some of the guys who had been in country for a while stopped bothering to learn their names.

Anyway, we got intel that some Vietcong were using this spot to cross a river to bring supplies to their troops, so Lieutenant Ferguson and me went to find a good place to set up an ambush. Then that night, our squad spread out on the shore so that right before dawn, when Charlie crossed the river, we would take him out, nice and easy. There were three men to my left, then me, then two men to my right, then the lieutenant, the radio man, and two more men to his right. It was raining, so it was a really dark night. It was going to be a good ambush.

But even though the lieutenant had told everybody to hold their fire until he gave the signal, one of the FNGs—the one farthest to the right—got too hyper. Probably took one of those stupid amphetamine pills the army gave out. As soon as he heard something moving on the river in front of him, he opened fire. It turned out to be a Vietnamese junk—one of those little wooden ships Charlie sometimes used to move supplies. By the time he stopped firing, the junk was all busted up, but we weren't going to ambush anyone else that night.

Then, all of a sudden, everything went bad. Instead of all that noise scaring off a few VC, like I thought it would, suddenly there's this flare flying through the air, and for a minute I can see that there's not just a few VC moving some supplies. There's like a whole lot of them. Like forty or fifty. Maybe even more. And then the shooting started.

These guys weren't crossing the river into our ambush—they had already crossed the river farther upstream onto our side, and were coming right down our right flank. We were going to get overrun, or surrounded. And just as the lieutenant went to call for support, another flare went up, the radio man got hit, and he spun around and then the radio got all shot up. We couldn't call anyone. We were dead.

By this time, bullets were flying all over the place. The kid who shot up the junk panicked, gave away his position, and was killed in no time. I didn't know it at the time, but the guy next to him had been hit too, and couldn't move his legs. The radio man was screaming, and we looked like we were going to eat it. The only thing keeping us alive was the fact that it was so dark, the enemy couldn't really see us. The lieutenant ran over to my position and told me to hold all fire and take the rest of the squad and retreat. He said that he was going to lay down some cover, and that he would follow with the radio man and the other guy that was still alive.

So the lieutenant started opening up on the VC with his big machine gun, and that slowed them down and diverted them from our position. I started to fall back with the five men at my end of the formation. We had to really move to keep from getting outflanked and pinned against the river. Even if we wanted to, we couldn't shoot, because the lieutenant and those other guys were between us and the VC. That probably saved our lives, since if we'd opened fire, the VC would have been able to find us and kill us.

The last I saw of the lieutenant was muzzle flashes from his machine gun. The VC must have thought there were ten of him, because he would fire off a few rounds, then run like crazy to another spot and fire off a few more. He knew that if he stood in one place, they could fire at where the muzzle flashes were coming from, and he'd be dead. But he could move like a ghost in the darkness, and they never knew where the bullets would come from next.

Carlos looked through the windows of the French doors into the Oval Office as President Ferguson spoke excitedly to his Chief of Staff on the phone. He didn't have any problem imagining young Lieutenant Ferguson, rain dripping off his helmet, single-handedly holding off an enemy force ten times greater than his in the middle of the jungle night, while his men escaped.

So by the time we made it back to camp, it was already late morning. I knew that I had to get back to the lieutenant with backup. But meanwhile, Charlie had started this big offensive away from where our ambush had been set up—a diversion to allow the troops we had met to move down the river with no problem. All the air and river support we had was helping out with that fight. I had to wait until that afternoon before I could get a small boat to go back up the river. What I saw when I found them I will never forget for the rest of my life.

The lieutenant was swimming right down the middle of the river, far enough from shore that the VC couldn't hit him from land. He was doing like the breast stroke, with the radio man on his back. He had tied the radio man's wrists together, and looped his arms over the lieutenant's head from behind, so the lieutenant could keep his hands free to swim, and so the radio man's head would stay out of the water. I don't know how the lieutenant kept swimming. I can't swim for shit. I would've drowned in two seconds.

But that wasn't all. The lieutenant was pushing the paralyzed guy down the river with him, too. He had taken his belt off and tied the guy to a piece of the busted-up wooden boat that the FNG had shot up. It was like a little private raft, keeping him afloat, because he couldn't move his legs.

By the time we reached them, the lieutenant was just about finished. He was so tired that he couldn't pull himself into the boat. We had to drag him over the side. And that's when I saw that he had been hit in the back with about ten pieces of shrapnel from a hand grenade.

Later, I figured out that altogether, the lieutenant swam about five miles, with one unconscious guy on his back, and pushing along another guy, after getting hit in the back from a grenade. It was the most incredible thing I've ever seen in my life. And if you ever ask him what happened, he'll tell you that I rescued him. I'm telling you, he's a great man, Carlos. The greatest man I've ever met.

The French doors opened, and the President came out of his office holding a small piece of paper. "Sorry to keep you waiting, Carlos," he said, as they walked several paces away from the guard who stood at the Oval Office entrance. They sat down on a bench, out of earshot of the guard, and the President looked down at the paper in his hand and then up again at Carlos. He looked a little tired, or maybe sad.

"Carlos," he said, "I'm sorry that I have to ask you to do this for me, but I can't think of a way that I can do it myself."

Worcester, Massachusetts

WHEN SERGEANT PETE VANDERWALL'S PAGER went off, he was having his usual end-of-the-tour cup of coffee at the Double V on Main Street. It wasn't that Vanderwall really needed the coffee so much—it was just something he liked to do before coming in from his shift. Like making sure that the kids were covered in bed before going to sleep at night.

He checked the number on his pager before returning the call. He didn't recognize it. It was unusual for him to be paged. Normally, dispatch would just get him by radio. It was probably a wrong number.

As he waited for whoever it was to answer the phone, he watched the owners of the Double V Sandwich Shop, Maria and Joe, cleaning up. They were in their fifties or sixties, but Pete had never seen them apart. They came to work together and left together. Pete thought of the last time he had spent the whole day with Vicki, and got a little envious.

Earlier that week, Maria had cut herself slicing a tomato, and Joe wasn't letting her get her new bandage wet. "It's nothing," she insisted with a smile, as Joe gently pushed her away from the sink. Joe knew better. Coming from Maria, "It's nothing" meant anything from a head cold to a dislocated shoulder. She once went two weeks limping around on a sore foot until Joe and their son finally threw her in the car and took her for X rays. Turned out she had a stress fracture.

A friendly, gentle male voice finally answered Pete's call. "This is Pastor Rick Reid."

"Pastor Reid, this is Sergeant Pete Vanderwall of the Worcester P.D. You paged me?"

"Yes, Sergeant, thanks so much for returning my call," the voice replied. "I'm the new pastor at the First Congregational Church over on West Street. I wonder if I could speak to you for a minute about a member of the congregation here."

A few years ago, Pastor Dunleavy had retired, but Pete hadn't heard anything about his replacement. "Sure, how can I help you, sir?"

"Actually, I'm calling with some news about Natalie

Reggio. Apparently you were involved in bringing her to the hospital after she suffered a head injury in a fight at Rockets."

The kid with the cracked skull who wouldn't make a statement until she had apologized to him? "Sure," Pete said. "I remember her."

"Unfortunately, Natalie's condition has taken a turn for the worse," the pastor said, "and she had to return to the hospital. She's back in ICU, because last night she slipped into another coma. The doctors aren't quite sure what happened, but at least she's stable now, thank God, and they're listing her condition as 'guarded.' "

Pete swallowed. That didn't make any sense. When he went to see the kid, she seemed like she was going to be fine. And why was her pastor calling him? "Doesn't she have any parents?" he asked.

"Actually, she does, but they haven't spoken to Natalie for years. I've left messages for them, but they haven't returned my calls."

Parents who gave up on their kid. Pete could feel his blood pressure rising. "Well, I'm real sorry to hear about Natalie. I'll make a note of it in the report," he said. If the kid died, and they learned that she had been hit, this thing would turn into a murder investigation.

"Thank you, Sergeant, but that's not really why I was trying to get in touch with you," the voice said. "Just by chance I was over to see Natalie last night, before she went back into the coma, and she gave me a letter to give to you." This whole thing wasn't making any sense at all. "She called me yesterday because she was very nervous. She said she wasn't feeling well, even though the doctors were telling her she was getting better. She was scared that something bad was going to happen to her, and she asked me to give you this letter if her condition deteriorated."

* * *

ALL THE WAY TO THE CHURCH, PETE COULDN'T get the image of his daughter, Donna, out of his mind. This kid Natalie was seventeen, and hadn't spoken to her parents in years. Now she was in a coma thanks to a drunken barroom brawl. Who was Donna hanging out with? What was going to happen to her when she started drinking?

Pete pulled up to the front of the church office, got out of his cruiser, and went to the mailbox. Reverend Reid had left the letter there, because he had to leave for an appointment. The envelope was sealed, and was addressed in a loopy handwriting to "Police Sergeant Peter Vanderwall of the Worcester Police Department." Pete got back into his cruiser and opened it.

Dear Sergeant Vanderwall,

I asked Pastor Rick to give this letter to you only if I died or got a lot worse, so if it's not too much trouble, can you please check to see if I'm alright? If I am, you shouldn't read this letter, because that would be really embarrassing, okay?

What was it about this girl? Pete had seen kids hurt and even kill themselves, drinking and driving mostly, but in other ways, too. Why was this one getting to him so much? Why did it feel so wrong that at this very minute, she was lying unconscious in some hospital bed, with parents that wouldn't even return a phone call?

I guess if you're still reading this, that means it's bad news for me. The doctors keep saying that there's nothing wrong, but I really don't feel right. I can't figure out what's wrong. All I know is that I'm really scared. But I'm writing this because there's something I needed to tell you which I didn't think of when you came to see me.

Actually, that's not true. I'm sorry for lying. I did think of it when you were there. I was just so embarrassed about what I had done, and so totally embarrassed about crying all over the place and making a fool of myself, that I couldn't bring myself to talk to you about this. I could only answer your questions about what happened. (By the way, I hope your investigation is going all right.)

I know that this is going to sound strange, because the first time you met me I was so drunk and out of control, but I have been leading this young person's alcohol awareness group at First Congregational for the past two years. (It's okay if you don't believe me, you can ask Pastor Rick.) And there's this girl named Julie Keenan that I am real worried about. She seems a lot like I was when I was about thirteen which is when I started drinking (she's actually only twelve but she talks like she's about twenty-five). She's been coming to the meetings and staying away from alcohol, but I think a lot of that might have been her having a kind of hero worship thing about me. (I know that sounds conceited, but I'm not saying it to make myself sound great. I just mean that she follows me around a lot, and stuff like that. I think she thought I was cool.)

Anyway, if I die, or get brain damage, or something, I don't know what she's going to do. And she's really young. I mean she acts like she's done everything, but I think Julie's really inexperienced, and I wouldn't be surprised if she hears about me drinking and being taken to the hospital and all that and totally loses it. And then if she acts out, and starts drinking and going completely wild, I think she could really hurt herself.

So I'm a little embarrassed to ask you to do this,

because you're a sergeant and all, but I was wondering if you could look out for Julie if I die, or if I can't because I get worse or something. I mean, Pastor Rick's a great guy, and he really tries, but I think Julie might not be able to see that right now. And her parents are completely clueless. I just get the feeling that if nobody's there watching over her, she might do something stupid, and then I would really feel bad. (I know AA tells you that you're not responsible for anyone but yourself, but I can't help it. That's just the way I feel.)

Pastor Rick just came in, so I'm going to give this to him now. But I really hope he doesn't have to give this letter to you. But just in case he does, thank you again for everything you did for me, and thank you for watching out for Julie, if you can.

Sincerely,
Natalie Reggio

FIFTEEN

SPEAKER #1: *. . . and with God's help our work continues.*

SPEAKER #2: *I heard that you have obtained another method with automobiles.*

SPEAKER #1: *I am sorry, but we were not able to. It is our greatest desire and objective. With the help of God we will find another way. Right now, our method is with an airplane.*

SPEAKER #2: *Our brother has sent a package to you. Perhaps this will help your holy work.*

SPEAKER #1: *Praise God. I pray that this summer, [inaudible] many newspapers from Boston. I will attend the biggest celebration on July 4.*

SPEAKER #2: *Perhaps we will meet July 5, and you will show me [inaudible] of your airplane. [laughter, inaudible]*

SPEAKER #5: *Our brother arrived yesterday, thanks always to God.*

SPEAKER #6: *Did he bring you a gift?*

SPEAKER #5: *He told me that there was going to be a great celebration this summer, and then there was* *going to be a loud cry from heaven, and then with God's help there would be another celebration even greater than the first.*

SPEAKER #6: *Praise be to God.*

SPEAKER #5: *And he said that fire and the praise of God would rain down from the summer skies . . .*

SPEAKER #8: *Our sisters have created beautiful things which will make our work easier.*

SPEAKER #9: *Have they been used?*

SPEAKER #8: *We have used them and they work well. God is smiling on our holy work.*

(Excerpts of transcripts of telephone conversations from [phone number and dates omitted])

May 2—Northampton, Massachusetts

TERRY TOSSED HIS COPY OF THE PHONE TRANscripts down on the table and said, "I should have asked that translator to make something up." He started walking around Zack's office, clicking the pen he was carrying. "This stuff is so boring I want to kill myself, never mind anybody else. 'With God's help, our holy work will continue.' 'With God's help, my brother got here yesterday.' 'With God's help, I wiped my nose.' Something tells me God's got better things to do. At least I hope so."

Zack didn't answer. Something was cooking in his big brain. "Did you happen to notice whether any of the voices on the phone were female?"

"No," Terry said. "Only men. Dr. Lanouche had mentioned that."

"And what were the names of the male victims?"

Good question. "Uh, let's see. There were a couple of

brothers, Nathenson, I think. And the other two . . . wait, I'll check." He went over to the file and pulled out one of the police reports. " 'Marc and Mitchell Nathenson, Rudolf Lange, and John Bercher.' So what?"

"So if Cal hadn't told us these guys were terrorists, how many of them would you expect to speak Arabic?"

Holy shit. Nathenson, Lange, and Bercher. Not exactly the most common names in the Cairo telephone book. "So you're thinking aliases?"

"I don't know what I'm thinking," Zack said, turning to his computer and keying something in. "But it seems a little unusual for every single phone conversation on that tape to be in Arabic, given the names of these guys."

Of course, having non–Arabic-sounding names and speaking on the phone in Arabic didn't prove anything. And neither did spending half your time thanking God for this morning's Dunkaccino. But the situation was beginning to get a little stink on it. Terry looked over Zack's shoulder at his computer screen. " 'Al Qaeda telephone transcripts'?" he read out loud. "What the hell are you doing, Zack?"

"I thought I remembered reading something about some transcripts that came out after 9/11." Zack was scrolling down a list of headings the search engine had listed. He clicked on one and said, "There was something really cryptic about the way these people were talking. I'm not sure if it was a code, or just some cultural thing, but I wanted to see if any of the stuff on our tape sounded like—whoa." He grabbed his copy of the phone transcripts and flipped the pages frantically.

"What?" Terry said.

"Check this out," Zack said, looking back to his computer screen. "In this Al Qaeda conversation intercepted in Italy, one of the terrorists said to another, 'I hope, God willing, that I can bring you a window or a piece of an airplane the next time we see each other.' Then they laughed, like that was some kind of big joke. That was before 9/11."

"And you're thinking that's a little like our conversation about cars where our guys said . . ." Terry looked at the page Zack had opened to. " 'Perhaps we will meet on July fifth, and you will show me whatever of your airplane.' And then they laughed."

"Yeah."

Not exactly the most compelling evidence, but the stink was getting a little stronger. "So here's a question," Terry said. "If these guys were really Muslim fundamentalist terrorists, then what the hell were they doing hanging out with two women? Doesn't that violate Rule Number One in the 'How to be an Islamic Whacko Freak' handbook? No women."

"Yeah," Zack said. "I don't know about that stuff. But I do know that the cops didn't bother doing a whole lot of checking up on these victims, because as far as they were concerned, this thing was open-and-shut from the time they showed up. Cal went nuts and blew the poor kids all away. Case closed."

Which was pretty understandable. Cops had better things to do than make work for themselves. Why make an easy case a hard one? There're six dead students in an apartment, and Cal sitting in the hallway, waiting for them with a confession and the murder weapon. Do the math. "So we don't even know how these women were connected to the four guys?"

"Right. All we know is that they all went to school together. I think one of the newspapers said that the women lived in a different apartment, but I didn't really pay much attention. Didn't the tapes say something about the women?"

"Yeah," Terry said. "Or sisters. Let me see." He looked back at the transcripts until he found the right passage. "Here we go. One guy says that they created beautiful things that the men used for their holy work. Hmmm."

"Maybe if we see where the women used to live, we can find out what that means," Zack said. "What do you think?"

"I think I got about zero other ideas," Terry said. "So let's check out the ladies. Praise God."

JUDGE COTTONWOOD DIDN'T WANT TO PICK up the phone. He knew it was Harold Baumgartner on the other end, and he knew what it was about.

It was The Phone Call.

Cottonwood exhaled deeply and picked up the phone. "Harold. How are you?"

"I'm well, Richard. How's the hip holding up?"

"Oh, you know the drill. Some good days, some bad." He steeled himself for the inevitable. "What can I do for you today?"

"No matter how many times I make this phone call, I never seem to know how to start it. So I'll just get right to the point, I guess. In a couple of months, you'll be celebrating your seventieth birthday, and, as you know, that means that sometime before then, you'll need to step down from the bench."

Judge Cottonwood imagined that many who received this call looked forward to it. Lots of people enjoyed retiring by the time they turned seventy. And for Massachusetts judges, the pension was quite generous, and it didn't prevent you from taking on other work if you wanted it. He personally knew several former judges who had returned to private practice, or had become involved in mediation or arbitration. Many also taught classes at the local law schools.

But for Richard, being a judge was all he'd wanted to do. It had become his entire life, starting twenty-six years ago. Despite the arthritis and the bad eye, retirement for him was little more than a death sentence. Which is why he hadn't thought about it seriously, or planned for it in any way, even though the rational part of him knew of its inevitable arrival.

"How about the Thompkins case?" Richard said. "Will I have enough time to do that trial before I go?"

"As far as I'm concerned, that shouldn't be any problem," Harold responded. "According to my records, you'll need to stop work on or before July twenty-second. I've got a pretrial on that case scheduled for the week after next, and I think we'll be picking a trial date then. I was thinking mid to late June. From what I can tell, I think it's going to go one to two weeks. I know you've been cleaning up your calendar. How does that look for you?"

Richard took a quick look at his appointment book. "I've only got a couple of trials set for later this month, and June is wide open. I'm not scheduling anything else except the Thompkins case, so even if one of the May trials goes into June, I should be fine."

"Terrific," Harold said. "So what are your plans after you retire?" he asked. "I've got to start thinking about that myself. I'll be the one getting this call in about four more years."

"Oh, I don't know," Richard said, opening the top drawer of his desk and looking at the bottle of Percocet. "I was thinking maybe of just relaxing for a while."

Maybe a very long while.

Detroit, Michigan

WAITRESSING ON FRIDAY NIGHTS WAS HARD work but good money, so it was tough when a local power failure forced the owners to close early that night. Lena had plenty of savings, but she could always use more, so she hated to give up the opportunity to earn a couple hours' more tips. But she had to admit she'd welcome the extra sleep.

As she rode the bus on the way home she checked her cell phone's voice mailbox. The only message was from her mother—something about vacation plans that she and Daddy had for the next several weeks. They were going to rent an RV and drive around some of the national parks in Utah, Arizona, and New Mexico.

Lena shook her head as she got off the bus and began to walk the few remaining blocks home. Utah, Arizona, and New Mexico. To them, a vacation. To her, a never-ending *National Geographic* special with bad cell phone coverage.

The message Lena was hoping to receive would have been from Captain Pisani. She'd started calling the captain the minute that Sergeant Kanteros had warned her away from the case.

It didn't take any experience at all to recognize that Sergeant Kanteros's message was as good as a note from heaven saying "Lena, you are finally on to something." Now she just had to hang on and find out what.

Of course, that was still the big problem. Lena had no idea why anyone cared about her questions. After all, what had she uncovered? A discrepancy between a little girl's memory and a police officer's report? An altered transcript of a phone call in an attempt to hide an unsuccessful burglary? As far as Lena could figure, there was no motive for any of it.

Luckily, the electricity was working where Lena lived. She opened up the door to her building and headed up the stairs to her apartment. And speaking of motive, why didn't the thieves take the rare coins that were all over Mr. LeClerq's den? Why did they take computer CDs instead? Even if they had been startled by Mr. LeClerq, they'd had time to at least grab something valuable on their way out. None of it made any sense.

It was after Lena had taken about three steps into her apartment that she realized something was wrong. She stopped dead, terrified.

She could hear somebody moving around in her bedroom.

And then she heard a man's voice say, "Did you just hear something?"

Before she could turn to run, she heard footsteps in the bedroom, heading for the door toward her. She wouldn't have time to make it out of the apartment before he emerged. She spun frantically, saw the bathroom door was open, and ducked inside. Stepping into the tub, she hid behind the shower curtain as she heard somebody come out of her bedroom into the living room and walk toward the apartment door. The man's voice spoke again. "Lena?"

Her heart was pounding so hard she was certain whoever was out there would hear it. Luckily, if he looked into the bathroom, at least the shower curtain would hide her, unless he actually came into the room and pulled the curtain back all the way. Then she looked up at the mirror over the sink, and shit! The way the tub, the mirror, and the open door were positioned, depending on where he was in the living room, if the man looked through the open door into the bathroom, he could see her reflection in the mirror!

Another voice came from the bedroom. "She's still

at work, Jack. Remember we checked the schedule on the counter."

Whoever was in the living room opened the apartment door and then, a few seconds later, closed it. As he returned to the bedroom, Lena got a quick glimpse of him. He was wearing a very dark rain slicker. "FBI" was stenciled in giant yellow letters on the back. And he was holding a gun in his hand, which he slid back into a holster.

Oh my God. Had he been planning to shoot her?

"You almost done?" Jack asked, now out of sight.

"Yeah," the man in the bedroom said. "I just gotta put a little into the closet."

A little what? Lena's chest started to hurt. Her heart was hammering. Was she having a heart attack? No. She was holding her breath. And she was still wearing her winter coat and a hat. She was way too hot. Her armpits felt damp.

"Well, hurry up. I wanna be long gone by the time the cops come in and bust her."

Trying to breathe soundlessly, Lena opened her mouth wide and let the air out slowly. She was cowering in her own bathtub, listening to the FBI describe how she was going to be arrested. She was sweating so much that she felt streams of perspiration running down her legs.

She started to shiver uncontrollably. Would they hear her? What would they do to her if they found her? Would they shoot her? Lena had always imagined that if she were going to die a violent death, she would go down fighting. Would they just walk into her bathroom and blow her away?

"All set," announced the bedroom man. "Let's go." And then the sounds of footsteps approached again from the bedroom. Lena was shaking. She didn't look into the mirror, fearing that the terror that was buzzing through her body would give her away.

"You sure this'll do it?" asked Jack as they reached the door.

"Shit, it better," said the other man. "This place is littered with so much stuff that even uniforms won't be able to fuck it up."

Then the apartment door opened, and a few seconds later, it closed.

For several moments, Lena just listened to the silence, still trying to breathe without making any noise. A part of her feared a trap, but sooner or later, she knew, she was going to have to move. Holding her breath again, she stepped out from behind the shower curtain, out of the tub, and tiptoed out of the bathroom into the living room. They were gone. Thank God.

And then Lena saw it.

All over her coffee table. On top of all of the other junk that she'd left there. A Baggie half filled with pot, a couple of roaches, and some matches. Another Baggie, spilling white powder out onto the floor. And another, sticking out from under one of the cushions on the couch.

She ran into her bedroom. More drugs. A scale. White powder spilled on her dresser.

Jesus. This would take forever to clean up. If she could even find it all.

And then she remembered what the men had said. The cops were coming to bust her. And even the uniforms won't be able to fuck it up.

Then she heard a siren.

Lena grabbed her laptop and ran.

SIXTEEN

DEFENDANT'S MOTION IN LIMINE RE: VICTIMS' BACKGROUNDS

Now comes the defendant in the above-captioned matter and hereby moves this honorable court in limine for leave to introduce evidence of the background of the victims. Specifically, the defendant seeks leave to introduce evidence that such individuals: 1) were members of a group of terrorists; 2) had each wrongfully killed innocent persons in incidents prior to and unrelated to the case at bar; and 3) were planning, at the time of their deaths, future wrongful killings of innocent persons . . .

As grounds therefor, the defendant states the following:

1. In August 1998, the defendant's wife and five-year-old son were killed in a terrorist attack in Kenya . . .

(Trial Paper Number 24)

May 3—John's Crossing, Saskatchewan

WITH GOD'S HELP, THIS WOULD BE THE BEGINNING of the end of the world.

The small plane had been serviced, fueled, and loaded with the cargo. It waited for El Amin in the cornfield near the border.

The infidels made such big noises about homeland security and protecting themselves, but they shared thousands of miles of border with Canada, and they did almost nothing to monitor crossings by air. Flying small planes over the corn and wheat fields of Saskatchewan and Manitoba wasn't necessarily the fastest way to transport explosives into the United States, but he had several weeks remaining before he needed his cargo to be on site in Boston. So flying this last crate of grenades into an abandoned field in northeastern Montana was hardly under any time pressure.

As he gathered speed through the field, and the plane slowly rose into the gray sky, drops of rain began to fall. El Amin was pleased. Even though the region was remote, they tried to fly only during rain, when the chance that their activities would be observed was even lower. God was smiling on them again.

God knew that the mission this July 4 was very important. Perhaps even as important as the one carried out by the martyrs on September 11. He had chosen El Amin and had kept him safe even when the infidels had sent an assassin to kill them all. He would show the infidels that there would never be peace until they were wiped from the face of the earth.

The plan was simple. This was the last flight for materials. He would land in about thirty minutes on the other side of the border and meet the car that Karim would bring to him. Although Karim had many shortcomings, he was good at buying inexpensive and inconspicuous used cars and making sure that they were reliable enough to make the four-day drive back to Boston. They would load this last crate of cargo into the trunk of the car, and then Karim would fly the plane back into Canada. At the same time, El Amin would begin his cross-country drive back to Massachusetts, staying carefully under the speed limit at all times. His trip would be uneventful.

There were only a few details to work out before the plan for this summer's attack was fully operational. Flying the plane at the correct altitude and activating and dropping the grenades was easy. What he needed to practice was taking into account the speed of the plane as he dropped the grenades, because he wanted to drop the first one precisely at the exit of the park. And he also needed to become more adept at turning the plane around quickly so that he could make several passes over the crowd of people in a short amount of time. If the first drop was accurate, the exit would become a place of chaos, and the remainder of the crowd would be trapped like sheep in a pen. Then he could make several passes over the crowd, dropping two grenades per pass. Three, with God's help. He had done enough research to know that a grenade's maximum kill radius was five to ten meters. The plan was to have each grenade explode a few meters above the ground. If the crowd was dense, over two hundred people would be in each grenade's killing zone. With God's help, the death toll would be extreme.

And then he would strike his final blow.

He checked his bearing and saw the small lake that served as his landmark. He banked around to properly orient himself for the approach, dropped into his descent, and landed smoothly. He taxied to the meeting spot, got out of the plane, and unloaded the crate of grenades onto the ground under the wing. Karim was sure to be late again, which is why he never received an assignment with great glory.

But to his surprise, about a minute later, an inconspicuous blue car came into El Amin's view, heading right for the plane. As it slowed, however, he realized that Karim was not the driver. Karim had a fat face, with a heavy beard. This was an older man with a thin face, wearing a baseball cap.

El Amin froze. In his worst nightmares he had not expected that a stranger would simply drive up to him this way. If he got into the plane and tried to fly away, at the very least, he would draw attention to himself. The last thing they needed was for people to be looking for him. The driver of this car would be able to give a description of the plane, and if he had a cell phone, a search might start quickly. El Amin worked best in total anonymity, out in the open, blending in. He did not do well on the run, looking over his shoulder at every turn.

Before the driver got a chance to pull around to the side of the plane where the grenades sat, El Amin took one, put it into the pocket of his jacket, and strolled to the other side of the plane, so he was in full view of the driver. The car pulled up to him. If something went wrong, El Amin would try to use the grenade. But as he peered into the driver's window, he could see that there was no immediate threat. The driver looked like an old farmer, not some government official. The window rolled down, and the driver took a lit cigarette out of his mouth, smiled, and said in a strange accent, "Howdy, there. Run into some trouble?"

At first, El Amin couldn't comprehend the meaning of the question. But then he understood. This man thought he had made an emergency landing, and came to offer help. He had to get him away from here, but without raising suspicion.

"Yes, I got surprised by the weather, and thought it would be best to set it down here, wait for the storm to pass, and then fly back," he answered, hoping that would satisfy the man.

The man nodded. He looked up toward the cloud cover. "Makes sense," he said. Then he turned back to face El Amin directly. A troubled look was in the stranger's eyes. What did he see? El Amin slid his finger into the ring of the grenade. The man said, "You're getting soaked. Wanna hop in, wait it out for a while? I'm in no big hurry."

The rain was coming down steadily now, and El Amin was very wet. That, of course, didn't matter. He was prepared to make far greater sacrifices for this holy mission. But he couldn't tell that to this silly old man. He smiled. He couldn't think of a way to refuse the offer without sounding suspicious. "Thank you," he said. "That is very nice of you." He walked around to the passenger side of the car and got in.

The car smelled like an airless ashtray, but it was warm and dry. "Bob McAllister," said the driver, with another smile, holding out his hand.

El Amin released his grip on the grenade, withdrew his right hand from his pocket, wiped it on his pants, and shook the old man's hand. He'd stay until the rain lightened, then he'd leave the stranger's car and wait for Karim. "Hello, Bob," he said. "My name is Fred Smith." He put his hand back in his pocket.

It turned out that Bob was simply a lonely old man. His wife had died two years earlier of cancer. He had been a farmer for most of his life, but had flown single-engine planes for a while in the sixties. Driving over to see if his fellow pilot was all right was at least half motivated by a desire to talk to someone. The old man reminded El Amin a little bit of his father's younger brother. The deep rumble of the car's idling engine, the rhythmic swishing of the windshield wipers, and the monotonous drone of the man's voice made it hard to stay awake.

A tapping on his window startled El Amin, and his hand tightened on the grenade. "Who's that?" Bob asked. A hooded figure stood outside in the rain. Karim.

"I'll see," said El Amin, opening the door and stepping out into the rain. As soon as he did, Karim grabbed him with both hands and threw him to the muddy ground. "What are you doing?" El Amin sputtered, scrambling to his feet, only to see Karim dive into the car. He was lying across the front seat, with his legs hanging out of the open passenger door. The automobile suddenly lurched forward and began driving erratically into the field, still with Karim's legs hanging out of the doorway. The car started to turn to the left, and then there was a loud bang, and some of the car's windows exploded. The car continued to drift toward the left, but slower now. It rolled to a stop fifty meters from the plane.

El Amin didn't know what to do. The rain continued to beat down steadily. He nervously fingered the grenade in his pocket and reluctantly approached the car from behind. As he got closer, he could hear the car's engine still running. Exhaust was coming from the tailpipe. And Karim's legs were still hanging out of the open passenger door. They were not moving. When he got close enough to look through the rear window, he could see blood splattered on the inside of the windshield. The wipers continued to work against the rain.

He crept carefully around to the passenger side of the car and looked inside. It was a sight of horrible carnage. Bob was dead. He still sat in the driver's seat, but his face and chest were so badly hit with shrapnel and so bloody that they were scarcely recognizable.

Karim was lying with his head and right arm at Bob's feet. His left hand and arm were gone. The left side of his neck had been hit by shrapnel, and blood was still pouring out of him. If he wasn't dead now, he would be in moments.

Obviously, Karim had martyred himself. He was such a fool! Apparently, while El Amin and Bob were talking, Karim had driven behind them, to the plane. He had seen that El Amin was in the car and, fearing that they had been discovered, decided that he had to kill the driver. So he took a grenade from the plane, pulled El Amin out of the car, dove in, and pressed the gas pedal with his right hand while holding the live grenade at Bob's chest.

Yes, now Karim the fool was a martyr. And now El Amin had a tremendous problem on his hands.

Detroit, Michigan

LENA WAS INSTANTLY WIDE AWAKE.

As well as terrified and alone.

After she had run from her apartment, she had gone to an ATM and withdrawn five hundred dollars—the maximum. Then she found a local motel, checked in under the name Amy Kurasawa, and paid in cash. She tried to call her parents, but there was no answer, which meant that they had already started on their trip. She left a message on their cell phone, saying that she was going to be out of touch for a while but that she was okay.

Then she'd tried to call Becca, but she always turned off the ringer on her phone when she went to sleep, so

Lena had only been able to leave a message to meet her at room 206 of the Sunset Motel as soon as she could get away from work the next day.

The good news was that she was on to something. Reporters didn't get drugs planted in their homes by rogue cops if they weren't doing something right.

The bad news was that Lena didn't know what she was doing. And she was scared to death. Suddenly everything and everyone was suspicious. Those men had been in her apartment before. She hadn't really moved those newspapers onto the already-read pile in her bedroom the other day—they had. That was the same day she found the remote on top of the TV—the one place she never put it. If they hadn't been there to plant the drugs the first time, what had they come for? What would they have done if she had been there when they broke in the first time?

The second break-in had come just a few days after Lena had ignored Sergeant Kanteros's warning and tried to call his boss. So the Detroit Police Department had to be involved, along with the FBI. Which meant that Lena had to be extremely careful about who she went to for help. She had no idea who in the police force was behind this, and therefore no way of knowing if she went to the police for help whether she'd just be going to a person involved in—what? Covering up totally lame burglaries?

So here she was. Hiding in a seedy motel room at 11:45 in the morning, all alone with her fifty-third cup of terrible coffee. Jumping eight feet into the air every time one of the maids knocked on any door within two hundred feet of her room.

At five minutes after noon, Becca finally arrived.

"So what's the big mystery?" she demanded, as Lena let her into the room, closing the door hastily behind her. "I came as soon as I could." Then she looked at Lena's face. "Hey. Are you all right?"

"I'm fine," said Lena, and then, just to make things perfect, she burst into tears.

AS LENA CAME THROUGH THE FRONT DOOR OF Becca's apartment, she came face-to-face with the gigantic poster of Jimi Hendrix that Becca had gotten last week, staring at her from the opposite wall of the tiny entryway. And as soon as she turned into the living room, she had to duck out of the way of the branches of Becca's ficus tree, Ernie, whose tremendous pot sat on a low dolly, which Becca rolled around the apartment, depending on where the light was.

Becca turned on the CD player, which started blasting out a Barenaked Ladies tune. Then she crossed over to her bedroom. "Make yourself at home," she called over the music. "I'm just going to change my clothes." Then she closed the door, and another gigantic face, this one of Einstein, stared out at Lena from the back of the door.

In fact, everything about Becca's apartment was oversized, except the apartment itself, which was smaller than Lena's.

But what mattered was that it was a place where Lena could hide and try to figure out what to do. She set down her laptop and slumped onto the couch.

What do you do when you can't go to the police? It had always been a pet peeve of Lena's when characters in the movies got into terrible trouble because they tried to handle things alone instead of just calling the police. What should you do if your house looks like it's been broken in to and had its power shut off? Don't call the police—just blunder around in the dark, until the dangerous bad guys grab you. What should you do if you get accosted by a stranger and told about a terrifying set of things that are going to happen unless you perform some impossible task? Don't call the cops—go ahead and try to disarm the nuclear weapon.

And then smile prettily when Bruce Willis comes crashing through the door seconds before the bomb goes off.

That, of course, was one of the problems. There was no Bruce Willis waiting in the hallway, ready to come save her. And the other problem was that the police were the dangerous bad guys. Which meant that Lena really did have nowhere to turn for help. She was going to have to take care of this on her own.

Becca emerged from her bedroom, wearing jeans and a T-shirt that was so big it came down to her knees, with a message printed across the front: THAT'S RIGHT—IT'S ALL ME. DEAL WITH IT. Then she sat down next to Lena on the couch and said, "I think I figured out what to do."

SEVENTEEN

Dear Kev—

There's a lot that I never got to tell you before you died. I used to regret that. I felt like I got cheated out of so much. I never got a chance to talk to you about girls, and getting married, and having kids. About colleges, and what kind of career you wanted to have.

After the bombing, I did a lot of research and then a lot of investigation into terrorism. And then September 11 happened. Now I wouldn't know what to tell you if you were still alive. It would have been so hard for me to try to explain to you how people can be so single-minded. How can the lives of innocent children be expendable? How can it be acceptable that they are intentionally taken? How would I have explained that to someone like you? No matter what age you were.

I wasn't very sure of myself as a parent. I didn't know how I was going to talk to you about things like the racism and hatred that this country still manages to generate, and death, and war. But the terrorism that is alive now is so horrible that if somebody cast a magic spell on me, and I could have a normal life with kids again, I don't know if I'd want to have them.

But I'm glad I had you. Even though it was for much too short a time, I'm so glad I had you.

Love, Daddy

(Letter #41 from Calvin Thompkins to deceased son, Kevin)

Two Killed in Bizarre Collision

Glasgow, Montana. Police discovered the burned bodies of two men today in a field 12 miles north of Glasgow, Montana. The men apparently died in a freak collision between a car and a small airplane, which caused an explosion and a fire that extensively burned both vehicles and the bodies of both victims.

Although neither victim has been officially identified, authorities have stated that the car involved in the accident was registered to Robert McAllister, age 64, a native of Glasgow. The plane was registered to the Yellow Aviation Flight School, which is based in Moose Jaw, Canada. Corporate records indicate that it was last rented to an individual named Morris Humphries, of Regina, Canada, four days prior to the discovery of the accident. Authorities have not been able to locate either McAllister or Humphries since the discovery of the bodies.

No official determination has been made as to the cause of the collision, but local law enforcement officers believe that it was little more than very bad luck and possibly bad weather which led to the freak collision. "There's no artificial light anywhere near the field," Police Sergeant Ed Qualls said, "so the accident must have happened at night, or else they would have seen each other coming and probably would have avoided the crash." Qualls did not speculate on why a plane and a car would have been in that field, although he did indicate that there was no evidence that either vehicle or operator was involved in any illegal activities.

Authorities from the National Transportation and Safety Board have been sent to investigate the crash.

(*Los Angeles Times*, May 6, page 65)

May 7—Washington, D.C.

CARLOS OLIVEIRA SHOOK HIS HEAD. A CAR-and-plane collision in some field in Montana. He'd save that one. He carefully cut the article out of the newspaper, mounted it on a three-hole-punched piece of cardstock, and placed the card into the daily news binder. As a part of the normal White House routine, the Chief of Staff gave the President a daily briefing on major news stories. But President Ferguson had told Carlos that he thought the best presidents were the ones who remembered that day-to-day life in America was very different from day-to-day life in the West Wing of the White House, so he asked Carlos to put together what he had started to call "The Oliveira Times."

If this had been a normal week, Carlos wouldn't have had a chance to keep up with that particular chore, because he would have been traveling with the President and the First Lady these past few days. They were attending an educational conference in St. Louis, and then they were making a few stops in Texas to promote an education reform bill that the President was trying hard to get through the Congress.

But when President Ferguson heard that Carlos's sister's law school graduation was smack in the middle of the trip, he refused to allow Carlos to do anything but attend the graduation. It was too important an accomplishment to miss, he said, so Carlos went, and was now impatiently waiting for the President's return tomorrow.

He didn't like it when the President was away. For one thing it was too quiet, and for another, Carlos needed to ask for some help, because he still couldn't figure out what do to about the Charley Cullhane thing.

The President had asked him to contact Charley's family. He was supposed to try to ask them whether they could provide any details regarding the special project Charley had been handling for President Graham. It was a long shot, since it was obvious from the way that Charley had disappeared, and from the contents of the memos, that he didn't want any of this to become public.

But instead of learning anything about the memos, Carlos learned that both of Charley's parents were dead, that he had no brothers, and that his only sister never returned phone calls. If the number Carlos had called ten times over the past week was even hers.

Carlos took a break to check his e-mail and noticed a subject line that read simply "Charley." He opened it and read:

Dear Mr. Oliveira,

My name is Nancy Nissenbaum. I am Charley Cullhane's sister. I'm sorry that I haven't returned any of your calls and that I am contacting you this way, but ever since Charley's disappearance, I have been terribly afraid that something bad is going to happen to me or my family, so I have been in hiding.

The reason I am writing is because the day after President Graham died, Charley came to see me. It was the last time I saw him. He told me that he had quit his job, and that he was going to go away for a while. Then he said something very strange. He said that he didn't want me to worry, but if anything should happen to him, it was extremely important that I should get in touch with you and to tell you to speak to a guy who works at the I.R.S. named Boris Staley . . .

Before he even finished the letter, Carlos was looking for the phone number of the I.R.S.

Northampton, Massachusetts

AS ZACK ENTERED THE MAIN OFFICE OF THE Stone Gate Apartments in Northampton, he was somewhat surprised at how neat it was. He and Terry had met for lunch and then come to investigate the apartment shared by the two female victims of Cal's rampage. The manager was on the phone when they arrived. While Zack stood at the counter, Terry grabbed a magazine and sat down to wait.

Earlier that day, Zack had spent a little time playing "Driving" with Justin. This consisted of pushing tiny toy cars around the floor of the playroom, occasionally moving close enough to the other player's car so that you could ask for directions to the swimming pool or the grocery store. Justin had chosen his own outfit today, and was dressed in a red-and-white horizonal-striped T-shirt and blue-and-white vertical-striped shorts. If the poor kid looked at himself in the mirror, he'd probably have an epileptic seizure. After Zack's third visit to the post office in about five minutes with a fire engine, he took a break, sat with his back leaning against the couch, and started the conversation he was dreading.

"So, Justin, when the trial comes up for Mr. Thompson, I'm going to be working for lots of days in a row."

Justin, who was in the middle of a trip to the video

store with his cherry red vintage Corvette, said without looking up, "Okay."

Zack took a deep breath. "So I've been thinking that it would probably be good if, just during the week or two that the trial is happening, you stayed at Aunt Claire and Uncle Tyler's house with them, okay? I'd visit you on the weekends, and we could talk every day on the phone. Would you like to do that?" Zack and Justin hadn't spent a night apart since Justin had come home with him almost five years ago. It was anybody's guess how Justin would react.

Zack wasn't overjoyed about the idea himself. Not that Claire and Tyler were a problem—his sister and her husband were ideal babysitters, except that their stupid cell phone never seemed to work for more than two minutes at a stretch. It just felt a little irresponsible putting Justin into someone else's care for such a long time.

The Corvette had been replaced by a blue 1966 Mustang convertible for a spin to the dentist's office.

Justin looked at him. "Aunt Claire and Uncle Tyler?" he said.

"Yeah. They were thinking that maybe you could help them when they took Spikey for his walks, and—"

"All *right*!" shouted Justin, breaking into a huge smile and then jumping up and running into Zack's arms. "I *love* Spikey! Can I feed him, too?"

Spikey was a little black terrier that urinated more than any living creature on earth. "I think you should probably ask Aunt Claire and Uncle Tyler about that."

"Okay," Justin agreed, jumping up. "Let's go."

For the next few minutes, Zack and Justin worked a little bit on the concept of time, and agreed that Justin would continue to play "Driving" while Zack called Claire and Tyler and checked on the Spikey question.

So much for Justin's reaction.

The manager hung up now and walked over. He was about sixty years old and still wore a military-style flat-top haircut. Justin had a theory that people who wore that style hair liked to carry trays on their heads. The man looked as if at one point in his life he had been very strong. Right now, he looked a little out of breath, a little mean, and a lot overweight. He slapped his meaty hands down on the top of the counter, displaying a tattoo on each forearm. The one on the left read *Back off*, and on the right, *Cuz I said so*. He looked first at Zack, then at Terry, and then said, much too loud for the room, "How can I help you gentlemen?" Great. *All those within the sound of my voice tremble with fear. Now drop and give me twenty.*

Zack looked over at Terry, whose smile was far too broad. In about fifteen seconds, he was going to rent an apartment here just so he could sue this dumb-ass on a weekly basis.

"I'm Zack Wilson—" Zack began, but the manager cut him off.

"Right," he said, with a look clearly meant to be intimidating. He was probably really something with the elementary school crowd. "The lawyers. Lemme get the file." He lumbered back to his desk, pulled out a manila folder from the bottom drawer, and brought it over to the counter. "Let's see, you wanted to know about number forty, right?" he said, opening the file. Inside there was only a lease, a copy of a receipt, and a photocopy of a check. The manager spun the folder around so Zack and Terry could see it. "Only thing strange about this is that the apartment is rented right through the end of the summer."

The term of the women's lease ran from September 1

through August 31. "But isn't that normal?" Zack asked. "A year's lease?"

"Yeah, the lease is normal, but they paid already," he said. "For the whole year. When they signed this, they gave me a check for the whole thing, plus a month's security." He pointed at the photocopy of the check. "See? Nobody ever does that."

The check was for $13,000. It was signed by Leon Lamere. "Can we get a copy of these?" Zack asked, handing him the check and the lease.

The manager scowled. Did he practice that in the mirror? "Yeah, all right." He walked over to a copy machine and turned it on.

Terry showed Zack the magazine he had been reading. On the cover was a picture of Calvin's horrendous mug shot, and the article inside was titled "Dealing with Demons—The Death Penalty—Whether Vengeance Is Cost-Effective." Below that was a picture of the bodies of Calvin's victims being taken out of the building on stretchers. "Impartial jury of his peers?" Terry said. "Piece of cake."

"You lookin' into Leon?" the manager asked from the copier. "Didn't give me any problem. Him and the two girls all signed the lease. That's the nonnegotiable policy around here." While the manager's back was to them, Zack glanced at Terry, who had closed his eyes and was pressing his fingers to his head. Pompous wore him out. "They had no beef with that."

"So the apartment is unoccupied, but technically, since it's rented to Leon, he's got it through the summer?" Zack asked.

"You got it," the manager grunted, returning with the copies and slapping them down on the counter. "Even if I wanted to rerent it, which I don't, it's Leon

Lamere's place until next September 1. I tried to call him after I heard them girls got killed by that black guy, you know, your client, but his number's been changed. Nobody got in touch with me for weeks after they died, so I went in there myself and, you know. Cleaned the food out of the refrigerator, took out the garbage. Stuff like that." Because good apartment managers do stuff like that. And if there happened to be some cash lying around . . .

"When you were in there, did you notice anything unusual?" Zack asked.

Once again, out came the scowl. *I am the most terrifying apartment manager in all the land.* Zack suppressed the laughter that began to bubble up inside of him. "You wanna take a look yourselves?" the manager said. "I got no problem with that."

"Absolutely," Zack said, exchanging a glance with Terry as the manager went back to his desk, opened the top drawer, and grabbed a large ring of keys.

ZACK HADN'T REALLY EXPECTED MUCH TO come of a search of Apartment 40. So when he entered, he wasn't disappointed.

The place was predictably stuffy. As the manager opened some of the window blinds and Terry turned on some lights, Zack could see clouds of dust drifting in the air. A few flies buzzed around. It didn't smell or feel dirty. Just unlived in.

The front door to the apartment opened into a sparsely furnished living room. The most remarkable thing about it was the lack of any clutter. No magazines, no junk mail, no books, no pictures. Nothing. Talk about spartan.

At the far end of the living room a half wall separated it from the kitchen. As they entered, the manager said, "I took out some garbage that was in here, and emptied out the refrigerator, but that was it. They kept the place really clean." He was right. The countertops were bare. Other than the fact that the cupboards and drawers contained very few plates, cookware, and utensils, there was nothing unusual about the place.

"Did Leon ever come by after the lease was signed?" Zack asked, as they turned into a hallway that led to the bathroom and a couple of bedrooms. "If you see him, I'd like him to know that we're trying to get hold of him."

"Nah," bellowed the manager. "The only time I seen him was when he came with the check. Tall, skinny guy. Didn't say much. Kinda weak-looking." *I almost killed him with my powerful handshake.*

And then, just as Zack reached the bedroom on the right, Terry said from the other one, "Hey, boys and girls, here's some nifty things."

Aside from a twin bed and a dresser, the room contained a workstation, with a computer, a printer, a scanner, and a large flat metal box with a glass top. Small pieces of electrical tape had been stuck to the glass, outlining several rectangles and squares of different sizes on its surface. Some razor blades, X-Acto knives, pens, pencils, a glue stick, a bottle of rubber cement, another of nail polish remover, and a booklet from the Massachusetts Registry of Motor Vehicles were sitting on the desk to the right of the box. Zack turned on the computer while Terry went over to the glass-topped box.

"It's a light board," he explained, reaching around behind it to flip a switch. The glass top became a very bright, white surface. "I used to use one when I worked on the school newspaper in college." He pulled open the top drawer of the desk. "I bet we find something fun in here."

Sure enough, there were about fifteen or twenty driver's licenses, from many different states, held together by a rubber band. In another part of the drawer was a stack of passports. Two were from Egypt, three from the United States, and two from France. One of those was clearly in the process of being altered—the photo had been stripped off.

The monitor to the computer flickered on. Zack took a look at some of the more recently used files, while Terry rummaged through the rest of the desk. The contents of the computer confirmed that whoever was using this stuff was doing some pretty sophisticated artwork. On documents that looked very official.

Terry had found strips of photographs of a young man that had been taken at some photo booth in a mall somewhere. Terry laid one of the strips on top of one of the squares that had been created by the electrical tape, and the outline of the light square showed clearly through one of the photos. "Let's say you needed a picture of a face that was, oh, I don't know, exactly two inches by two inches, because Uncle Waldo got you that Little Suzy Passport-Maker kit you always wanted for your birthday. You'd just take your trusty X-Acto knife here"—Terry picked up one of the knives—"and presto." He cut the photo along the line created by the tape, picked it up, and placed it exactly into the space on the passport where the photo had been removed. "Congratulations, you are the newest citizen of France."

The computer made a noise. Zack looked over at the monitor. "Holy shit," he said. The computer was systematically deleting all of its files.

"What the fuck?" Terry said, reaching over and

hitting some keys on the keyboard, as if that were going to do anything. Zack flipped the switch on the computer itself. There was no change. The files kept disappearing. He lunged for the power cord and yanked it out of the wall. But the computer was on battery backup by now. The evidence was disappearing.

"Would you mind telling me what the hell you guys think you're doing?" the manager asked. His game face was back on.

Terry had had enough. "What we're trying to do is preserve evidence that would be admissible in a murder trial, but unfortunately, this computer's been rigged to wipe itself clean if anyone turns it on wrong. So I guess that means you'll need to be a witness this summer at the trial. We'll be in touch."

"Listen, fellas, I had no problem with these girls," the manager said, backing away from the desk, and Terry. "I had no idea what they were up to. If we gotta call the cops, that's fine with me. But I got nothing to do with this. We need to get going." *Since it's time for me to run and hide under my bed. Cuz I said so.*

"Yeah, okay." Zack was pulling open the dresser drawers. Nothing but clothes. Whoever was using the setup in this room was obviously in the business of creating false identities. That much was clear. Did that prove that they were terrorists? No. Did it justify blowing them away? No.

Did it make Cal's story start to look even more credible? Yeah. A lot.

After they left the apartment, the manager nearly broke into a sprint to get back to his office. "We really might need him to testify to what he saw on the monitor before the computer erased itself," Terry said, as he and Zack left the apartment grounds.

"I know," Zack said. "And he's going to be the world's shittiest witness, too."

"Maybe," Terry said, "but we better stand next to each other when we question him, because if he makes his scary face in court, one of us might faint."

EIGHTEEN

Dear Kev—

The people I shot weren't that old, you know. Most of them were in their twenties. That's how old your mother and I were when we had you. I think about that sometimes. And sometimes I think about their parents.

(Letter #45 from Calvin Thompkins to deceased son, Kevin)

DIST. ATTY. O'NEILL: *Directing your attention to January 14, at approximately 3:30 that afternoon, did you respond to a call at 214 Main Street?*

OFFICER MARANOWSKI: *Yes, sir. Me and Officer Tommy Clarke were the first officers on the scene.*

Q: *What did you observe when you arrived at the apartment?*

A: *Well, when we got there, we drew our service revolvers and ran upstairs. As soon as I saw the defendant lying on his back in the hallway, bleeding, I called for an ambulance.*

Q: *When he saw you, did he say anything?*

MR. WILSON: *Objection.*

THE COURT: *Overruled. You may answer.*

A: *He kind of laughed and said, "I can't believe they didn't kill me."*

(Trial Volume VII, Page 112)

May 8—Austin, Texas

MATT WAS BEAT. HE HAD JUST SPENT MUCH OF the afternoon and evening in discussions regarding education reform. It was ridiculous. Surgeons could perform heart operations in utero, astronauts could live for months on a space station orbiting the earth, but nobody on the planet could figure out how to teach kids to read as well as they could thirty years ago.

The limo pulled into the private drive of the Texas governor's mansion, where he and Sammy were staying for two days before returning to Washington. Secret Service agents waited for the motorcade at the entrance to the guest suite. Matt wondered if Alvin wished he hadn't invited them to stay, now that he saw what the Secret Service did to a place before the President got within ten miles of it.

Matt went right to the kitchenette, to find a beer. Sammy was already there, sitting at the table, reading a computer printout and writing something on a legal pad. "You know what?" she said, as Matt came in. "I'm really glad I married you, but this thing is driving me crazy."

She was wearing a T-shirt and shorts. It was good to see her. "Hang on one second," Matt said, as he got a couple of bottles out of the refrigerator, gave one to Sammy, kissed her, sat down next to her at the table, and said, "I'm glad I married you, too." He took a swig of the beer and closed his eyes as the cold liquid ran down his throat. As soon as they had a chance, he was going to take Sammy to some Caribbean island for a vacation. No, first he'd take her bathing suit shopping, then they'd go on vacation. She'd look good in something blue. An image came to mind. Maybe a little less of the blue, a little more of Sammy. A better image. He smiled, opened his eyes, looked at his wife, and said, "Okay. Now what were you saying?"

Sammy closed the printout, looked briefly at the legal pad and then up at Matt. "All right. Carlos got me all this background information about the judges who were on that list," she said. "I was sure that if we could find something linking them, we could figure out why Graham wanted Charley Cullhane to dig up all of this dirt on them." She looked back to the pad. "Most of them seemed to be in New York and Michigan, but I figured I'd start with the judges from North Carolina."

"That's funny. You're from North Carolina."

She just gave him a look. "Ha ha," she deadpanned. "I just wanted to see . . . you know."

"Whether you knew anyone that might have been on the list."

"Yes," Sammy said. "But I didn't." She looked down at the pad. "There were only three: Gary Mills, Claire Cath, and John Wynott."

"Where'd they go to law school?"

"Stanford, Boston University, and Duke. Yuck."

Sammy went to the University of North Carolina. Everything about Duke was a problem for her. "Does the University of North Carolina even have a law school?"

"Of course it does. It's very highly respected by judges and lawyers across the country."

Continued discussion on that topic promised disaster. Matt shifted back. "Who appointed them?"

"Mills and Cath were appointed by Reagan, and Wynott by Bush. The father."

"Is it a Republican thing?"

"No," she replied. "When I checked the judges in the other states, I found lots on the list appointed by Clinton. There were even a couple who were appointed by Carter."

"What about undergrad?"

"They went all over the place."

There had to be a common thread running between these judges. They didn't just accidentally end up on that list. "Did you get a chance to look at what they were doing before they were appointed?" Matt asked.

"That's the one thing that I was sure was it." Sammy flipped open the legal pad. "The first six people I checked all worked as Assistant U.S. Attorneys or for the Attorney General's office before they were appointed. But then I found others who didn't. There wasn't any pattern."

That was no surprise. Matt had read somewhere that more than half of the judges in the country had worked as prosecutors of one kind or another. He took another swig of beer. "What about their jobs? Are they all the same kind of judges?"

Sammy turned to another page. "That's the only one that seemed not completely and totally hopeless," she said. "But that might just be wishful thinking." She read from the pad. "Of the fifty-nine judges on the list, fifty-five were magistrate judges. They do the unimportant stuff, like pretrial motions and scheduling conferences. Except these four: Aubrey Seaver, Craig McDonald, Bonnie Wescott, and Francis Constantino. They're District Court judges."

Fifty-nine judges, all magistrate or district court judges? "No Bankruptcy Court judges?"

"No."

"How about judges on the Circuit Courts?"

"Nope," she said. "And no one on the Supreme Court, either, thank God."

"Wait a minute," Matt said. "Did you say Aubrey Seaver is on the list?"

"He was one of the District Court judges."

"He retired late last year," Matt said, "very unexpectedly. He was a young guy, seemed to like what he was doing, and then, poof. Quits. Just like that."

"Just like that," Sammy repeated, looking through some of her papers. "Let's see. Right here. Seaver retired into private practice, in Los Angeles, last November. And I just happened to have looked up his phone number," she said, reaching over and taking Matt's hand. "Can I assume that I'm authorized to make an unofficial phone call to Attorney Seaver?"

He kissed her. "I'm glad you use your powers for the forces of good," he said with a smile.

She smiled back. "I'll call him tomorrow." She kissed him, hard. "Let's go to bed, Mr. President," she said. "I'm tired of saving the world."

Worcester, Massachusetts

"BY NOW, YOU ALL KNOW THAT DRINKING AND doing drugs is a very dangerous way to live your life."

Pete was bombing. He never should have agreed to do this. He wasn't good at speaking to strange teenagers. He wasn't good at speaking to his own daughter. Hell, he wasn't good at speaking to anybody. "Not only is it illegal, it's a good way to get yourself killed."

Pastor Reid had talked him into addressing the young people's meeting that Natalie Reggio had been leading for the last few years. What a dumb idea. The kids were squirming in their seats. A boy with really greasy hair was staring at something out the window. Julie, the girl that Natalie had asked Pete to look out for, was writing something on another boy's hand. Pete might as well have been speaking in Chinese for all they cared. Oh, well. He tried. It was time to finish up and get home.

"I was with Natalie Reggio on the night she went into the hospital."

And just like that, everything went quiet. It was eerie, like the sound of her name had some kind of magical power. Was this what they wanted to hear? Didn't they already know about this?

"You saw what happened? You saw her get hurt?" asked one of the girls.

"Well, I wasn't there, but we finally learned what happened," Pete said. "Natalie had been drinking. A lot. When she reached the hospital, her blood alcohol level was over point two-oh."

"Shit," said one of the kids quietly.

"Anyway, apparently she and some friends had gone to a bar, and were drinking, and a fight broke out. Natalie was involved."

"Natalie was in a fight?" asked the boy Julie was writing on.

"That's right," Pete replied. "Not what you expected from Natalie, I guess."

"No way," the kid responded. "She was like, I don't know. She just wasn't into that," he insisted.

"Well, alcohol can change people," Pete said. "It sure changed Natalie that night."

"I thought she just fell," said another.

"She did fall," Pete said, "but probably not like you think. The bartender who was there said that in the middle of the fight, Natalie decided to climb up on a table, I guess to jump on somebody or something. Anyway, she steps onto a chair, and then puts her foot on the table, and it's wet, and her foot slips off the table, and she falls backward and lands right on the back of her head on the ceramic tile floor of the bar. It fractured her skull." The kids were hypnotized. "I must have gotten there just after that, because even though she got up from the fall, about a minute later she lost consciousness, and we rushed her to the hospital. That's when she went into the first coma."

Julie's eyes looked like they were too big for her face. Was she scared? Was this what Natalie had hoped would happen? "Anyway, as you probably can tell, I don't usually do these talks. Officer De Luca runs the D.A.R.E. program out of our station, and she's the expert on this kind of thing. I can tell you this, though. I spoke to Natalie at the hospital, and I know that she is a brave, smart young woman. And I know that when she started drinking that night, she knew she was making a mistake, but she never thought she'd end up in a fight, or in the hospital, or in a coma. Nobody ever does."

Pete wasn't quite sure how to end, but it didn't seem to matter. As he looked out into the troubled eyes of the teenagers, he felt for the first time in a long time a sense of real accomplishment. He was getting through to some of them. Out of the corner of his eye, Pete saw somebody come into the room and hand Pastor Reid something, and then saw Pastor Reid approaching him. He stepped back, assuming that the pastor would have something to say to conclude the meeting.

Instead, he came over to Pete and solemnly handed him the phone message that he had just been given.

Natalie Reggio was dead.

Wilton, Massachusetts

TERRY NUDGED THE SPEEDOMETER OF HIS Lexus up to eighty. He and Zack were on their way out to meet with Leon Lamere. For such an obviously hopeless case, they were sure doing a lot of driving.

"It's jury nullification, isn't it?" he asked. "That's all we've got."

Zack was quiet for a minute. "Yeah," he said, exhaling loudly. "That's it, unless we can convince Cal to let us try insanity. There's no way we're going to stop O'Neill from proving that Cal murdered those people. But if we can show that they were terrorists, then maybe we've got a shot at having the jury look the other way."

Look the other way. *Ladies and gentlemen of the jury, we all know that our client is guilty, but he killed some very bad people, so can you please vote not guilty?* "That is so fucked up," Terry said, "even for us. The value of human life, the rule of law . . . Is there anything we aren't taking a potshot at in this case?" He flashed his brights at the idiot driving sixty-five in the left-hand lane. "If we win this thing, something is very, very wrong."

Zack remained silent. The idiot switched lanes. *Thank you, God.* "Oh, come on," Terry continued. "Don't tell me you actually believe we should win. You know I don't think Cal should be executed. But he's about as guilty as you can be. And according to the Constitution-bashing psychos at *The Boston Post,* about ninety-three percent of the world agrees with me."

"Yeah," Zack replied. "I know. But I've got to tell you, something happened when Justin and I were down in Florida, and it's been bugging me ever since. I was getting him an ice cream, and when I looked up, he had disappeared. For about thirty seconds, I thought I'd lost him." He took a deep breath. "And that feeling, when I thought he was gone . . . I've been thinking a lot about how Cal must have felt when he lost his little boy."

Terry couldn't imagine ever even having kids. The idea of losing one was so far out of his experience that thinking about it made no sense. He'd seen the haunted look of families who had lost a child to crime. It was as close as he ever expected, or wanted, to get. "Yeah, but, Zack, we can't just start handing out Get Out of Jail Free cards to the parents of every missing child so they can go hunting for bad guys. That's crazy."

They drove in silence for another minute. Then Zack asked quietly, "Is it any crazier than blowing up a five-year-old boy and his mother?"

IF LEON LAMERE WAS A TERRORIST, HE WAS THE frickin' jolliest terrorist Terry had ever met.

They had tracked down the address from the check used to rent the apartment. It was the home of Leon Lamere, in Wilton. Leon was the owner of Lamere's Furniture Palace, a gigantic furniture and carpeting outlet, and he had agreed to meet them at his store. He was a short, stocky man in his forties, who wore an expensive suit over a patterned silk shirt that was open at the neck. Leon never seemed to stop smiling. And he really liked gold jewelry. Loads of necklaces, bracelets on both wrists, a Rolex, rings on both hands. But despite the disco-king aura, Leon had a very friendly, genuine manner. Go figure. "Have you ever been to my store?" he asked, somehow smiling even more. "Come on in, I'll show you around while we talk."

The place was mammoth, and a lot of the furniture actually looked decent. They were only there for a couple of minutes before Zack's eyes began to glaze over. He didn't know a Stickney rocker from a Barcalounger. And couldn't care less. That was okay. Zack would live. Terry had been looking for a half-round end table for his living room for a long time. This just might be the place.

"So," Zack said, "we were hoping that you might be able to tell us whatever you could about Marianne Duhamel and Helene Ghazi."

A puzzled look crossed Leon's face. "I don't recognize either of those names—" he began, but then a cell phone rang. Lamere made an apologetic gesture and pulled a phone out of his pocket. "This is Leon," he said.

While he spoke, Terry walked a few steps away with Zack and sat down on an impressively uncomfortable couch. "Tall, skinny, and weak-looking. You think Mr. Tough Guy Manager was jerking us off?"

"I don't know," Zack replied. Another cell phone rang, and while still speaking on the first call, Leon reached into his other pocket with his free hand and pulled out another phone. He looked pretty embarrassed as he tried to juggle two phone calls and somehow indicate to Zack and Terry that he would be right with them. "He said it before he saw all the forgery stuff and got scared. I don't think he had any reason to lie. Maybe he just forgot what Leon looked like."

"Forget a guy who hands him a check for thirteen thousand bucks? I don't think so."

"Maybe Leon wrote the check, and some other guy delivered it," Zack said.

"Nope," Terry said. "I looked at the signatures on the check and the lease. They're identical." He reached into his jacket pocket and fiddled with a little electronic gadget. "You know, besides ads for Viagra and once-in-a-lifetime opportunities to refinance my home, I get more e-mail from Judge Cottonwood than anyone else," he said, handing the thing over to Zack.

It was a BlackBerry, a portable Internet device, and it was displaying an obviously bogus e-mail from someone purporting to be the judge, inviting Terry to clarify his position on some of the issues on the case, "so the trial would run with maximum efficiency." Zack handed it back. "Good thing you have one of these," he said.

Terry turned it off and said, "I'm telling you, one of these days, you're going to thank me for buying all this shit."

Finally, Leon was through with his calls. He came over to them, still holding the phones. "I'm so sorry," he said, sitting on a chair across from them. "I am turning them off." He put the phones back in his pockets. "Now, where were we?"

Zack held out a copy of the check and the lease to Leon. "We were hoping you could tell us anything you knew about this apartment lease, and the two women who signed it with you."

"Apartment lease?" Leon repeated, taking the papers. If he was lying about his confusion, he was a whiz at it. He looked exactly like somebody who had never signed an apartment lease with two women who forged passports. He reached into his jacket pocket to put on a pair of small, rectangular reading glasses. He looked first at the check and then at the lease. Then he shook his head. "Will you come with me to my office?" he said, standing. "I did not sign these things, but I think I know who did."

NINETEEN

DR. HAAS: *Victim One suffered six gunshot wounds. One bullet entered his right thigh from the rear, one entered the area of his right pelvis, one entered the right side of his rib cage from the rear, piercing his right lung, and three entered in a very small area in the center of his chest from the front.*

DIST. ATTY. O'NEILL: *Were you able to determine which, if any, of these gunshots caused the victim's death?*

A: *Well, two of the bullets that entered the front of his chest shattered his sternum and struck him directly in the heart. Either would have caused death within a matter of seconds. The third bullet that entered his chest severed his aorta, the principal artery carrying blood from the heart. That wound would have caused death within three to four minutes from exsanguination—basically, bleeding to death. Essentially, any one of those three wounds was the cause of death.*

(Trial Volume IX, Pages 70–71)

May 12—Wakefield, Massachusetts

AS SOON AS ZACK SAW CAL'S FACE HE COULD SEE that his client wasn't expecting any good news. That was fine, because he and Terry didn't have any.

They were visiting Cal in one of the tiny attorney/client rooms at MCI-Wakefield. Usually, by this time in the process, even in the most hopeless of situations, Zack had turned up something that he felt he could use to create a chance, even if just a slim chance, of some success at trial. This case was proving to be the exception.

"So," Cal said, sitting down at the table across from them. "Where are we?"

Terry snorted and looked away. Zack looked over some notes he had made. He spoke first.

"Well, we're pretty much in agreement that at this point, the only thing we can argue is jury nullification."

Cal nodded. "Tell them the whole story and hope that they won't convict me, even if it is technically murder."

"Yeah. Technically," Terry said.

"So have we hired one of those experts on picking juries?"

Terry closed his eyes, shook his head, and said, "Experts on picking juries. Oh my God." He looked like he had a headache.

"That kind of thing shows up on TV a lot more than in real life," Zack explained to their client. "We're court-appointed lawyers. I get fifty-four dollars an hour for working on your case, Cal. Because he's helping, Terry only gets thirty an hour. We had to beg the court for the five hundred dollars we spent having that tape translated into English. Defendants without tons of money don't get to hire jury selection experts."

"You don't, by any chance, still have tons of money lying around?" Terry asked. His eyes looked bloodshot.

"No," Cal answered cheerfully. "I gave it all away after I found the terrorists and decided what I was going to do."

Terry sighed. "Of course you did."

"So how do we pick the jury?" Cal asked.

"We look at the questionnaires they fill out, look at their faces, and guess," Zack said. "For what it's worth, I'm pretty good at picking juries," he added. "But in your case . . ." He trailed off. He didn't need to say that whatever jury was picked wasn't going to make the slightest difference.

Cal got the message. "Won't it matter who's on the jury when we start to talk about why I killed these people?"

"Well, we've been having a little problem running down the evidence that these people were who you said they were."

"What happened when you checked into how the women paid for their apartment?" Cal asked. "I actually never knew about that."

"Yeah," Zack said. "We went to see the person who we thought had paid, but it turns out it was probably his son."

"I don't understand," Cal said.

Terry jumped in. "The guy who we thought had signed the check has got so many bank accounts he can't keep them straight. He owns this mansion in Wilton, and this monster furniture store. He's like the king of the sofa beds. He's also the king of the shitty fathers. His wife's an alcoholic, his daughter's in some rehab halfway across the country, and his son, last time anyone saw him, was some religious freak wandering around Egypt."

"So what does this have to do with the women in that apartment?" Cal asked.

"It looks like the son forged the check," Zack said. "Apparently he knew that the father would either overlook it—"

"Overlook it," scoffed Terry. "Yeah, right. If my father caught me trying to rip him off for thirteen thousand dollars, he'd have taken the check and stapled it to my forehead as a gentle reminder not to try that again."

Angry Dad would have taken that kind of misbehavior as an opportunity to bail out of Zack's life even sooner than he actually did.

"Anyway, what ended up happening was that the father just assumed that the son was renting an apartment for himself," Zack explained to Cal. "The family apparently doesn't communicate very well."

"If stealing thirteen thousand dollars and then disappearing halfway around the world doesn't count as communicating," Terry said.

"So the son gave the money to the women," Cal mused. "And now they're dead, and we can't find him. So that's sort of a dead end."

"Right," Terry agreed. "Which makes this the total of what we've got so far: Some of the men that you shot spoke Arabic on the phone, and one of their conversations sounded like an old Al Qaeda conversation about pieces of an airplane. The two women you shot lived in a different apartment which was paid for by the fucked-up kid of a rich guy, and a year and a half ago, the kid was into religion in Cairo, but now he's Allah knows where. And in the women's apartment, there was a setup for forgery." Terry shook his head. "Man, you must have had more than that to be convinced that these people were really terrorists."

"I did," Cal said. "You should have seen the stuff the private detectives found."

"I'd love to," Terry replied, "but wouldn't you know that every single private eye we spoke to told us that he destroyed every single record he ever had about this case. So that kind of sucks."

Cal nodded. "I thought that might be a problem."

" 'Might be,' " Terry said through clenched teeth, rubbing his forehead.

Cal's gaze was steady. "I know I messed up. I wasn't thinking straight at all." He took a deep breath and let it out slowly. "All I knew was that when I went into that apartment, only one of two things was going to happen. Either I'd die as I succeeded in killing the terrorists, or I'd die as I failed to kill the terrorists. So it never crossed my mind that I'd need any of that information. I already knew these were bad people and they needed to be taken out. And since I figured I was a dead man, I didn't think I would need to prove anything about my motives for my actions."

"But what about if you didn't kill them? You weren't going to bother telling the world to look out for these guys?" Terry was still pretty angry.

Cal merely smiled. "No. I did have a plan for that."

"Which was . . . ?"

"I had written Steve Doctorow a letter—"

"I *knew* he knew more than he was telling us," Terry interrupted.

"I really didn't tell Steve anything," Cal said. "I just said that if something happened to me, he needed to open an envelope I sent with the letter and do what he thought was appropriate."

And there it finally was. The information they needed was in the envelope with Doctorow. They had found it in the most roundabout way imaginable, but they had found it. The question remained whether Cottonwood would allow it in, but at least—

"Unfortunately, when I survived the attack, I asked Steve to destroy the envelope."

Unfortunately. Terry squeezed his eyes shut and said, "I don't fucking believe this."

"I couldn't let anyone who had this information just sit there with it," Cal said. "I told you I wasn't thinking clearly. It never crossed my mind that it would be important to prove they were terrorists. All I was thinking was that sooner or later some Al Qaeda cell would learn that this information was in Steve's hands or some poor private detective's hands and then they'd kill them."

Cal was so busy protecting everyone else that he never stopped to think how thoroughly he was screwing himself.

"Quick question," Terry said. "Is there anything in the past six months that you *haven't* destroyed?"

Cal just sat there, staring at him. Then he turned to Zack. "So you're telling me that this is over?"

Zack said nothing.

May 19—Detroit, Michigan

IT WAS GOOD THAT LENA WAS SO PATHETICALLY short, and way good that she wasn't claustrophobic, because Mrs. Cyr from next door had come to visit Becca. That meant that Lena had to hide in the back of Becca's closet, crouching behind the humongous framed *Star Trek* poster that Becca hadn't had a chance to put up yet.

The first time someone knocked on Becca's door,

Lena thought she was going to vomit. She dove into the back of the closet and thought about all of the ways that she could give herself away. A sneeze. A leg cramp. A cough. What would happen to her if she were caught?

After that, hiding at the first hint that someone might be coming became part of Lena's routine. She tried to make it efficient, and not so terrifying.

But it was hard to feel anything but frightened when she was crammed into a closet, one forgetful moment from exposing herself to whatever awful fate awaited her at the hands of the police and the FBI.

There was something more to the LeClerq case than a high school teacher having a heart attack while calling 911. Lena was sure of that.

Unfortunately, that was about the only thing she was sure of.

Becca's theory was that the LeClerq case was, as she had called it, the tip of the nightmare, and that Lena had innocently stumbled onto something much bigger and badder than she could imagine, which was why she'd been threatened and then framed.

If that was true, then all Lena had to do was figure out what the bigger and badder thing was. Without getting herself or anyone else killed in the bargain.

Becca was fully involved now, spending whatever spare time she had checking into reports of break-ins where nothing but computer disks were taken, or reports of discrepancies in 911 tape transcripts. She was determined to find a pattern, or a name running through them all—some link that she could use to contact the FBI in Washington, D.C.

That was Becca's big plan. Contact the main office of the FBI and tell them the whole story. Lena had a little problem with that.

First, what exactly was the whole story? A dispute about who made a call to 911, and whether the caller reported a break-in or a heart attack. A police file that didn't mention the alleged break-in, during which, by the way, nothing valuable was stolen. The break-in at Lena's place. But she didn't even want to think about trying to convince an FBI agent in Washington that all of the drugs all over her apartment were planted there by FBI agents here in Michigan.

Oh, and the amazing disappearing Officer Halsey. And the veiled threat from Sergeant Whatever His Name Was.

Like anyone would ever believe her.

What it all boiled down to was that Lena was going to have to stay in hiding at Becca's place. She had had to stop going to work, and Becca was supporting both of them. Lena had done some research online from Becca's apartment and had noticed an unusual number of break-ins in Dearborn. She was going to have to figure out a way to speak to these victims without exposing herself to whoever was threatening her. It was hard to believe that there was a connection, but if there was, Lena was going to find it.

The idea that somebody had broken into her apartment and was trying to frame her was awful, and yeah, she was scared. But as time passed, something began to take root beneath her fear. Something that drove her to continue to try to connect the dots, to find out what was going on here—who was terrorizing her, who was coming into people's homes for reasons she still hadn't figured out.

Who had taken her life from her.

Camp David, Maryland

BORIS STALEY WAS USHERED INTO MATT'S OFfice.

The young man wore a suit that was remarkably ill-fitting and had the worst haircut and the largest glasses Matt had ever seen. He was blinking at an alarming rate. He looked scared to death.

Matt could only imagine the poor guy's confusion. His day had probably started just like every other day. First breakfast, then a ride on the train to his job as a computer programmer—"information technology specialist"—for the I.R.S. But on the way home, things went very differently. As soon as Boris left the building, a couple of big guys pounced on him, hustled him into a car, stuck a phone in his hand, and suddenly he's being driven to Camp David, for his own safety. What the hell?

"Hello," the young man stammered. "I'm Boris Staley, sir. I guess you wanted to see me." He obviously had no clue what was going on. Welcome to the club.

"I'm sorry about all the drama, Boris," Matt said, walking over to shake the young man's hand, "but I'm concerned that your life is in danger, and I needed to know that you are safe."

Apparently, the faster Boris blinked, the more his brain worked. Boris had gone to Cal Tech, and was as smart as you'd expect a computer programmer to be, but even he couldn't begin to make sense of this whole thing. "I'm sorry, Mr. President, but I can't imagine why anyone would want to hurt me. I'm just an I.T. guy who works for the I.R.S. I don't even get involved in anyone's taxes. I doubt that more than ten people in Washington know my name. Sir."

Matt smiled sadly. "Unfortunately, Boris," he said, "that is no longer true."

May 20

IT WAS A COMBINATION FAMILY GET-TOGETHER, picnic lunch, and emergency national security meeting. Seated at the conference table at the presidential retreat at Camp David with Matt and Sammy were Internal Revenue Service information technology specialist Boris Staley, strung about as tight as a ukulele, fearfully blinking away behind the giant windshield he wore as eyeglasses, and presidential body man Carlos Oliveira, who looked just about old enough to get into an R-rated movie.

Thomas Jefferson was probably turning over in his grave.

But then Jefferson hadn't discovered that his predecessor had set up a large-scale blackmail operation targeting federal judges. Matt needed help from people he could trust. And right now, these were the people he could trust. Sammy's phone call to Judge Seaver in California had been very unsuccessful. Matt was down to Boris.

Deli-style sandwiches, potato salad, soda, and iced tea had been served. Nobody seemed very hungry, though.

"Why don't we get started," Matt said, pushing away his plate. "The sooner I get this thing figured out, the sooner I can try to do something about it." He turned to young Mr. Staley, who was about five seconds from jumping out of his skin, and said, "Boris, were you able to get in touch with your folks?"

The question caught the anxious fellow entirely by surprise. For a moment, incredibly, the rate of blinking actually increased, but then he seemed to settle down a bit. He swallowed, gulped a breath, and spoke. "Uh, yes, sir. Yes, Mr. President, I did, thank you."

"Good. I didn't want there to be any unnecessary anxiety, in case you needed to stay put for a little while."

"Uh, yes, sir," Boris said. *Blink, blink.* "They said they were really excited to speak to you."

"Good," Matt said. Now that the poor kid was talking, there was a chance that he wouldn't hyperventilate himself into a heart attack. "So how about you tell us about your meeting with Charley Cullhane?"

The young man started to speak, but something must have gotten caught in his throat, and he started to choke. He reached for his soda with trembling hands and, coughing, he took a drink. It was anybody's guess whether that would calm him down, or whether he'd be the first person to drown in a glass of ginger ale at Camp David. But the storm passed, and he set the soda down on the table and got himself together.

"I don't remember exactly when it was, but about a year and a half ago, totally out of the blue, I got this e-mail from a guy who said his name was Charley Cullhane. He claimed he worked for the President, and he wanted to meet me for lunch to talk about something private—"

Sammy interrupted. "He said he worked for the President?"

Boris was nearly startled into another choking fit, but he hung in there. "I didn't save the e-mail, but it either said he worked for the President or for the White House. Anyway, we met for lunch, and he asked me for, well, the craziest report I ever heard of. He said it was a huge secret that had to do with national security. I checked his identification, and he even had a letter of introduction."

"From the President?" Sammy asked.

"No, from the Chief of Staff," Boris said. "Mr. Browning."

Creepy Vernon Browning. Matt looked over to Sammy, who kept her eyes on Boris. She never gloated about the serious things. He stretched out his leg and touched her shoe with his. He would apologize more formally later.

"It looked legitimate," Boris continued, "but I told him I would need clearance from my boss. He said that was all arranged. I figured he was nuts, but when I got back to work, I had the clearance to do the project."

"What did he ask you to do?" asked Matt.

"He wanted me to generate a list of names and addresses, sorted by zip code, of every taxpayer in the country that had a *q* in their name that was not followed by a *u.*"

The tension in the room was broken for a moment by some smiles at the absurdity of Boris's mission. "It sounds nuts," admitted Boris, "but imagine what that kind of a list would look like."

"It would look like a list of Arabic names," Carlos said quietly. And suddenly, the tension was back.

TWENTY

Dear Kev—

I had another bad dream the other night.

We were at the beach, playing, when suddenly I couldn't find you. I panicked, but then I saw you out in the water, and I relaxed for a minute. You wanted me to come out there with you and play.

Then this huge wave came up and just sort of crashed into you from behind, knocking you down. You got up, but you were so scared and hurt from the fall that you ran out of the water, and you wouldn't go back in.

I knew how much you loved swimming, so I got really mad at the ocean, and I started shouting at it. Then all of a sudden there was nobody on the beach but me, and while I was shouting at the ocean, I started throwing things into it. First I threw our cooler, then the chairs we brought down, then our beach blanket and all your toys. And I got madder and madder, shouting louder and louder.

Then suddenly, you're standing next to me again, and you're crying, and you say to me, "Daddy, stop!"

And then I woke up, feeling really bad.

I miss you.
Love, Daddy

(Letter #51 from Calvin Thompkins to deceased son, Kevin)

. . . It is therefore the order of this court that for the pendency of this matter, there shall be no communication of any nature regarding any facet of this matter, either direct or indirect, from the defendant, the defendant's attorneys, any member of the defendant's attorneys' staffs, or from anyone working for or associated with the Office of the District Attorney for Hampshire County, to any member of the public, including but not limited to any member of the television, radio, or print media . . .

Further rulings on live coverage of court proceedings are deferred until this matter is transferred to the trial judge.

By order of the Court,
Harold D. Baumgartner,
Justice of the Superior Court

(Trial Paper Number 16)

May 28—Northampton, Massachusetts

DISTRICT ATTORNEY FRANCIS X. O'NEILL couldn't believe his eyes. "This can't be right," he said out loud, in his empty office. "This cannot be goddamn right!" He stood up, holding the court order he had just read, and headed straight for Stacey Ruben's office. That stupid Judge Baumgartner couldn't permanently cut them off from all contact with the press. A temporary injunction was one thing. But a permanent injunction? A gag order? How was he supposed to spin any publicity out of this case if he couldn't *talk* to the damn press?

Stacey was on the phone when he stormed into her office, so he sat in a chair in front of her desk to wait until she was through. What the hell was he supposed to do when the press called? Ignore them? That was idiotic. And unconstitutional. Whatever happened to freedom of the press? It was right there in the Bill of Rights, goddamnit. They'd appeal this, right to the SJC if they had to. The people had a right to know what was going on here. And he had a right to get some goddamn publicity out of the biggest case in the Commonwealth in the last fifty years, for the love of God.

Finally Stacey hung up. "What the hell is this?" F.X. demanded, holding out the order to Stacey. "Can he do that? Can we appeal it? This is the goddamnedest thing I've ever seen."

Stacey took the order from him and began to read it. She didn't have political aspirations, which was a good thing, because she was Jewish, and in western Massachusetts Jews had about as much political clout as blacks. But Stacey was book smart. They needed her kind in the office. There were a lot of book-smart defense attorneys out there, and you had to have somebody on your side to handle that part of the case.

Stacey finished reading the order and handed it back to him. "I don't know, F.X.," she said. "This kind of thing is almost always left to the discretion of the trial court. We can appeal, but I think it might be spending a lot of time for nothing. I don't see how we can show that this order is an abuse of discretion. That's a pretty high standard to make on appeal. And besides, the trial is only a month away."

This couldn't be happening. Having press conferences during the trial was vital. The media coverage would be huge. What was he supposed to do? Sneak in and out of the courthouse with a trench coat over his head? "Yes, but, Stacey, for God's sake. When this trial starts, the place is going to be hip-deep in reporters. How are we supposed to avoid any contact with the press?"

She looked at the order again. "It just says that we

can't make any statements to the press during the pendency of this matter. But Judge Cottonwood is handling the trial, isn't he? Judge Baumgartner specifically left the decision to televise the trial to him. He'll probably let it go, won't he?"

Thank God for small favors. Dick Cottonwood knew how to try a case. And he wasn't going to be afraid of a few cameras in the courtroom. "Yes, but sweet Jesus, what about the pretrial coverage?" F.X. asked. "There are going to be an awful lot of phone calls between now and then."

"Well, it's not as bad as it could be," Stacey told him. "He could have ordered the press to stay off the case entirely. They can say whatever they want. We're the ones who can't talk. At least for now."

That sounded promising. "What do you mean 'at least for now'?"

"Well, when the file gets transferred up to Judge Cottonwood, we can always ask the court to reconsider its ruling. There's a much better chance that Judge Cottonwood will reverse Judge Baumgartner's order than the SJC would on appeal."

Whatever. At least there was a chance he could get back in front of the microphones. F.X. had some serious business to do in this case, and it was business he needed to do in public. He didn't just plan to ride Calvin Thompkins's guilty ass into the execution chamber. He planned to ride it right into the Governor's Mansion.

June 10—Dearborn, Michigan

LENA FELT LIKE SHE WAS DRESSED UP FOR Halloween.

She was sitting in the passenger seat of the two-hundred-year-old car that Becca had rented, wearing a full-length gown and a headdress with a veil over her face. Becca was dressed identically, except her veil was pulled up so she could drive without getting them killed.

Becca Spellman and Lena Takamura—undercover Muslims.

Curiously, all of the break-ins that Lena had discovered had taken place in Arab households in Dearborn. The only way she could possibly go out in public was in disguise. So Becca took a day off, and she and Lena, dressed as Muslim women, drove out to Dearborn, to meet with three of the burglary victims—Ria Khalil, Mirene Qafar, and Mona Muqqar. Ria and Mirene were friends, and agreed to drive together to Mona's house, where they would all meet.

The Muqqar house was a small ranch, on a street featuring small ranches. After Becca and Lena entered the house, they joined Ria, Mirene, and Mona in the modest living room and tried to figure out why anyone would want to take their computer equipment.

"I never even used the computer," Mona told them. "My husband was the one who bought it, but he just used it to play video games. We weren't even connected to the Internet."

"Did they actually steal the computer?" asked Becca.

"No, they just took the little case of CDs that came with the computer, and some disks that my husband had bought," the young woman replied. "Back when he thought he was going to do more than play Donkey Kong." The three women laughed.

"And how do you know each other?" Lena asked.

Mirene answered. "Ria and I met at a PTO meeting in the elementary school where our children go. We had lived in the same neighborhood for a few years, but we hadn't met before then."

"And how about you, Mona?" Lena asked. "Do your children go to the same school?"

"My children are in college now," Mona answered.

"So you have no connection to this school?" Becca asked.

"No," Mona said. "We only moved here from Cleveland about two years ago. I had never heard of Mirene or Ria until Lena called me and told me about how the break-ins at their houses were like mine. They only took worthless computer stuff and messed around in our file cabinets. I was so angry when I found out someone had been inside my house. It was like, I don't know. It was like a violation."

Just then, Becca's cell phone rang. She went into the kitchen so that the others could continue their conversation. The three women were all very willing to discuss possible connections between them, but in the end, it seemed that the only common threads were their religion and the fact that they lived within a few miles of each other.

About fifteen minutes later, Becca came back into the room. She had her cell phone in one hand and a tissue in the other. It was obvious that she had been crying.

"Becca, what's the matter?" exclaimed Lena, standing with the others.

"We have to leave right away," said Becca. "I'll tell you about it in the car." Then she turned to the Muslim women. "And you should all go home, too," Becca said. "Don't tell anyone about this conversation. We all could be in very serious danger."

ON THE DRIVE HOME, BECCA ALTERNATED BEtween intervals of verbal outbursts and silent seething.

"Those motherfuckers!" she yelled, banging her

hand on the steering wheel. "They will not get away with this. I am going to sue the shit out of each and every one of them."

According to Becca's neighbor, Mrs. Cyr, about an hour ago, two men from the FBI walked right into the apartment building and started banging on Becca's door. When no one answered, the men broke the door down and tore the apartment apart. Belongings were scattered everywhere, the couch was ripped open, and even Ernie the tree had been turned over and broken. When they saw Mrs. Cyr watching from the hallway, they told her that Becca had been selling drugs from her apartment and was in serious trouble, and that she should call them if she saw Becca or knew where she was.

Mrs. Cyr knew that Becca would never do anything illegal, so as soon as the men from the FBI left, she called her.

While Becca drove, Lena struggled to make sense of it all. Somehow, the men who had planted the drugs in her apartment must have discovered she was staying with Becca. Someone at Becca's workplace must have found out about her extracurricular investigation and reported it to whoever was doing this.

And by the way, why were they doing this? The talk with the three Muslim women had left her more bewildered than ever. Aside from the fact that all of their homes had been broken into by thieves who took only computer CDs and disks, there was nothing that linked their households except that they were all Muslim. And that didn't line up with Phillipe LeClerq, the Detroit schoolteacher who had died during the burglary of his home. He was Catholic. The types of computers were different. They simply didn't share any common history.

The only thing which caught Lena's attention

was that Ria thought that she'd heard about a mosque somewhere in Ann Arbor that had had a rash of these kind of incidents about a month ago.

As soon as Becca turned down her street, she abruptly pulled her veil down over her face and hissed, "Jesus, there's Ira and Manny in an unmarked. I can't believe they've got my apartment staked out. Oh my God. Put your veil on. We can't stop here. Oh my God."

Becca drove right past the dark blue Ford that was parked three doors away from her apartment. She knew most of the cops who worked in her neighborhood. Her hands were shaking as she made a left turn and drove away from her home. "What do they think I'm going to do? Turn myself in? For what? Hiding somebody that they're trying to frame? Is this crap supposed to scare me?"

Lena turned to check if they were being followed. "Well, it's scaring me," she told her friend. "And now I'm scared for you, too." The street behind them was empty. How did this get so out of control? Why was this happening?

Becca turned again and headed north on Lincoln Avenue. "All I know is that I'm pissed. You never did drugs in your life, I never did drugs in my life, but according to Mrs. Cyr, we're like Detroit's newest cocaine kingpins. This morning I drive you to meet with some crime victims, and this afternoon I'm a fugitive. This is bullshit."

"I'm so sorry I got you involved in all of this. I can't believe any of it."

"You didn't get me involved in anything," Becca said, turning left onto Elm Street. "Whatever I did, I wanted to do. These assholes have no right to do this. And they aren't going to get away with it, either."

"Well, I think we should just find another FBI office,

turn ourselves in, and get some kind of protection from whoever these crazy people are." Lena started digging around in her bag, looking for her cell phone. "I'm sorry I didn't do that when you first suggested it."

Becca turned down First Avenue, toward the entrance to the interstate. "I don't trust anybody anymore," she said. "The FBI planted drugs in your apartment. Then they came and busted my place up. Now the Detroit P.D. has staked out my street and are ready to arrest me for drugs and harboring a fugitive and God knows what else." Becca merged into the acceleration lane of the interstate, heading north. "You've got your laptop, and I've got an idea." She signaled left and got into the fast lane. "We are so out of here."

TWENTY-ONE

An Open Letter from a Fugitive

My name is Lena Takamura. Not quite two years ago, I graduated with honors from the University of Michigan in the field of journalism, and with high hopes of becoming an investigative reporter.

Today I am in hiding, because the police and the FBI are seeking to arrest me on false charges for crimes I did not commit. Indeed, the very publication of this column might subject the newspaper printing it to retribution from whoever it is that is attempting to intimidate me with my own government's legal system.

These people want one thing: for me to stop investigating why the homes of so many families throughout Michigan, most of them Muslim or Arab, have been burglarized by thieves who are apparently interested only in stealing computer software and electronic storage media. And why, in at least one of these cases, police attempted to tamper with witnesses' statements, police reports, and emergency phone transcripts to cover up evidence of such a burglary when it led to the death of Phillipe LeClerq, a beloved high school teacher from Oak Park . . .

(*Ypsilanti Sentinel*, June 17, page 1)

June 15—Northampton, Massachusetts

TERRY COULDN'T BELIEVE HIS EARS.

"Anyone with half a brain would know that the only chance you had for jury nullification is if you tried the case in the press," Zack's father said, with a strange smile on his face. Terry, Zack, and his dad were in the kitchen, getting more drinks for some of the guests. Zack was having a birthday party for Justin, and had invited his parents and his sister and her husband out to his house. "But you just got the court to issue a gag order! Talk about shooting yourself in the foot. Christ, Zachery, what were you thinking? Were you thinking anything at all? Now you've got absolutely zero chance to win."

Terry wondered what would happen if he just hauled off and smacked the old man right in the mouth. Was there a special criminal statute which prohibited bitch-slapping a federal judge at his grandson's birthday party?

"Dad, could we talk about this some other time?" Zack asked, as he reached into the refrigerator for another bottle of root beer. Justin loved root beer. The kid had taste. "I was hoping we could keep this day just about Justin."

"Oh, yeah, of course," the old man said, taking a sip of his drink. "I just can't believe that your guy's been telling you he killed these people because they were terrorists, and Franny O'Neill's the one who's been playing the media like a two-dollar banjo."

Zack got a couple of paper cups out of a cabinet and started pouring the soda. Anybody who knew him could see that he was getting steamed, but he just kept pouring while his father kept spewing.

"Why the hell weren't you leaking this terrorist nonsense to some of your buddies at the *Globe*? You know

Dick Cottonwood's never going to let you get that stuff in at trial. He'll rule that it's irrelevant, and he's right. Nobody on the jury's ever going to know why this guy shot those people."

Zack didn't say a thing. He just took the cups of soda and left the kitchen. So Judge Wilson turned on Terry. How was it that he could say all this shit and keep smiling? Was that supposed to make it friendly? Or funny?

"Am I missing something here?" the judge continued. "This trial is hopelessly lost, isn't it? And your client's a big colored guy, to boot. Oh, the jury's really going to love that."

A long time ago Zack had told Terry about a Buddhist saying that was supposed to work when someone was pissing you off. How did it go?

"I don't know what kind of case you think you're going to put in, but as far as jury nullification, you can forget about that," Zack's father continued.

If a guy offers you a gift—

"I mean, talk about a bungled opportunity." The old man just wouldn't quit. "You two are diddling around at a birthday party, and about a week from now your guy is going to get hooked on murder one. I was reading the *Post* the other day, and I swear to God, that electric chair poll they're running is about ninety-five percent guilty—"

—and you really don't want the gift—

Terry put down the bottle of beer he was drinking so that he didn't crush it into sand. Maybe it hit the counter a little hard, because Zack's father jumped. "Judge Wilson," he said, careful to keep his voice even. "You did a lot of trial work before your appointment, didn't you?"

"Oh, yeah," the old man said. The smile was back.

"Spent close to thirty years trying cases before President Bush put me on the bench."

"Wow," Terry said. "Many of those criminal trials?"

"Over a hundred," the judge said with pride. "The district attorney's office knew me pretty well, I can tell you that."

"I'm curious. How many of those cases did you win by jury nullification?"

Bang. Good-bye smile, hello glare.

—take the gift and bash him on the head with it.

"That's what I thought," Terry said. "So how about you listen to your son for once in your life, climb down from the pulpit, come out into the other room, and have some of your grandson's birthday cake."

ZACK LOOKED OUT THE WINDOW OF HIS OFfice, watching Justin play in the yard. The boy seemed to be alternating between squatting down and looking quietly at some dandelions and chasing squirrels around like a madman.

Zack turned to Terry and said, "I think the quote you were looking for goes something like this: 'If someone offers you a gift and you refuse it, then to whom does that gift belong?' "

They were in the final stages of pretrial preparation. Not that there was much to prepare. Outside, Justin returned to the dandelions. "Oh, yeah, that's it," Terry said. "But mine works, too. In a kind of confrontational, non-Buddha-like way."

A bird landed on the lawn behind Justin. What would he do when he saw it?

Terry spoke again. "Your father was right, wasn't he?"

Zack turned back to look at his friend. Terry was reading the directions to a desk clock he had bought that would tell what day and time it was anywhere in the world. "About the fact that there's no way we can win this case?" Zack asked him.

"About that fact that the only hope we had of winning this case was to convince the jury that the victims were terrorists, and the only hope we had of doing that was of leaking it to the press before the trial."

Justin was doing somersaults. The bird was gone. "Yeah," Zack said.

Terry was quiet for a minute. "But you knew that back when you started working on that motion to shut the D.A. up, right? You just refuse to play those games, even though you know everybody else does."

Courtrooms were full of lawyers who promised to play by the rules and then broke every one they could get their hands on. They tainted jury pools by leaking and planting stories in the media, by holding press conferences to try to put whatever spin they could on a case, by giving their opinions, honest or not, about their chances of victory. They bribed court officers and assistant clerks with lunches and drinks to get information. They coached their witnesses by telling them what to say on the stand, without the least regard for the truth. They concocted alibis for defendants. They hid witnesses. They withheld evidence. They enhanced the stories of victims. They violated the letter and the spirit of court orders, laws, canons of ethics. They lied and they cheated, and they did anything they thought they could get away with, because they were in a bottom-line business. Win or lose. All or nothing.

Guilty or not guilty.

The phone rang. Zack let the answering machine pick it up. "This is Judge Cottonwood's secretary," a female voice said. "The judge was wondering if you could fax over a draft of any pretrial motions you had, including any updated witness lists." She gave a phone number and then hung up.

Zack looked over to Terry, who was still fiddling with the clock. Apparently, it was 11:32 P.M. in Shanghai. "You hear that Judge Cottonwood's suddenly looking to get pretrial faxes?"

"No," Terry said. "You hear that Roger Spinnelli, Judge Cottonwood's secretary, got a sex-change operation in the last five days?" He blew a burst of air from his mouth and took another look at the directions. "Those asshole reporters'll do anything to get a story."

Justin was now sitting down and doing some reading. Out loud. To the dandelions. "You know, if we knew that those people were terrorists, I'd have been really tempted to try that crap my father was talking about."

Terry put down the clock and looked up. "Man. You're the one always saying that the system would work if people didn't try to manipulate it." He joined Zack at the window. It looked like Justin was trying to get a dandelion to read to him. "You know that when the trial starts, I'm going to be in there swinging, because the Constitution says Cal gets to have a defense. But I know he did it, you know he did it, everybody on the planet knows he did it. Are you seriously thinking that it would be a good idea if he got off?"

Justin left the book out on the lawn, open and on its edges, like a tent, and ran into the house for something. "If those people really were terrorists, I'm having a hard time faulting what he did," Zack said. "And I'm having a really hard time thinking it would be a good idea to execute him for doing what he did. It seems that ever since September 11, all this country has been focused on is catching and killing terrorists. So Cal Thompkins catches and kills six terrorists and what are we going to do? We're going to convict him of murder, and then we're going to kill *him*."

"Call me crazy," Terry said, "but however smart or nice Cal Thompkins is, and whatever tragedy happened in his life, I'm just not comfortable with him wandering around town with his trusty AK-47, deciding who he's going to blow away. That's a little too *Wild Wild West* even for me, thank you very much."

They both watched as Justin reappeared and began to place tiny toy chairs and tables under the tent that he had made with his book. Apparently he was furnishing a home for the flower.

"What are you going to do with Justin during the trial?" asked Terry.

"He's going to stay with my sister and her husband in Boston," Zack said. "They promised that they'd take him to see the fireworks at the Esplanade on the Fourth of July."

"Sweet."

Washington, D.C.

MATT WAS HAVING BREAKFAST WITH SAMMY IN the residence when Carlos brought in a newspaper article. Matt had asked him to keep a eye out for stories just like this one—a Michigan reporter was claiming that she had to go underground because authorities were trying to keep her from investigating illegal searches of Arab homes. And in the middle of the article, there was a single name circled: *LeClerq*. The *q* was underlined. And suddenly, everything made sense.

He turned to Sammy. "What do magistrate judges do, again?"

"Hey, where are you going?" she said. "You haven't finished eating—"

"Remember you said magistrate judges don't do the important things," Matt said, handing her the article. She looked down at it and then back up at Matt.

"Yes. Like pretrial motions and scheduling conferences."

"And applications for search warrants?" Matt was shrugging on his jacket.

Sammy just stared at him. And then she jumped up and followed him into the hall. "Exactly like applications for search warrants."

TWENTY-TWO

Dear Kevin,

Well, tomorrow is the big day. The beginning of the trial.

The judge has decided that the television cameras can stay, so the whole world will be watching. It doesn't really matter to me. The only opinions I really care about are yours and Mommy's.

A few days ago I realized something which made me sad. When I killed these people, I made a mistake. It's not that they weren't bad people. They had done horrible things in the past, and they were planning to do horrible things in the future. And I'm not sorry that they are dead. But when I first learned how dangerous they were, I didn't have to shoot them. I could have gone to the police and tried to have them captured, instead of just shooting them in cold blood. I let my own feelings of loss and pain blind me to the fact that what I was doing by hunting them down was tying your memory to more violence, more killing. I shouldn't have done that. I wish I hadn't.

It's pretty strange, actually, that now, after going through this whole thing, and finally really facing my feelings about what happened to you and Mommy, I am probably in much better shape to live a productive life than I was right after you were killed. Yet here I am, standing on the verge of a conviction which will end in my own death.

In many ways, by killing these people, I have failed you. You were such a kind, loving little boy. You wouldn't have wanted me to do that. I'm sorry that I did. I hope you can forgive me.

Because I know nobody else will.
Love, Daddy

(Letter #65 from Calvin Thompkins to deceased son, Kevin)

DIST. ATTY. O'NEILL: *Trooper Dragonin, I am handing you what have been marked as Exhibits 86 through 101. Can you identify what these are?*

TROOPER DRAGONIN: *These are the jacket portions of sixteen .30-caliber spent projectiles.*

Q: *Have you seen these projectiles before?*

A: *Yes, I recovered these projectiles on January 14 from various locations within Apartment 3C at 214 Main Street, Northampton.*

Q: *And directing your attention to Exhibit 75, can you identify that for us, Trooper?*

A: *Yes. That was the modified AK-47 that I recovered at the same time as the projectiles, from the hallway immediately outside Apartment 3C.*

Q: *After you recovered these projectiles and the AK-47, Trooper Dragonin, what, if anything, did you do with them?*

A: *At the request of my supervisor, I made several test firings with the AK-47. I then made a microscopic comparison of the projectiles I had recovered at the scene with the projectiles that I obtained by test-firing the weapon.*

Q: *Did you form an opinion about the projectiles that you had recovered at the scene?*

A: *My opinion was that the projectiles at the scene had been fired by the modified AK-47 I had recovered in the hallway outside of the apartment.*

(Trial Volume XI, Page 63)

June 19—Worcester, Massachusetts

AS HE PULLED INTO THE DOUBLE V FOR HIS last cup of coffee of the day, Pete Vanderhall thought about quitting—just walking away from the job. It was about the tenth time he had thought about it just that day.

The funny thing was that when he first became a cop, it was a dream come true. Pete had been working toward it since ninth grade, and when he finally passed through the academy, he felt like the proudest rookie in his class.

And even though the first years were tougher than he had imagined, and the moments of excitement and pride were far outnumbered by the moments of sadness and frustration, he was still convinced that what he did mattered. That if he stayed true to the job, and did his work right, he'd make a difference, even if only a small one, in the world.

But lately, he was starting to doubt that. Sure, he'd stayed true to the job and done his work right. The fact that he'd made sergeant bore that out. And the men who worked for and with Pete respected him. He knew that, too. But as far as making a difference . . .

As stupid as he felt about it, young Natalie Reggio's death had had a profound effect on him. He had attended her funeral and had even tried to look out a little bit for her friend, Julie. But Pete didn't need any special ability to predict the future to see where the girl was heading. The youth officer at Julie's school had told Pete that Julie was just another disaster waiting to happen. Pete had even gone to talk to her once, but it had backfired completely. He'd seen her hanging out at the 7-Eleven down by Grossman's, and he'd pulled into the lot to say hello and ask her how she was doing. But as soon as he did, she and the five kids she'd been with scattered. He knew that meant that they were carrying, probably alcohol, maybe weed, but he didn't chase them. He had wanted to speak to her, not bust her.

Pete walked into the diner and sat at his regular spot at the counter. Joe was on the cell phone with his son, Carlos, the one who worked at the White House, but he didn't need to ask Pete what he wanted. Coffee, black with two sugars. He put the cup down in front of Pete and walked down toward the other end of the counter, where Maria was washing something in the sink.

Every day was the same. Pete got up, got into work by seven-thirty for his eight-to-four shift, had lunch and late afternoon coffee at the Double V, went home, talked to the kids and Vicki, had dinner, watched some TV, and went to sleep.

The next day, he did it all over again.

And that had been enough, when he thought his job meant something.

So why wasn't it enough anymore?

Northampton, Massachusetts

JUDGE COTTONWOOD COULDN'T BELIEVE IT. He wasn't listening at all to Fran O'Neill drone on and on about the Commonwealth's theory of the case. All he could think about was that in the last trial of his career, he was going to have to put up with Terry Tallach.

Following his normal practice, His Honor had called the attorneys into his chambers for an informal, pretrial conference on the Thompkins case just to ensure that everything would run smoothly. He knew O'Neill and his assistant wouldn't give him any problems. And even if Zack Wilson was a little too smart for his own good, at least the guy followed the rules. But Wilson's partner, Terry Tallach, was a pest. Despite the fact that anybody who read the papers knew how this trial was going to turn out, the judge had been looking forward to being a part of the historic guilty verdict. Now he wasn't so sure.

Tallach was fool enough to try anything, and with a courtroom full of cameras, that made the judge uneasy. He had no qualms about throwing the loudmouth into a cell for contempt if necessary. But who could guess how that might play on television? The judge had no desire to give the defendant something to complain about on appeal. No, he'd have to be a little careful with Tallach.

The district attorney finally finished talking. Then Wilson said he wasn't comfortable revealing anything about his client's case until the trial actually started. That just confirmed what Judge Cottonwood had already suspected: The defendant had no case.

It was time for the speech.

"As those of you who have tried cases before me know, I don't like surprises," the judge began.

OH GOD. THE SPEECH. TERRY COULDN'T BElieve he had to sit through it again. No surprises, rules were made to be followed, everyone's goal is to discover the truth and to participate in a fair trial, blah blah blah. If the Big Dick hadn't so completely established his reputation as the judge most likely to go out of his way to screw defendants, it might have been a little easier to swallow.

But every defense lawyer knew that a criminal trial before Judge Cottonwood was nothing less and nothing more than a big, fat, five-alarm boning. And as he got older, Judge Dick would do everything in his power to make sure you lost not only at trial but also on appeal. Lately, simple cover-your-ass motions at the end of trials had become golden opportunities for Cottonwood to make completely bullshit "factual findings" on the record, which would be sure to doom any hope of a new trial.

Like that time in one of Cottonwood's robbery cases, when the defendant suffered a concussion in a car accident on the way to the courthouse and began the trial dizzy and with a blinding headache. Midway through the trial he actually fainted, right in front of the jury, but thirty minutes later, after a nurse took his vital signs and determined that he was conscious and not having a heart attack or bleeding internally, the trial was resumed.

After losing, the defense attorney filed a motion for a new trial, claiming that his client hadn't been able to assist his attorney during the trial.

Judge Cottonwood issued a ruling that read "While it is true that the defendant lost consciousness during the trial, the trial was suspended at the moment that he fainted, and resumed thirty minutes later only after he was thoroughly examined and cleared by a health-care professional." Then Cottonwood wrote exactly what he knew would totally fuck the defendant's appeal: "I observed the defendant at all times during the trial, and he was consistently and actively helping his attorney throughout."

Yeah, sure. What Cottonwood really observed was the defendant occasionally whispering to his lawyer. For all Cottonwood knew, the guy had been singing the "Macarena." But it was enough for the Appeals Court. Appeal denied. Next case.

"One final word before we get out there and begin." Cottonwood was finally in the homestretch. Thank God. "I will be retiring at the end of the proceedings in this case. So it is my hope that we can all work together to be sure that this is a fair trial . . ."

A few empty platitudes later, everyone stood up, and the lawyers returned to the courtroom to await Judge Blowhard's grand entrance.

Except for the seats in the gallery which had been reserved for the prospective jurors, the place was packed. Countless reporters and freak-show junkies who wanted a firsthand view of the impending train wreck were squeezed into every available seat. Three television cameras complete with geek crews were obnoxiously conspicuous. Every court officer on the payroll was somewhere in the room, clustered in twos and threes, all trying to look vitally important.

And sitting by himself, at one of the two long tables set up in the front of the room, was the guest of honor, the main event, the big black guy whose mug shot had been scaring the shit out of America for months. Cal Thompkins. For somebody who was about to go through a few weeks of hell on earth while everybody and his uncle gawked, he looked like the most relaxed guy in the place.

Thanks to a typical screwup, before Zack and Terry had even reached their places next to Cal, one of the court officers opened the doors at the back of the room and began to usher the fifty prospective jurors into the seats that had been reserved for them, and another officer at the front of the room shouted, "Court! All rise!" and Judge Cottonwood made his entrance. The reporters and the gallery didn't know where to look and whom to pay attention to. But Terry did. He watched the jury pool enter the courtroom like they were on a Hollywood red carpet.

Picking juries wasn't really that hard if you used your common sense. The idea was to try to choose people who would have an easier time relating to your client than to the other side's client. So there were a few rules of thumb in picking juries for criminal trials if you were a defense lawyer and your client was black. One was that you never let a family member of somebody in law enforcement near the case, and the other was that you tried to get as many minorities onto the jury as possible.

A quick look at the prospective jurors and their questionnaires—the little forms that told the lawyers tiny bits of information about them, like their occupation, or if they'd ever been involved in a criminal or civil trial before—confirmed that Cal's incredibly bad luck was holding firm. Of the fifty-seven people in the jury pool, over twenty were related to someone who worked either with the police or with the prison system.

And the total number of minorities on the panel was four. Naturally, one of them was married to a cop.

Getting a jury of Cal's peers out of this panel was going to be a joke.

But then again, the number of people in any jury pool who had blown away six students with an automatic weapon was likely to be small.

* * *

EL AMIN WAS PERFORMING THE FINAL MAINtenance check on the airplane before the mission. Everything else was ready. Even the weather reports were looking favorable.

He had done his research and his tests. The plan was simple. He would take off in the mid to late afternoon of July 4 from the airfield and fly directly to the Esplanade. The park would be swollen with half-naked, drunken infidels, who would have no inkling of the wrath that was about to descend upon them from the sky.

He would make his first approach from the west and north, because that would give him the greatest amount of time to establish the proper altitude. After studying maps and taking careful measurements, he knew the exact moment he should begin dropping grenades.

The first would hit at the pedestrian entrance to the park itself. It would explode a meter or two above the ground, spraying deadly shrapnel in a circle approximately ten meters in diameter. Depending on how dense the crowd was at that point, many dozens would be hit by the grenade. There would be a scene of panic and chaos, blocking the only exit from the Esplanade.

Then El Amin would fly back and forth over the park, raining grenades down on the unsuspecting heads of the infidels. They would stampede toward the blocked exit like frightened cattle and then create an unmissible target of teeming humanity for his final act of martyrdom.

With his plane packed full of fertilizer and ammonia, El Amin would dive into the thick of them, exploding a hand grenade just as the plane hit, igniting the explosives that would create a devastating ocean of flame, terror, and death.

It would have been better if his comrades had survived the attack in the apartment, so that El Amin's actions were not the only ones to pour infidel blood into the ground. But even though he was now acting alone, he was confident that starting next year, foolish Americans would not be the only ones to celebrate the Fourth of July.

TWENTY-THREE

(Court in session at 9:50 A.M.)

THE COURT: *Before we begin today, Mr. Thompkins, I understand from your attorneys that you intend to testify on your own behalf. I am now advising you that you have an absolute right to take the witness stand if you choose, and you have an absolute right to not take the witness stand if you so choose. The decision is entirely up to you.*

I am further advising you that your decision as to whether to testify should be made in consultation with your attorneys.

If you decide to testify, you will be subject to cross-examination by the Commonwealth, under the rules of evidence.

And finally, if you decide not to testify, and if your attorneys request, I will instruct the jury that absolutely no adverse inference, no suggestion negative to you in any way, could be taken by them as a result of your choice not to testify.

Do you understand these rights, sir, as I have explained them to you?

THE DEFENDANT: *I do, Your Honor.*

THE COURT: *Very well. We'll take a ten-minute recess.*

(Trial Volume XII, Page 5)

June 20—Northampton, Massachusetts

YESTERDAY AFTERNOON, AT THE END OF THE second day of the trial, Cal had asked Zack and Terry how they thought things were going.

Zack said, "Pretty much as we expected—not too bad."

Terry said, "You want to know how you're doing, keep an eye on the earring ladies."

By some crazy coincidence, two of the female jurors always wore long, and sometimes very elaborate, pierced earrings. And they were also the most expressive people in the whole group.

One of them was a divorced retired health-care administrator, somewhere in her sixties with long gray hair pulled back in a ponytail. She seemed kind of nervous, but she was quick to smile whenever she interacted with any of the other jurors or the court officers. And she was completely focused on the case, taking meticulous notes throughout, concentrating intently on the witnesses' testimony, reacting freely to whatever they said.

The other earring lady sat to her left. She was about half the age of the first earring lady, but twice her weight. She was single, she worked for one of the telephone companies as an emergency service dispatcher, and she was the only black person on the jury. But Terry said to focus on her because her facial expressions were so obvious that you would have to be blind not to know what she was thinking.

And now, at the end of the third day, using the

earring ladies method, Cal couldn't help but feel a little optimistic.

They were both hopelessly in love with Zack.

Cal didn't know how he did it. Zack wasn't that much to look at—he had a nice smile and looked okay in his dull suits. Maybe it was his relaxed manner, or the confidence with which he spoke to the judge and the witnesses. Or maybe it was some female thing Cal would never understand. But right now, Zack had at least those two jurors, maybe more, eating out of his hand.

The white-haired lawyer for the Commonwealth seemed a little bumbling. He tried to come off like the wise, experienced prosecutor, but his questions sounded like he was trying to make himself the most important person in the room at all times, regardless of what he was asking. "And can you please tell Judge Cottonwood and the jury, Ms. Washington, that afternoon of January 14 when you stayed home from work because you were sick, was there anything in particular that happened that you made note of, such that you might conclude that it was unusual, or notable, or otherwise memorable in your mind in terms of being different from a typical, or, let's say, normal afternoon?"

On the other hand, Zack seemed like he was the calm voice of reason, honesty's best friend, making sure that the witnesses were at ease, making sure that they had a chance to describe precisely what they had seen or heard, making sure the jury got a complete picture of everything they needed. So on cross-examination, Mrs. Thelma Washington, who was on the stand solely because she had happened to glance out her window and see the biggest terrorist coming into the apartment building earlier that afternoon, had a chance to tell her story without being interrupted by dumb, ten-minute questions from the district attorney.

And as Mrs. Washington left the witness stand, and the judge instructed the jury not to discuss the case with anyone, the earring ladies both looked at Zack with such gratitude and admiration that Cal actually thought he might have a chance.

June 26—Washington, D.C.

THERE WAS A KNOCK ON THE DOOR, AND THEN the Chief of Staff walked in. "You wanted to see me, Mr. President?"

Matt was very good at spotting liars, which meant that since he hadn't recognized Vernon Browning's falsehoods, the man was a terrific liar.

To be fair, Matt had never really directly confronted Browning about the Cullhane memos; he'd merely asked him to look for them on President Graham's laptop some weeks ago. Technically, the Chief of Staff hadn't lied when he reported back that he hadn't found the memos on the computer. It was true—they weren't there.

The lying part had been earlier, when he'd said he wasn't aware of any memos about judges.

As Matt's commanding officer in the army used to say, that was going to require a discussion.

"Yeah, Vernon, sit down for a second," Matt said, waving him toward one of couches at the center of the room. Matt was disgusted. He didn't have much respect for liars. But he was still missing some crucial information about what went on under President Graham. And the only way he was going to find it was to get Browning to admit it and to talk about it.

"Listen, I've been keeping something from you," he continued, taking a seat opposite Browning in an armchair, "and I need to let you know about it so I can get your input." Don't worry, Vernon old buddy, we're all on the same side here.

The Chief of Staff was the picture of the loyal servant. Sitting forward, actively listening, ready to spring into action at the smallest command of his leader. "Whatever I can do, Mr. President," he said.

Matt nodded. "Good," he said. He measured his next words carefully. "I stumbled onto a counterterrorism program that you and President Graham were using, which, for obvious reasons, had to be kept secret." If the Chief of Staff ever took up poker, he'd be a millionaire. Browning's face was a masterpiece—concern, respect, and a touch of confusion thrown in for added flavor. It was time for that to disappear. Matt raised his voice a little. "I'm talking about the Cullhane memos, and the searches of those Arab Americans."

And just like that, the facade cracked. Browning had been caught, and he knew it. "Now I'm certain all you were trying to do was get early intel on any terrorist activity that might have been brewing," Matt said, "but what I don't know"—and now he couldn't keep the anger out of his voice—"is when you were going to tell me about it. Wasn't I entitled to know? How can I possibly be effective in protecting the American people if I don't even know what kinds of operations we've been conducting to ensure that protection?"

Browning really looked contrite. And then he abruptly stood up. "Will you excuse me for a moment, Mr. President, I need to get something to show you." And he walked through the door that connected their offices and returned with a thick file folder, which he handed to Matt.

It was all there in black and white. It had started during President Graham's administration, but it was still in full swing. For months while Matt was President, the government of the United States was systematically, secretly searching its citizens. It had come to this. Incredible.

"This operation was instituted by President Graham as an ongoing series of searches of various Arab Americans for evidence of terrorism, sort of like a random traffic stop to search for evidence of drunk driving," Browning explained. "The President wanted to be sure that he did everything possible to avoid another September 11. It was code-named Operation: Iron Vigilance."

Operation: Iron Vigilance. Good God. "I understand," Matt said, continuing to leaf through the folder of information. The idea that terrorists could be plotting another September 11 from within American borders was maddening. But that didn't keep images of German storm troopers ransacking Jewish homes from running through Matt's mind. Which were then replaced by images of airliners exploding into the World Trade Center. He began to feel sick.

"So you got together a list of magistrate judges who were vulnerable, and then asked them for search warrants, or to authorize wiretaps, or whatever. And if any judge gave you trouble, you'd just show them the, uh, research you'd done on their own private lives. And since the target was Arab Americans, you focused on getting judges in New York and Michigan—"

"And California."

"And California," Matt continued, "because that's where the majority of Arab Americans live."

"I know it might sound a little heavy-handed, sir—"

"Oh, I understand the reasons behind the program," Matt interrupted. "But why keep me in the dark?"

"Plausible deniability, sir," Browning replied with a

smug smile. "We wanted to be sure that if the lid ever came off this thing, and it began to go bad politically, you could honestly assert that you had no knowledge of the operation."

Of course. It wasn't about taking responsibility for one's own actions. It was about winning the next election. "Is that why Charlie Cullhane was involved?" Matt asked.

"Exactly, sir. If word somehow got out, we knew that Charlie would accept the responsibility for writing those memos. If it didn't stop there, I was the next line of defense. Obviously, I would have taken full responsibility, and would never have let it get to President Graham. But after he died, I figured that since the operation was already under way, the most effective way to protect you was to keep you totally out of the loop." Browning took his own dramatic pause. "Which I know now was a mistake, sir."

No shit. Matt took a deep breath. Stay cool. "Tell me, Vernon, where are we in this thing? Have we had any success? Some of these searches seem to be focused on, what, more blackmail material?" In a couple of cases, sex videos and toys had been confiscated. Matt's disgust was changing into something like anger. At former President Graham. At Browning. At the terrorists that had started this whole mess.

"That was something that a couple of the agents came up with on their own," said Browning proudly. "Naturally, there was no immediate intention to use it against anyone. But if a later investigation required some . . . leverage against these people, that evidence would be available to persuade them to cooperate."

Matt's head began to ache. So they weren't just blackmailing judges, they were blackmailing anybody. When would it be okay to use this "leverage"? To get whatever information was available at any time, or only when a threat was imminent? "But what about actual terrorism?" he asked. "Has the operation turned up anything to help us prevent some kind of future attack?"

"Yes. We've confirmed two cells," Browning said, reaching over and pointing to a set of papers at the back of the folder Matt was holding. In Oakland, four men, none of whom Matt had heard of, were under surveillance, suspected of plotting an attack on the Golden Gate Bridge. And in Massachusetts, Maliq Ansaar, aka John Bercher, Ahmad El Amin, aka Rudolf Lange—why did these names sound familiar? "We were planning on moving against both cells simultaneously after we ascertained whether they were working together, when out of nowhere that computer programmer up in Massachusetts stormed the apartment like Rambo and took them all out."

That's it. The case had been all over the news lately, but Matt had forgotten the names of the victims. He had read them in the press clippings that Carlos had given him. "Isn't the shooter facing the death penalty?"

"Yeah," said Browning with a smile. "Our friends in Massachusetts have finally decided to join the fight against crime."

"But I haven't heard anything about the fact that the victims were terrorists."

"We decided that it would be better for the public not to know, as long as the threat had been eliminated. One of the things President Graham and I were working on was to try to restore the confidence of the American people. We thought it would do far more harm than good to have the press filled with stories that while we're telling everyone that we've got the terrorist threat under control, six terrorists were living right in the middle of

Northampton, Massachusetts, plotting some horrible attack on July 4."

We decided that it would be better . . . We thought it would do far more harm than good . . . More presidential decision-making without the President anywhere in sight. Matt's head was throbbing. "So what are we waiting for in Oakland?" he asked. "Why haven't we moved against that cell?"

Browning looked down quickly, and then back up at Matt. "We were hoping to maximize the impact of the capture—" he began.

"Jesus Christ, Vernon, are you telling me that you were *timing* the raid against these guys in Oakland for some political—" Matt stopped abruptly and slapped the folder shut. "Okay, I've heard enough." He looked across at Browning. "I know I wasn't elected to this position," he began, "and believe me, I sure didn't want the job. But for reasons that must be obvious even to you, starting immediately I'm going to be doing the job without your help."

"But, Mr. President, these are extraordinary times—"

"That's right," Matt cut in. "They most certainly are. But whenever I'm in charge, in ordinary or extraordinary times, I need to trust the people who work for me." He shook his head and stood up, looking down at the lifelong bureaucrat. "If we've got to play the kinds of games you've been playing to keep our people safe, God help us, that has got to be my call. The fact that this has been going on without my knowledge for as long as I've been President . . ." He trailed off. It was going to be hard going without Browning, but it was going to be impossible going with him.

Browning stood up. "I assure you, sir—" he began, but Matt cut him off again.

"I'm so sick of the double-talk," he began, but then stopped himself. This conversation needed to end. "As long as I'm in this office, I'll do what I think is right for the people of this country, regardless of whether it serves your political agenda or anyone else's. I'll expect your resignation in an hour."

June 30—Northampton, Massachusetts

WHILE ZACK WAITED FOR A FEW MINUTES TO try, for the third time, to get through to his sister's cell phone so he could say hi to Justin, he wondered if Cal Thompkins really knew how bad things had gotten.

The court was in the midafternoon recess. The medical examiner was testifying. It wasn't a surprise that his testimony was damaging. It was a surprise that it was as damaging as it was.

Fran O'Neill had finally decided that it was more important for his witnesses to actually testify than for him to ask questions that sounded important. And the medical examiner was a relatively young man whose manner, somehow, had managed to amplify the horror of the violence that had been done to the victims.

When he first started to speak about the destruction that just one of these bullets did to the first victim—one of the women—all of the goodwill that Zack had built up with the earring ladies just vanished. He must have been making eye contact with the pair at least ten to twenty times per day in the first few days of the trial. But from early this morning, when the medical examiner first began to describe how Cal's bullet had shattered Marianne Duhamel's skull and ripped through her brain, the only eye contact Zack had made with the ear-ring ladies was a single glance he exchanged with the older one, in which she had silently told him, in no uncertain terms, that she no longer loved him, because he represented someone who had done something unforgivable.

Claire's phone finally started ringing, and after she said hello to Zack, she handed the phone to Justin.

"Hi, buddy, how are you doing?" Zack asked.

"Great. Daddy, can we get a dog?" was the reply. Spikey the incontinent black terrier had apparently made a very good impression.

"Remember we were going to talk about that when you came home with me next week, right?"

"Oh, yeah," Justin said, somewhat subdued. Then he brightened right up. "Okay. Bye, Daddy!"

"Wait! Justin!" The little guy was adjusting much better to this arrangement than Zack was. "Are you having a good time? What did you do today? Did you play with Aunt Claire?"

"Uh-huh. We're walking Spikey now, and then me and Spikey are going to play ball."

"Sounds like you're having fun."

"Uh-huh."

"Well, I can't wait to see you. You remember I'm coming this weekend. For the you-know-what."

"The fireworks?"

"Does that sound good?"

"That sounds great!"

Just then, Claire's phone died, and Terry came out to get him. Court was back in session.

July 2—Washington, D.C.

"WELL, I CERTAINLY HOPE YOU'RE NOT WORried about Vernon Browning," Sammy said, as they pulled away from the White House gates toward the Kennedy Center. They were in the back of the limousine, headed to a performance of a piece by Mozart that Sammy really loved, by a dream string quartet, including Yo-Yo Ma on cello and Itzhak Perlman on violin. "He'll have plenty more chances to be a big-time political hack after you leave the White House. Or maybe he'll just write a book and get disgustingly famous. Lord."

But Matt's thoughts were elsewhere. "Remember that article about that reporter who's hiding in some basement somewhere, afraid to go to the grocery store because she thinks they're going to throw her in jail?"

"The one in Michigan."

"Yeah. That's right. The same place where Judge Stanton committed suicide. The same place where that man died when they were searching his house illegally. What do you want to bet that the search warrant for that fiasco came from Judge Stanton? I bet you a dollar that when we check, we're going to find that he killed himself after he learned that the unconstitutional search he authorized led directly to the death of a perfectly innocent man."

But wasn't that just part of the price of staying safe? Of national security? Sure, there were plenty of innocent people whose houses were being searched. And in a tragic accident, one of them died. But thousands and thousands of innocent people died on September 11. And how many thousands more suffered from injuries of every kind from that attack? Loved ones without spouses. Children without mothers and fathers. How far would Matt have gone to stop those fanatics that day? He certainly would have searched a random home, or a handful of them, or gladly authorized an entire program devoted to random searches.

But what if he didn't *know* there was an attack coming? What if he just feared one? What would he be willing to do then?

"I still can't decide how to handle this whole thing," he said to Sammy. The motorcade moved painfully slowly through the city. Every time Matt went anywhere he felt like issuing a blanket apology for fouling up the traffic.

"You mean you're not sure whether to stop the searches?" asked Sammy.

"Yeah, I know they're unconstitutional, but . . ." He shook his head. "I'm just afraid I'm going to let the country down."

Sammy sighed. Then she leaned over and kissed him, gently, and then wiped away some lipstick with her finger. "Don't worry," she told him quietly. "Whatever you decide, you won't."

East Jordan, Michigan

IT WAS SMALL, AND THE ROOF LEAKED. THE bathroom didn't work, and no matter how many windows they opened, the cabin still smelled like stale beer, mildew, and dirty socks.

But the moment that Lena stepped over the threshold of the ramshackle lodge deep in the northern woods of Michigan, she had never felt so good about anywhere in her life.

Two years ago, Becca's brother, Tad, and his friend, Kyle, had decided to spend a week at an old hunting lodge that Kyle had inherited from his grandfather. But when their car died, Becca had driven up to rescue them.

Luckily, Becca had a great memory for directions, so when it became clear that neither she nor Lena was safe in their homes, she got on Interstate 75 heading north, and about a million hours later, they pulled off a dirt road in front of Kyle's inheritance.

On the drive up and on the following day, Lena wrote "An Open Letter from a Fugitive" on her laptop, and then drove forty minutes into the tiny town of East Jordan, where Lena mailed the diskette containing her column to Mr. Olafsen at the *Ypsilanti Sentinel* with a letter, telling him what had been happening. Then they bought some food and supplies at the general store, and right as they left, a miracle happened. They discovered that for about a fifty-yard stretch of Maple Street in front of the store, they had cell phone coverage. So they both called their families and let them know they were okay.

A month later, the euphoria of fleeing Detroit had begun to wear off. Canned food sucked, black flies sucked, wearing the same clothes day after day sucked. Lena and Becca were going crazy. They needed help to escape their exile, but they didn't know whom they could trust. They knew that Lena's letter had been published and picked up by wire services around the country. Lena felt it was just a matter of time before they'd be able to return to Detroit in safety, but she was still terrified of the police.

They couldn't survive through the holiday weekend without supplies, so Lena and Becca went back into town. While Becca went up and down the aisle of the general store putting food into a basket, Lena drifted toward the front of the store, drawn by the small television playing near the cash register. A headline beneath a news anchor read, "Arson Suspected in Local Newspaper

Blaze," and then, to her horror, Lena watched video of the offices of *The Ypsilanti Sentinel* burning to the ground.

Now she knew that she'd never be able to return home.

TWENTY-FOUR

THE COURT: *The record will reflect that the defendant and his attorney Mr. Wilson are present, but Attorney Tallach is not present. Are you prepared to proceed, Attorney Wilson?*

MR. WILSON: *Actually, Your Honor, Mr. Tallach was called away on unavoidable business. He will be here as soon as possible. The defendant respectfully moves for a brief recess pending his return.*

THE COURT: *Mr. Wilson. We recessed for lunch at approximately 12:30. It is now almost 2:30. We have waited long enough. I am not going to delay this trial one minute longer, and I am going to assume that you are ready to proceed. Mr. District Attorney. Are you ready for cross-examination?*

DIST. ATTY. O'NEILL: *Thank you, Your Honor. (Cross-Examination of Calvin Thompkins)*

Q: *Mr. Thompkins, isn't it true that on direct examination, you admitted that on January 3, you rented Apartment 3B at 214 Main Street?*

A: *Yes.*

Q: *And isn't it true that you also admitted that you did so because you knew that that apartment was* *directly across the hall from the apartment of the victims?*

A: *Yes.*

Q: *And you knew that the victims were renting that apartment at that time that you rented Apartment 3B, did you not?*

A: *Yes.*

Q: *And isn't it also true that you admitted that you obtained an illegally modified AK-47 machine gun, with ammunition, specifically for the purpose of going into the victims' apartment and shooting them with the machine gun?*

A: *Yes.*

Q: *And isn't it also true that on January 14, at approximately 3:00, after ascertaining that the SIX victims were in their apartment, you took the machine gun and the ammunition, and you went across the hallway to Apartment 3C, and you shot and killed Marianne Duhamel, Helene Ghazi, Marc and Mitchell Nathenson, John Bercher, and Rudolf Lange?*

A: *Yes.*

Q: *And you meant to do this?*

A: *Yes.*

Q: *And you had planned to do it?*

A: *Yes.*

DIST. ATTY. O'NEILL: *I have no further questions, Your Honor.*

THE COURT: *Any redirect, Mr. Wilson?*

[No response.]

THE COURT: *Mr. Wilson?*

MR. WILSON: *Yes, Your Honor.*

THE COURT: *Do you have any further questions for this witness?*

MR. WILSON: *Actually, Your Honor, no, I don't.*

THE COURT: *Fine. Mr. Thompkins, you may take your seat. Mr. Wilson. Anything further, or is the defense resting?*

MR. WILSON: *If I might have a moment, Your Honor.*

THE COURT: *Please, Mr. Wilson—*

MR. TALLACH: *[inaudible] late, but he's here, Zack.*

THE COURT: *Excuse me, Mr. Tallach.*

COURT OFFICER: *[inaudible] . . . clear a path.*

THE COURT: *Mr. Court Officer, what is going on back there?*

MR. WILSON: *I apologize, Your Honor—*

THE COURT: *Mr. Tallach. Unless someone can give me an explanation of what the disruption is, I will hold you directly responsible, and hold you in contempt—*

MR. TALLACH: *I really don't think you're going to want to do that, Judge.*

(Trial Volume XII, Page 111)

July 3—Washington, D.C.

THAT MORNING, MATT WALKED TO THE OVAL Office nursing a large mug of coffee. He had slept badly.

After the string quartet performance, Matt had a dream that Yo-Yo Ma and Itzhak Perlman were in the World Trade Center, playing a concert, on September 11. The cellist made it out alive, but the violinist, because of his physical disability, did not. In the dream, Yo-Yo Ma came into the Oval Office carrying the lifeless body of

Itzhak Perlman, both men still covered with the gray dust and ashes of the catastrophe. Then the cellist morphed into Carlos, and he placed Perlman's body on Matt's desk. Carlos said to Matt, "Here is the information you asked for," and pointed to the Jewish violinist's arm, which had been marked with a concentration camp tattoo.

When he got to his desk, Matt opened the file he had been discussing with Browning a week ago. The dossiers of the terrorists who had been killed by that guy in Massachusetts were chilling. The brothers, Khalid and Nemetallah Wali, had apparently been working together for some time. The high points of their extensive criminal careers included complicity in the Bali nightclub bombing, convictions in absentia of a mass murder in Egypt, and direct involvement in the bombing of the U.S.S. *Cole.*

The two women were also something of a team. They had been key players in the kidnapping and murder of a French businessman in Algeria six years ago during which over a million dollars had been extorted from the victim's family.

And the last two were no better. One had been caught on tape in an Iraqi marketplace running from a car that then exploded, killing eight and wounding sixteen. The other had been seen hanging around with two of the September 11 hijackers when they were attending flight school and had been indicted for the murder of a family of seven in Turkey. And he was linked to three other murders—one directly, and two through his association with the Wali brothers.

Matt felt restless, so he got up to ask Mrs. Wittenour to schedule a meeting as soon as possible with Homeland Security Director Francks. But just as he reached the office door, Carlos appeared. "Excuse me, Mr. President, but there's a story on the news that you should see, sir. It's on CNN right now."

Matt followed him into the outer offices. The television screen showed video of an office building on fire. The voice-over was saying, "—arson took place less than two weeks after the Michigan newspaper ran a story on their front page titled 'An Open Letter from a Fugitive.' The reporter who wrote the letter, who faces various drug charges, predicted that the paper might suffer retaliation just for printing her story. The reporter claimed . . ."

But Matt was no longer listening. He was thinking about the six terrorists who had been killed in Massachusetts. And the reporter who was running for her life. And the burning newspaper office. And what Browning had said a few days ago: "*We decided that it would be better for the public not to know.*"

And suddenly Matt realized what he had to do.

Northampton, Massachusetts

"THE DEFENSE CALLS CALVIN THOMPKINS."

As Cal took the stand, Terry marveled at the fact that somehow, things were just about to get worse.

The trial was already an eye-bulging, hair-pulling, blood-boiling, feather-flying duck-fucking.

And Cal hadn't even gotten up there yet and personally admitted to everything.

"Can you please identify yourself for the jury?"

"My name is Calvin Edgar Thompkins. I'm the defendant in this case."

"Can you tell us a little bit about your background? Where you went to school, your profession, where you lived before this incident?"

Terry didn't need to check the earring ladies to read this jury anymore. It wasn't even close. There wasn't a sympathetic face in the bunch.

They'd probably already filled out and signed guilty verdict slips yesterday at lunch.

Which wasn't exactly a surprise. After all, this was a case charging a gigantic black man with walking into an apartment and lighting up six people with an AK-47.

Actually, the trial had gotten off to a relatively benign start. The early witnesses weren't too damaging. One neighbor heard a lot of shooting and banging upstairs and had called 911. Another had seen one of the victims as he went into the apartment building.

But then the witnesses who saw the crime scene began to testify. The jury was transfixed, and horrified. The photos of the apartment and the autopsies were devastating. As they were passed through the jury box, the younger earring lady had started to cry. The man to her right passed her a tissue and squeezed her hand in sympathy.

It was beyond bad.

The witnesses who testified to Cal's confession and the ballistics that conclusively tied him to the killings were just icing on the cake. The case was hopelessly lost.

But like he always did, Zack kept slugging away. He managed to get in the fact that Cal's wife and son had been killed by terrorists in Kenya. Terry watched carefully to see what effect it had on the jury.

Zero. The earring ladies had given up making eye contact with Zack or anybody else at the defense table. The skinny postal worker sitting two seats to their left even looked a little put out that he had to be bothered with the information.

There wasn't anything left to do now except for

Calvin to finish telling his story, and for the jury to find him guilty. The conviction was a lock.

"So you are admitting that you shot these people?"

"That's right. I am admitting it."

"But can you tell us why you did it?"

O'Neill was ready. "Objection, Your Honor! May we be seen at sidebar, please?"

"There's no need for that, Mr. District Attorney," the judge said. "The objection is sustained. This concerns the issue we discussed before trial. The record will reflect that the defendant's appellate rights are protected in accordance with the motion *in limine* he filed on the topic of motive. Please move on to a different line of questioning, Mr. Wilson."

And that was it. Calvin's entire defense—that he killed the victims because they were terrorists—was wrapped up, nice and neat, never to be even heard about by the jury.

The problem was, Zack played by the rules. He knew that Calvin's motive for the killings was an issue, and rather than springing it on the prosecutor or the judge in the middle of the trial without any warning, he had filed a motion *in limine,* a pretrial motion, seeking permission to put this evidence before the jury. This was the proper way to try a case. It alerted all sides to the presence of an issue, and allowed for a thorough and careful analysis by the trial judge, and then a ruling. And if the ruling was to be challenged on appeal, the appellate court would have a full record of the debate to consider in rendering its decision.

What made playing by the rules so tough in this case was that there was never any question that the judge would rule against them and that the judge would be technically correct. Whether or not these people were terrorists was not the least bit relevant as to whether Calvin murdered them. So any other lawyer in Zack's shoes would have gotten the information, or at least a hint of it, in front of the jury by asking a question that would never be answered.

Were you aware that the victims in this case were terrorists?

What led you to believe that the victims in this case were planning a terrorist attack?

How were the victims in this case connected with the terrorists that killed your wife and child?

Each of the questions was completely inappropriate and, according to the rules of ethics and evidence, should never be asked. But all a defendant needed was one juror to dig his heels in, and there would be no conviction. The jury needed to vote unanimously, one way or the other, guilty or not guilty. Anything short of a twelve-to-zero vote, and the judge would declare a mistrial. So given the choice between having no chance of getting the information before the jury and having the tiniest chance that an improper question might instill a seed of doubt or sympathy in the mind of one juror, Terry knew plenty of lawyers that would ask it.

But not Zack. For better or worse, when he took the oath to be a lawyer, he promised to play by the rules, so play by the rules he did. Zack glanced down at his notes before continuing to question Calvin. Although how he was going to continue was anybody's guess. There really wasn't a hell of a lot left to ask. He looked up, and just as he opened his mouth, Calvin spoke. "I killed them because they were terrorists."

That woke everybody up. *Attaboy, Calvin.* Cottonwood shot Terry a venomous glare. Uh-oh. Had he said "Attaboy, Calvin" out loud?

O'Neill leapt to his feet and bellowed over the murmuring courtroom. "Objection, Your Honor! Move to strike!"

Cottonwood was about to have a stroke. But he managed to squeeze out through his clenched teeth, "The objection is sustained, and the jury is instructed to ignore the last remark from the defendant, which is to be stricken from the record." Old Dick knew that this conviction was in the bag. He also knew that the bigger he made this issue, the more questions it would raise in the jurors' minds. That certainly wasn't in the prosecution's best interests, so Cottonwood tried to play it off as if nothing important had happened, despite the fact that his head looked like it was going to explode. "Please put your next question to the witness, Mr. Wilson."

But Calvin wasn't done quite yet. "Your Honor," he persisted, "there's no way I can get a fair trial if the jury is supposed to ignore the fact that these people were terrorists."

This time when O'Neill jumped up and started shouting, the noise from the courtroom almost drowned him out. The jury looked bewildered. Judge Cottonwood looked like he wanted to dive off the bench and start pounding Calvin on the head. Instead, he picked up an old paperweight that he had and started slamming it on the bench, shouting, "Order! Order, or I'll clear the courtroom!" Then, when things quieted down a little, he actually rose from his chair, took a step toward Calvin, and looked down at him. "Mr. Thompkins," he said, in a voice that had surely intimidated many a witness over the past decades, "I have already ruled on the issue you are trying to raise. Once before trial, and once during the trial. I now instruct you again. Confine your remarks to the questions that are put to you by the attorneys, or I will be forced to—"

"What?" Calvin interrupted, standing up to face the judge. "What will you be forced to do?" he shouted. "Execute me *twice*?"

And that did it. The courtroom went ballistic. Four court officers jumped on Calvin and wrestled him to the ground. Cottonwood started banging his paperweight again, which did absolutely nothing except add to the chaos. People in the gallery were shouting, court officers were calling for help, reporters were scribbling so fast it looked like their pads were going to burst into flames. Any questions that had been in the jury's mind from Cal's remark about terrorists had completely gone out the window when he jumped ugly with the judge. They weren't sympathetic toward him—they were scared to death of him.

At some point, the judge just gave up, shouted to no one in particular, "Court is in *recess*!" and left the bench, followed by his clerk, the court reporter, and a court officer. One of the other court officers had already started to hurry the jury out of the courtroom while the rest of the officers continued to scuffle with Calvin until they finally hauled him up and hustled him away, in handcuffs.

As soon as the theatrics at the business end of the courtroom was over, the reporters bolted. Minutes later the rest of the stunned gallery finished exiting, leaving just Terry and Zack, who sat alone at their table.

"Well," Terry said, "at least Court TV is going to be happy about the way this thing is turning out."

Zack smiled a little. "Want to walk over to The Red Onion and get a sandwich?"

"Always," Terry said, and the two friends got up and headed out of the courtroom, and down the stairs to the basement entrance. It was the only way to avoid the media feeding frenzy that had become a daily event on the front steps to the courthouse.

Almost as soon as they left the building, Zack's cell phone rang. He took it out of his pocket and answered, "Zack Wilson." He waited for a minute, then said, "Oh, come on. Nice try, but you know the rules." And he hung up.

"Who was that?" asked Terry, as they reached the sidewalk.

"That," Zack said, putting the phone back in his pocket, "was either the President of the United States with a bad head cold, or some lame reporter doing his half-assed Matt Ferguson impression, trying to get a story. God almighty."

They continued down the street and turned down toward The Red Onion. It was a beautiful, sunny day, just like the weather goofs had promised for the entire July 4 weekend.

Zack's phone rang again. At first Terry thought he wasn't going to answer it, but after five rings, Zack sighed, pulled it out of his pocket, and opened the connection. "Zack Wilson," he said, and all of a sudden he stopped walking and stood absolutely still for a full minute, listening intently. Then finally he said, "Yes, sir," and, slowly and quietly, closed the phone and put it in his pocket, looking over at Terry.

"So," he said finally. "It looks like the President's got a sinus infection."

Worcester, Massachusetts

FOR SERGEANT PETE VANDERWALL, THIS WAS A pretty damn big day.

Joe had called him from the diner, and specifically asked that Pete be in charge of a very special detail. If Pete hadn't known Joe for ten years, he never would have believed it.

But it was true. Joe, back when he called himself José, had been the staff sergeant for then Lieutenant Matt Ferguson when the two young men served in Vietnam. And now President Ferguson was coming to Massachusetts, so he decided to drop in for lunch at the Double V.

What a scene. Pete had arrived at about noon with five other officers. They immediately cleared the dining area of three very startled patrons and then set up roadblocks all around, allowing for an unimpeded route from the airport to the diner.

Pete stayed at the restaurant, coordinating the local police detail, while the place was descended upon by Secret Service agents and White House staff members. And then, at 12:32, in walked President Ferguson himself. He and Joe and Maria hugged, and sat down for sandwiches. It was surreal.

Pete had been given special instructions that one car was allowed to pass through the roadblocks, and sure enough, this big lawyer rolled up a half hour later in a Lexus. The lawyer went through about six different searches to be sure he wasn't armed before he was allowed to approach President Ferguson. He handed the President a piece of paper, shook his hand, took a folder from him, made a quick call on his cell phone, got back in his car, and left. Five minutes later, the President was on his way to Springfield, and Pete was riding lead car in the motorcade, calling ahead for traffic control.

As they pulled up in front of the Superior Court in Northampton, Pete wondered what the hell the

President of the United States had to do with the Thompkins trial.

Northampton, Massachusetts

AS JUDGE COTTONWOOD SAT AT HIS DESK, HE wondered what the hell the President of the United States had to do with the Thompkins trial.

As soon as he realized that the commotion at the back of the courtroom was because President Matthew Ferguson had come into the building, he had called another recess, and was now sitting in his chambers. The President was being made comfortable in a spare courtroom, surrounded by the necessary security. The lawyers were on their way in. How this had gone from a simple, straightforward homicide trial to a three-ring circus in such a short time was really aggravating. Every news station in the country knew that the President of the United States was here to testify. The judge had to regain control of this thing before it got completely out of hand.

Finally, the lawyers found their way in. Fran O'Neill looked furious. With good reason. His assistant looked worried, but she was nervous to start with. Wilson was a little hard to read, but Tallach looked like he had just won the lottery. A pain shot through the judge's left hip. Goddamn him for thinking this whole thing was a big joke.

"All right." Judge Cottonwood turned to Attorney Wilson. "Before anybody says anything, I'd like to know what you think you are doing springing a new witness on the Commonwealth this late in the trial."

"Well, Your Honor," Wilson began. Good thing it was him, because if Tallach so much as opened his mouth, five seconds later he'd be headed for a jail cell. "This witness came as a total surprise to us today. I received a cell phone call at twelve-thirty, right after we recessed for lunch. President Ferguson apparently had just recently received information that the victims in this case were, indeed, terrorists. He was aware of the case, and thought that the information was important enough to call us and tell us about it."

Damn it all to hell. Under these circumstances, there was no way an Appellate Court would uphold him if he were to refuse to allow the witness to testify because the guy wasn't on the original list. The judge turned to O'Neill. "And you had no idea about this?"

The district attorney was so furious he could barely speak. "None, Your Honor," he sputtered. "And I've barely had a chance to go through these reports—"

"What reports?" asked the judge.

"The President brought a detailed set of notes and reports with him, outlining the evidence that had been compiled against these people," Wilson said. "I provided a copy to the Commonwealth."

So they were in the middle of a trial that was headed directly toward the conviction and ultimate execution of a man for ridding the world of six terrorists. What a hell of a way to end a career. The judge turned to O'Neill. "Well, Mr. District Attorney. What is your position on all of this?"

Judge Cottonwood had seen that look on the district attorney's face before. O'Neill was utterly overwhelmed by what was going on. All he could do was to open his mouth and hope something good would come out. "First of all, Your Honor, assuming that the reports do confirm that these people were terrorists—"

And then the nervous assistant jumped in and saved her boss's bacon. "It's all irrelevant, Your Honor," she said. "Assuming that the defense can get around any hearsay problems, Your Honor has already ruled that any information regarding whether the victims were terrorists is irrelevant. All this information does is corroborate what the defendant was trying to testify to earlier. But whether the defendant was right or wrong about their being terrorists has no bearing on whether Mr. Thompkins is guilty of premeditated murder."

And, of course, she was right. They had all become momentarily distracted by the fact that the defendant's proposed witness also happened to be the President of the United States.

"But, Your Honor," Tallach broke in. Wilson had stopped paying attention. He had taken some electronic gadget from Tallach and was squinting at it like he was trying to read something on it. "The defendant has a right to present a case," Terry argued. "It's not exactly unusual for a jury to learn of the relationship between a defendant and his alleged victims."

"Let's get all our cards out on the table, shall we?" snapped the judge. "We all know why you want this evidence in. You're hoping for jury nullification. But you can't just throw whatever you want into the case hoping for some emotional response from the jury, no matter how dramatic your witness is. Ms. Ruben is right. The information is irrelevant, whether it comes from the defendant, the President of the United States, or God Almighty himself."

Tallach looked over at Wilson, who was now buried in some papers in his file. O'Neill knew better than to say a word.

"So that's taken care of," the judge continued crisply. "My ruling is that President Ferguson's proposed testimony that the victims in this case were terrorists is irrelevant."

There was a moment of silence, but then Wilson picked his head up. He said quietly: “I’m sorry, Your Honor, but you’re wrong.”

And fifteen minutes later, Judge Cottonwood had to agree.

TWENTY-FIVE

MR. WILSON: *Would you please state your name, address, and occupation for the record, sir?*

PRESIDENT FERGUSON: *My name is Matthew Ferguson. I live at 1600 Pennsylvania Avenue, Washington, D.C. My occupation is President of the United States.*

(Trial Volume XII, Page 112)

Northampton, Massachusetts

TERRY COULDN'T BELIEVE WHAT ZACK HAD just done. It was the biggest mistake Terry'd seen in his entire legal career.

Zack had gotten the case just where he wanted it. He had convinced Judge Cottonwood that he had the right to put the President on the stand. And that he also had the right, by the way, to call a parade of upstanding and serious counterterrorism experts from the FBI and God knows what other federal agencies, as well.

There was no way that even Judge Cottonwood could deny them the right to do it. And there was no way that Judge Cottonwood could continue to sit on the trial. They were going to need time to find and subpoena all these witnesses. And then the Commonwealth was going to need time to prepare its cross-examination. By the time it was all done, Judge Cottonwood would be months into his retirement.

So the Big Dick would have to declare a mistrial, and the trial would have to start over. With a different jury and a different judge.

Zack had done it. He had avoided a certain guilty verdict and Judge Cottonwood, all in one brilliant stroke.

And then O'Neill's assistant, Stacey Ruben, came up with this lame-assed suggestion that they just go ahead with the trial, stipulate that the victims were terrorists, and waive all hearsay objections to the President's testimony.

It was a last-ditch, bullshit offer, and they all knew it. There was no reason why Zack would choose to put evidence before the jury through a written stipulation rather than through live testimony of law enforcement officials. Especially when it meant that he had to keep going in front of Cottonwood.

And yet, here they were. No law enforcement officials, no terrorism experts, nobody at all that could put any emotion, any feeling at all into the most important part of their case. Instead, there was Zack, standing in front of the nastiest jury in the world, reading the stipulation, a cold, lifeless piece of paper. "*All of the six victims of Calvin Thompkins's shooting were terrorists, who had murdered innocent people in the past, and who were, at the time of their deaths, plotting to murder additional innocent people.*"

Yawn. The jury was barely moved. About three of them looked over at Cal when they heard the word "terrorists," but none with any sympathy in their eyes. The earring ladies stared straight ahead. This wasn't working. Zack had really misplayed this.

CAL HAD TO ADMIT IT. FOR SOMEBODY WHO hadn't spent a dime on his lawyers, he was really getting his money's worth.

The President of the United States was testifying on his behalf.

"Yes," Matt Ferguson said. "I took office as President on December 10 after President Graham died from an aneurysm."

"And, Mr. President, did you address the nation on that day?" Zack asked.

"Yes, I did. I felt that it was important for me to make a brief statement to the American people."

"Who prepared your remarks?"

"I did."

"By yourself?"

"Yes," the President replied. "I haven't been in politics for very long, and I've never been comfortable reading things that others wrote for me. I prefer to write my own speeches."

Zack was handing the President some papers. "Mr. President, are you familiar with the document that I just handed you, which has been marked 'T' for identification?"

The President looked at it and then smiled up at Zack. "Yes. This is the speech that I gave after I was sworn in as President."

"Would you mind reading to the jury the highlighted portion, please?"

The President looked down at the paper and began. " 'Ever since September 11, we have become painfully aware that our country is at war. Ask anyone who lives in New York, Pennsylvania, or Washington, D.C. . . .' "

What the hell did this have to do with his case? Cal grabbed a legal pad, scrawled a question mark on it, and pushed it in front of Terry. Terry glanced at it and then reached into a briefcase on the floor beside him, pulled out a book titled *Superior Court Jury Instructions,* and opened to a page that had been bookmarked. It was headed "Elements of First-Degree Murder." Then he slid the book over in front of Cal and pointed to a passage that read, "*The first element that the Commonwealth must prove beyond a reasonable doubt is that the defendant committed a killing that was unlawful. That is, a killing that was not justified or excusable. A killing is justified, and therefore not murder, if authorized by law, for example, when committed during a battle of war . . .*"

"Go on, please," Zack was saying to the President.

" 'This is an unusual kind of war, since our adversary aims to kill innocent people rather than to destroy military targets. But the actions of these aggressors constitute warfare, plain and simple.

" 'In that sense, every American citizen is a soldier in this war. Most of us do not wear uniforms, most of us do not have ranks or carry weapons, but we are all at war.' "

Zack was going to argue that Cal was innocent because he was a soldier fighting a war against terrorists?

Now, *that* was interesting.

While Zack asked the President about how he wasn't really a politician, and how he always said what he meant, Cal thought about this idea that he was a soldier in the war against terrorism. Was that what he was? Was that what he was thinking when he was waiting at the apartment door, waiting until it was the right time to walk over there and open fire? Waiting like a machine, until the right button was pushed, before going into action. Did soldiers think what he had been thinking? Was that what it was like for real soldiers just before they began a battle?

And then Cal realized that his opinion about the issue made absolutely no difference. The only opinions that mattered belonged to the fourteen jurors who were sitting in that box.

If only he hadn't shot those people.

It was ironic. Cal knew in his heart that what he had done was wrong. Not that the world wasn't better off now that those people were gone. There was no doubt about it. But no matter what anyone said in this courtroom, he knew what he had done was monstrous, and every time he looked at the jury, he just knew they were going to convict him.

He saw the horror in their eyes when they reviewed the pictures of the crime scene and the grisly autopsy photos. If he had been sitting in the jury box, he would have convicted himself. And when he got up in the judge's face, well, that was the end of it. No doubt.

Even the earring ladies wouldn't meet Cal's eyes now. Zack and Terry could put whoever they wanted to on that witness stand, and sing and dance like Broadway stars from now till the end of time, but Cal knew where he was going after this trial was over. And it wasn't out for a steak dinner.

Now it was the D.A.'s turn. He rose, smoothed down his painfully boring tie, and began his cross-examination.

"Good afternoon, Mr. President."

"Good afternoon."

"When you made the statement that every American citizen is a soldier in the war against terrorism, did you expect the people of the United States to start hunting down and shooting suspected terrorists?"

Terry looked like he was going to stand up and object, but before he did, Zack reached over and put his hand on the big man's arm. The two exchanged a look, and both remained silent. But Terry was not happy.

The President answered in a clear and strong voice. "Absolutely not. I do not support vigilante violence, and my statement was never intended to advocate it."

"I see." The district attorney could not have been more smug.

"You don't have any personal knowledge of the defendant in this case, do you?"

"No, I don't," the President replied. He had a good face. He didn't look like he had anything to hide, like so many politicians.

"And you don't have any idea whether Mr. Thompkins is now or ever was a member of the armed services of this country, do you, sir?"

The President looked calmly at the D.A. "No, sir, I don't," he replied.

The D.A. walked back and forth in front of the jury box. He was putting on a show. He wasn't bad at it. "Mr. President," he said, "you are the commander in chief of the armed forces of this country, are you not?"

"That is one of my roles, yes," the President answered.

"And you yourself were, at one time, an active duty officer in the U.S. Army, were you not?"

The President smiled. "Yes," he said. "I myself was, at one time, an active duty officer in the army."

The D.A. smiled himself. Whether he picked up the gently mocking tone in the President's answer was not clear. What was clear was that the D.A. was just about everybody's pal.

"In your experience both as an officer and as commander in chief of the army, can you tell me what the army's response would be if an individual who was not a member of the armed services walked onto one of their bases, wearing a T-shirt and blue jeans, and asked to see the commanding officer, brandishing an AK-47 and announcing that he was a soldier in the war against terrorism?"

Terry and Zack shot up as one. "Objection!" they both said at once.

"I'll withdraw the question," the D.A. said serenely, walking back to his seat. "I have nothing further for the witness. Thank you, Mr. President."

TERRY WATCHED AS ZACK GAVE THE CLOSING argument.

Zack was really good at this. If Cal was to have any chance, he was going to have to be.

Terry still couldn't believe that Zack had chosen to go forward with the trial in front of Cottonwood, with this jury. Not only did that assure them of every disadvantage when it came to any rulings the judge might make from now till the end of the trial, but it also squandered their opportunity to start fresh before a new jury, with a whole set of bright, shiny law enforcement witnesses on their side.

Instead, the evidence that the victims were terrorists was read to the jury from that dumb-ass stipulation, that insignificant scrap of paper.

And Zack was gambling that that scrap of paper, with the President's testimony, was enough to overcome their client's admission that he had been responsible for some of the bloodiest carnage that Terry had ever seen in a murder trial, not to mention Cal's ugly little outburst in which he all but punched out the judge.

It was one pretty big freakin' gamble, especially the way this jury looked. Maybe their faces were a little less implacable today, but they were a long way from not guilty. In fact, they looked shell-shocked. Which was hardly surprising, considering this morning's free-for-all and today's special guest star from Washington. The older earring lady kept looking out toward the courtroom doors, as if any minute someone else was going to burst in and turn the place upside down.

In the end, given the nature of this case, the bloody photos, Cal's confession, and his confrontation with the judge, the jury was likely to blame the defendant for everything. He was the reason they were here. He did this. He sure didn't look like he deserved any favors. And the jury sure didn't look like they were going to give him any.

Zack began to wrap it up.

"The decision is yours, and yours alone, ladies and gentlemen. You heard the evidence. The President of the United States, the commander in chief of the armed forces of this country, told us months ago from the White House, and he came into this courtroom and told us again today, that we are at war with terrorists and that we are all soldiers in that war. And as Judge Cottonwood will instruct, a soldier who kills an adversary in a battle is not guilty of murder.

"Calvin Thompkins isn't asking for a medal. He isn't asking for sympathy, or understanding, or even an acknowledgment of the unimaginable loss he suffered when terrorists took the lives of his innocent wife and young son. He is asking only that you do your sworn job, and that is to follow the instructions the judge gives you, and come to the inevitable conclusion that Cal

Thompkins is not guilty of the crime of murder. Thank you."

Massachusetts followed one of the more blatantly pro-conviction traditions in criminal justice, allowing the prosecutor to have the last word. The D.A. stood up and began to speak.

And this was where O'Neill was superb. He wasn't a brilliant lawyer, but he had rapport with juries, and this jury definitely seemed to like him more than Zack and Terry. Possibly because he wasn't representing the big, scary black guy who shot a bunch of people and who then screamed at the judge right before getting into a fight with four court officers.

O'Neill was naturally long-winded, but he had enough common sense to keep this argument short. The issues weren't complicated at all. He was making a great impression, damn him. And closing strong.

"We all know what's going on here," he told the jury. "No one believes that Calvin Thompkins was a soldier, regardless of whatever rhetoric his excellent attorneys were able to dig up from President Ferguson's old speeches. You know Calvin Thompkins isn't a soldier, and I know he isn't a soldier. He knows he isn't a soldier. The evidence is clear. He was angry because his family, in a horrible tragedy, was taken from him. But that anger doesn't give him or anybody the right to shoot his way into an apartment and murder six people, whoever they were—good, bad, or otherwise.

"Our country is governed by laws, not by angry people who have enough money to go around getting illegally altered machine guns and lying in wait until an apartment fills up with their prey before spraying over a hundred bullets into victims and the walls and the ceilings and the windows and the streets below.

"You know what the evidence has told you. The defendant knows what the evidence has told you. Put aside the shouting, and the fighting, and the fancy arguments that in the end don't make any sense at all, and you will see that there is only one just verdict in this case.

"That verdict, ladies and gentlemen, is guilty."

AN HOUR AND A HALF LATER, TERRY AND ZACK sat at the defense table. A court officer and a few people in the gallery were still in the courtroom. Otherwise, it was empty.

As soon as the closing arguments were made, Judge Cottonwood gave his final instructions to the jury, and at five minutes to four, they had begun their deliberations.

Because the following day was July 4, the judge explained that deliberations would continue only through five that evening, at which time they'd break for the long weekend.

"You going to tell me what you saw in this jury that made you decide to roll the dice with them?" Terry asked Zack. Normally he had absolute faith in Zack's judgment. But this time, he really believed Zack had screwed up. What were they doing here? They should have been celebrating the final exit of Judge Asshole, starting a long holiday weekend, and beginning to think about preparing for a brand-new trial in which Cal actually had a chance to win. Instead, they were waiting for the judge to come out at five o'clock and say have a nice weekend, and then come back next week, and sit around until the jury said, "Guilty."

Zack was quieter than usual. "I was playing a hunch," he said. The part of Terry that treasured their twenty-year friendship knew not to reply.

The other part of him wanted to jump up and down

on the table, screaming, "You don't play hunches in a capital murder trial, you idiot! This isn't a freakin' game show! We had a chance to disappear Cottonhead, and instead you decide to spin the verdict wheel with a bunch of people who clearly think Cal might open fire on *them*!"

Instead, he got up to go to the bathroom, only to hear the court officer's phone ring. The officer spoke briefly, then hung up the phone. He turned to Zack and Terry. It was 4:37. The jury had been deliberating for forty-two minutes.

"They've got a verdict," the officer said.

CALVIN HAD BARELY GOTTEN SETTLED BACK IN the holding cell before the officers came back and unlocked his door. "C'mon, Thompkins," the bald one said.

Ever since his outburst, the judge had insisted that Calvin be handcuffed and shackled at the ankles, so he had to shuffle into the courtroom, an officer on each arm. They settled him into the chair beside Zack and Terry. "What's going on?" he asked.

"Verdict," Zack replied.

"Is it a good sign that they came back so early?" Cal wanted to know.

"It sucks," Terry responded.

"Court!" shouted one of the court officers as the door behind the bench opened and the judge walked in. Everyone stood and remained standing as the door near the jury box opened and the jury entered. "Please be seated, court's now in session," the court officer said, so they all sat there, silent.

The judge started to warn people about reacting to the verdict, but Cal wasn't really listening. He was thinking about Cheryl and Kevin, and the last time he'd seen their faces. He thought about what he had done, the terrible bloodbath he'd perpetrated. He thought about the expressions on the faces of the terrorists as he had shot them. About how they had been planning to kill again. About how he had planned to kill them.

The judge's clerk interrupted his thoughts. "Will the defendant please rise?"

Cal stood. So did Zack and Terry.

"Ladies and gentlemen of the jury, have you reached a verdict?" asked the clerk.

The foreman stood. He was very nervous. "Yes, we have."

"In the matter of the Commonwealth of Massachusetts versus Calvin Thompkins, what say you? Is the defendant guilty or not guilty?"

The jury foreman hastily looked over at Cal and then down at the paper he was holding in his trembling hand. Then he cleared his throat and said, "Guilty. Guilty of first-degree murder. Premeditated murder."

Calvin just stood there. There was a tremendous swirl of energy in the courtroom, but he was having trouble focusing on any of it. His thoughts kept returning to Kevin and Cheryl. His face felt unusually warm. He thought there was an insect buzzing around his left ear, but it didn't matter. Nothing mattered. The jury had spoken. His execution was now a certainty. No matter what anyone thought of the people in that apartment, this jury was not going to allow Calvin to walk away from his decision to take the law into his own hands.

It was over.

But the insect kept buzzing into his left ear, and then Calvin felt a pushing on his left shoulder. Finally he realized that it wasn't an insect. It was Zack, trying to get his attention. Just like in the dream, Zack was whispering something in his ear. Calvin couldn't imagine what difference it made. Whatever Zack had to say was irrelevant. The one thing that was clear was that after the months of waiting, it was finally over. Nothing Zack could say would change that. It was over.

And then at last Calvin heard what Zack was saying.

"It isn't over."

TWENTY-SIX

THE COURT: *Ladies and gentlemen of the jury, I'd like to take this opportunity to thank you for your service in this case. I know that you all had to make personal sacrifices to discharge your responsibilities in this matter, and I also know that you are anxious to get back to your normal lives . . .*

(Trial Volume XII, Page 224)

CALVIN SANK TO HIS SEAT. AS HE STRUGGLED TO make sense of Zack's words, he became more aware of what was happening around him. The court officers moved in close, probably afraid he was going to try to escape.

Did you happen to notice a six-foot-five, two-hundred-fifty-pound black man wearing a bright orange jumpsuit, handcuffed and shackled at the ankles, shuffling toward the front door?

The judge was thanking the jury, the court officers were leading the jury out the door, the D.A. was shaking hands with just about everyone he could reach, the reporters were bustling around, the clerk was scribbling all kinds of things on various pads and file folders, passing things back and forth with the judge.

What could Zack have meant? This isn't over?

Everyone seemed frantically busy except Terry, who just sat there, his head hanging down, and Zack, who was staring up at the front of the courtroom. Then, still staring up at the judge's bench, Zack slowly rose and said something.

It was way too noisy to hear what he had said, but he just stood there stubbornly and said it again.

". . . Your Honor."

It was pretty weird. All this activity, all these people moving around, talking, writing things, and there was Zack, just standing there, staring up at the judge, speaking to him, without being heard. He said it again, and this time Cal heard the words ". . . the defendant, Your Honor." But that was it. There was still too much activity going on for anyone to hear anything. And the judge was completely absorbed in a conversation he was having with his clerk.

Finally, the judge looked up, and he saw Zack. And then he looked out into the gallery. And there was Zack, still standing there, determined to wait for his chance to speak.

After another moment the judge spoke, and the courtroom fell silent. "Mr. Wilson?" he said. "You wish to address the court?"

And then Zack was finally heard. "Your Honor, the defendant moves for a required finding of not guilty, notwithstanding the verdict."

WHEN TERRY HEARD ZACK SPEAK, HIS HEAD snapped up. As if this case weren't bad enough, now Zack had gone completely mad. Cottonwood was going to ream them. A few carefully considered postconviction findings on the record, and whatever minuscule chances Cal had on appeal would be gone. O'Neill must have thought it was Christmas in July.

But then Terry saw the look on Cottonwood's face, and suddenly it all made sense. Zack hadn't been gambling on the jury. He had been gambling on the *judge.* The best criminal defense lawyer Terry had ever seen had decided to place the fate of the most guilty defendant Terry had ever seen in the hands of the most anti-defendant judge Terry had ever seen.

Which just about guaranteed that this was the most fucked-up case Terry had ever seen.

WHILE THE DISTRICT ATTORNEY ARGUED against the motion, sputtering and posturing for the cameras one last time, Judge Cottonwood stared at Wilson. And he knew that Wilson knew.

This wasn't just going to be the last trial that Richard Cottonwood would preside over. Thanks to Zachery Wilson, it would be the most difficult.

In his early years in the district attorney's office, and then on the bench, Dick Cottonwood had watched defense lawyers confuse and manipulate juries into verdicts that were absolute mockeries of any decent person's understanding of justice. In his later years, he exercised his power as a judge ferociously, to ensure that he did whatever he could to make certain that violent and dangerous monsters were kept off the streets, regardless of how slick their lawyers were or how many times the ACLU wailed about constitutional rights. If Judge Cottonwood had had the death penalty available to him, he would have used it dozens of times to rid the world of the many murderous villains who had passed through his courtroom. The ones who selfishly and thoughtlessly killed and maimed the innocent.

And Zachery Wilson knew that. And he also knew that thanks to the evidence that President Ferguson had just provided, Judge Cottonwood no longer saw Calvin Thompkins as a large, frightening-looking black man who systematically and successfully executed a plan to snuff out the lives of six people. Judge Cottonwood saw the defendant as a man who had taken it upon himself to rid the world of six murderous villains. Six monsters who had killed innocent people before, and who were plotting to do it again.

So here he was, at the end of a long, hard career as a judge who stood proudly behind every long prison sentence and harsh judgment he had ever rendered. About to put the finishing touches on a trial that convicted and ultimately sentenced to death a man who, on a sunny afternoon in a small apartment in Northampton, had done exactly what the judge had been doing for his entire legal career.

O'Neill finally finished whatever the hell he was saying. The judge spoke to Wilson. "Do you have any rebuttal?" he asked.

"No, Your Honor," Wilson answered. "We waive argument, and press the motion."

The judge made a few notes on a pad. Then he put down his pen and spoke to the hushed courtroom. "As is my practice," he began, "I will now make some observations regarding the evidence in this case, in order that my decision on this motion is better understood in the event that there is any appeal." He glanced at his notes and then looked up again. "The President of the United States came to this courtroom and testified that he had publicly stated in his capacity as commander in chief that the country is at war with terrorists and that each citizen is a soldier in the war. He further testified that, as he has stated on repeated occasions in public, he does not speak in metaphor. He means precisely what he says. Nothing more, nothing less. Every citizen of this country, including the defendant, is at war. The testimony of the President was unimpeachable. His reputation for truth and honesty is impeccable. Nor was there any dispute of such by the Commonwealth."

The judge paused while the court reporter put a new cassette in her tape recorder.

"There is also no dispute that the defendant in this case premeditated his actions. He admitted killing the victims in this case, both in his statements to police and here in his own testimony. He also admitted that his actions were taken with the specific intent of killing these victims. He had the state of mind necessary for committing the crime of murder.

"But, finally, there is no dispute that the defendant killed the victims in this case because and only because they were terrorists. Although the defendant attempted to testify to that fact, I initially excluded that testimony as irrelevant. I now reverse that ruling, and find that the defendant's motives are not only relevant, but critical."

The courtroom was still silent, but if tension had a voice, its roar would have been deafening.

"That is because the definition of murder specifically *excludes* a justified killing. And the law of this Commonwealth is that a killing done by a soldier in a battle of war is a justified killing.

"The question then is put squarely to this court: Was the killing of the six people in that apartment justified, such that it was not, by the legal definition, murder?"

Judge Cottonwood looked out at the defendant. He met the gaze of a man who, in a very short time, would be sharing the very lonely and frightening fate that he knew he himself would be facing as soon as this trial ended.

"Taking into consideration all of the factors I have just outlined, the court rules that no reasonable person could find beyond a reasonable doubt that the Commonwealth proved all of the elements of the crime of murder, as there was no murder in this case—only justifiable killings. Accordingly, the defendant's motion for a directed verdict of not guilty notwithstanding the verdict is allowed. The defendant is to be released immediately. Court is adjourned."

East Jordan, Michigan

LENA WAS LEAVING THE GENERAL STORE AND headed over to meet Becca at the post office when her cell phone rang.

She answered it without thinking, which she realized was very stupid as soon as she heard the man's voice say, "Lena Takamura? If you are armed—"

And then, just as Lena started to run, everything around her went into slow motion. She heard a distant voice from the phone say, "Shit! She's running!" and she watched herself throw the cell phone down behind her, as if it were somehow going to harm her. And then she looked to her left and saw a man jump out of a dark blue car and start to chase her. She turned sharply to the right, heading down the only other street in the town, only to find another dark blue car parked across the street, totally blocking her way. Two men stood there.

They started to run toward her.

Lena had run track in high school, and thought she was fast. But these guys were way too quick for her. By the time she'd stopped herself and changed direction to get away from the two new men, the first guy was all over her. She struggled against him, but in a matter of seconds, he had wrestled her to the ground. As she fell she braced herself for the impact, expecting to be crushed. The guy must have weighed twice as much as she did. But somehow, she landed on top of him. She started kicking at his legs, but then he rolled over so he was on top of her. Now she *was* being crushed. She tried to wriggle out of his hold, but she was completely pinned. And she was gasping for breath and so terrified that she couldn't even scream for help.

So this was the way she was going to die. In the middle of Nowhere, Michigan, hunted down like a dog in the streets. Finally trapped by whatever horrible people were breaking into people's homes, and falsifying records, and burning down newspaper offices—

She summoned up the last of her strength and tried to break free again.

"Lena," the man who was crushing her said. At least he was out of breath, too. "I know this is going to be hard for you to believe, but we aren't here to hurt you. President Ferguson sent us to get you and take you home." He paused to take another breath, then said, "We're the good guys, Lena."

TWENTY-SEVEN

Perfect Weather to Accompany Boston Pops in Entertaining Thousands on Esplanade in Independence Day Celebration

The National Weather Service reports that Mother Nature will lend a major hand to the Boston Pops in ensuring that this year's Fourth of July celebration on the Esplanade will be one of the most memorable in history. Experts predict . . .

(*Boston Post*, July 4, page 1)

July 4—Northampton, Massachusetts

TERRY WAS HUNGOVER AND CLEANING UP, BUT the smile that he had been wearing all last night was still plastered all over his face.

He had been up way too late partying with Zack and some friends after the big verdict, and when he woke up, a lot the worse for wear, he decided that he would spend July 4 quietly, rather than drive in with Zack to join him and Justin on the Esplanade for the fireworks. Thanks to the perfect weather, the place was going to be packed tighter than normal for the Independence Day festivities, which meant there would be less than the usual seven and one-half square inches for each sunburned ass in the park.

On those rare occasions when Terry actually won a criminal trial, he enjoyed putting the file back in order before packing it up and putting it in storage. It helped him linger on the victory just that much longer. So he went over to Zack's house and began to put everything into boxes.

Sure, it was possible that the Commonwealth would attempt to appeal, but it was unlikely. O'Neill had come off relatively well, given what the case had turned into, and he probably didn't want to look like the guy who went out of his way to try to send a successful terrorist hunter to his execution. He'd had his big moment of victory in the trial when the jury returned their verdict, and he could blame the judge for the fact that the defendant got away with it.

So as Terry started to reorganize the file folders and label the boxes, he was pretty sure that they wouldn't be opened for a long time, if ever again.

And then he came across the folder that the President had given him yesterday at the diner in Worcester, and opened it to the first page—a memo listing the six dead terrorists with a brief summary of their history.

Khalid and Nemetallah Wali, Helene Ghazi, Maliq Ansaar, Ahmad El Amin, and Marianne Duhamel. These were the given names of Calvin's victims. The jury had never even known that the male victims had been using aliases. Was their verdict really a condemnation of vigilantism, however justified, or had they been so traumatized by Calvin and his acts that they seized upon the opportunity to put him away forever?

Terry would never know, and he was okay with that. He dropped the folder in the box and started to close it, but something stopped him. He reached back into the box, pulled out the file, and opened again to the front page.

Khalid & Nemetallah Wali, Helene Ghazi, Maliq Ansaar, Ahmad El Amin, & Marianne Duhamel.

Something nagged at Terry, like a forgotten phone message. He stared at the list of names. There were the two Wali brothers, who had used Nathenson as an alias—Marc and Mitchell. And the two women, who didn't use aliases. Ghazi and Duhamel. But when Terry got to the last two names, Maliq Ansaar and Ahmad El Amin, the nagging feeling grew stronger.

Terry flipped through the file until he reached the sections outlining each terrorist's dossier. Ansaar's alias was John Bercher. The pictures of him in the file revealed him to be the Elvis Costello terrorist: dark hair, thick, black-rimmed glasses. He was the one that Cal had shot while he was on the couch.

El Amin—aka Rudolf Lange—was the guy who crashed through the window into the courtyard below. The reconnaisance photos in the government's file showed him to be of average height and build, with dark hair, dark eyes, and a mustache. Terry didn't remember much about the way El Amin had looked after Cal's attack except that it was horrible, because he'd taken a bullet under his left eye and then had landed right on his nose down on the brick path three floors below. His face was so messed up that even Judge Cottonwood had allowed only black-and-white photos to be shown to the jury.

But as Terry flipped the page to read about El Amin's criminal history, his eye caught something at the bottom of the prior page: *C-shaped scar on back of left hand.* Maybe that's what Terry's subconscious had been trying to get him to remember. Because it was odd. Not that the identifications had been in question. There had never been any doubt about whom Cal had killed. But Terry had never noticed any scars in any of the autopsy photos. So he left the folder open on the table and pulled out the file containing the autopsy reports and photos of the victims.

He flipped through the pictures until he came to El Amin's. The dead man was lying on the examining table, on his back; his hands rested on the table, palms down. He was dark-skinned. He had a mustache.

But the back of his left hand was unscarred.

Terry turned to El Amin's autopsy report and started reading.

POSTMORTEM EXAMINATION: RUDOLF LANGE

External: *The body is that of a well-developed, well-nourished twenty-eight-year-old male approximately 64 inches long and weighing approximately 130 pounds . . .*

Terry put the report down and picked up the government's dossier of El Amin. *Physical description: Height: 5'8"–5'10". Weight: 150–170 lbs.*

Okay. Something was very wrong here. A guy could fluctuate in weight. But sixty-four inches was five feet four inches. How could the government's estimate of El Amin's height be that far off?

He flipped back to the reconnaisance photos and found one with El Amin standing next to one of the women—the one named Helene Ghazi. El Amin was a good half a head taller than she was. Terry quickly flipped to the autopsy report on Ghazi.

She was sixty-four inches tall.

Holy shit. The sixth guy that the government said was in this terrorist cell was five feet nine inches tall, weighed a hundred sixty pounds, and had a scar on the back of his left hand.

The sixth guy that Cal had killed was five inches shorter, thirty pounds lighter, and had no scar.

It was a different guy.

Ahmad El Amin was alive.

AS ZACK APPROACHED THE PARKING LOT BY the T station at Riverside, he realized that he was really screwed. Traffic had been butt-ugly for the last half hour of his trip, and there was no way that he was going to find a parking spot. He was going to have to dump his car somewhere far from the trolley stop, hike back, and—

Incredible. Just as he was pulling up to the part of the lot closest to the train, a car started up and pulled out of a beautifully legal spot about fifty feet from where Zack needed to stand and wait for the trolley.

It was like God was smiling on him.

EL AMIN CHECKED THE SKY AGAIN AS HE DROVE toward the airport and shook his head. The weather was absolutely beautiful. The crowd at the Esplanade would be huge. The number of people that would die would be at a maximum.

It was like God was smiling on him.

* * *

PETE DIDN'T KNOW WHY HE WAS DOING THIS.

Every July 4 since he started as a cop fourteen years ago, he volunteered for duty that day. At first, it was to get the overtime. Now that he had greater seniority, the overtime was easier to come by, and Vicki was really bugging him to take the day off.

But there was something about working that day that had become like a tradition for Pete, and it was hard for him to give it up. Even though he felt like nothing he did mattered anymore, he hadn't quite reached the point where he was able to chuck his whole routine.

Things were pretty quiet that afternoon, so Pete pulled into the Double V a little earlier than normal for his end-of-the-shift coffee. Carlos was there with his parents, and while they all shared some apple pie, he explained that even though the President had immediately flown back to Washington after testifying, he had ordered Carlos to stay in town for the long weekend with his family.

Joe told Pete that he and Maria were going to close up early and take Carlos home. Pete said good-bye, got into his cruiser, and headed for the entrance to the turnpike.

Five minutes later, Pete's cell phone rang. It was the lawyer that he'd given his card to yesterday at the Double V. He wanted to get in touch with Carlos.

Because he needed to speak to the President.

TERRY COULDN'T BELIEVE IT. TALK ABOUT screwups. How could everybody have misidentified the sixth victim in that apartment? More accurately, the one who fell *out* of that apartment.

But then it made sense. The victim's face had been almost completely destroyed by the bullet wound and the injuries suffered in his fall. The other three men who were shot were the ones who had rented the apartment. The coroner and the police had assumed that the fourth male victim had to be the fourth male occupant of the apartment. It fit with everything else, and whoever identified the victim no doubt assumed from the general description of Rudolf Lange—dark-haired, dark-skinned, with a mustache—that it was him. But if the sixth victim wasn't Rudolf Lange, who was he?

And then that feeling that Terry was missing or forgetting something started to play around the edges of his consciousness again. Was there a chance that the real Rudolf Lange, aka—Terry checked the dossier again—Ahmad El Amin—was going to show up? Not in a million years, now that the guy knew that the government knew he was a terrorist. Terry looked down at the file. El Amin had taken classes at UMass. Served as a teaching assistant. Worked part-time in a copy center.

And obtained a pilot's license to fly small planes.

Wait a minute. Didn't that transcript of the phone conversations include something about airplanes? Terry dug out the transcripts. He frantically flipped through the pages until he found what he was looking for.

. . . Right now, our method is with an airplane.

. . . I pray that this summer, [inaudible] many newspapers from Boston. I will attend their biggest celebration on July 4.

. . . Perhaps we will meet July 5, and you will show me [inaudible] of your airplane.

[laughter, inaudible]

. . . He told me that there was going to be a great celebration this summer, and then there was going to be a loud cry from heaven, and then with God's help there would be another celebration even greater than the first. . . . And he

said that fire and the praise of God would rain down from the summer skies in the fourth hour of the afternoon of the fourth day . . .

Jesus Christ. This guy was going to launch some kind of attack from his airplane at four o'clock on the Fourth of July at Boston's biggest party.

The celebration at the Esplanade.

Zack.

EL AMIN KNEW THAT ALL GLORY BELONGED TO God, so he tried hard not to feel anything but praise and thanks to the Almighty as he neared the exit for the airport. But in truth, he was feeling a little proud of himself. His was going to be a truly magnificent death.

When he got to his plane, El Amin would place the final crate of hand grenades within easy reach of his pilot's seat, then he would pack the rest of the plane as full as he could with fertilizer and ammonia.

He knew that he was going to have a great deal of success killing people with the hand grenades, but when his time for martyrdom arrived, it would be in a manner befitting the blessed nature of his mission.

God would be greatly glorified.

AS ZACK EMERGED FROM THE TROLLEY, HE heard his cell phone ring. Finally. Zack had been trying to get his sister on the cell phone for the past two hours, with no luck. Claire had told him that she, her husband Tyler, and Justin would be easy to spot. They were going to get to the park early and set up a blanket near the handicap area close to the Hatch shell. She'd assured Zack that he'd find them right away.

Sure he would.

Zack had asked Claire to call when they reached their final spot, so he would know exactly where they were. The call must have been from her.

But when Zack answered the phone, it was Terry's voice he heard. He listened for about forty-five seconds, and then he started to run.

IT WAS 3:44. THERE WAS A STRETCH OF THE LEFT lane clear ahead of him. Pete pushed the speedometer up past 100. There was no way that he was going to make it.

The little airfield that Abdul el Whatever was using was still five to ten minutes away. If he was going to be flying above the Esplanade at 4:00, he'd have taken off already.

And Pete was the closest cop anyone could raise.

He had called the staties for backup, but by the time he'd gotten through to somebody who had the authority to dispatch troopers on such a crazy-sounding call, Pete knew that there was no chance they'd make it before he did. It was on him. Either he was going to stop this madman, or there was going to be a major disaster.

Terry hadn't been able to get Carlos on the phone, and so he had told Pete everything. Pete was having a hard time believing it.

"Have you verified any of this with the FBI?"

"What am I supposed to do? Call the FBI and try to get them to believe this crazy shit? They don't know me from the next psycho. But if I'm right, and somebody doesn't stop this El Amin asshole, people are going to die today."

The surviving member of the cell had been flying a small plane, registration number XD4437, out of a little airfield in Westborough. He had been under surveillance until Thompkins shot that apartment up. Apparently somebody had mistakenly thought he was one of the victims. It looked like this killer was off everybody's scope.

There was a little stretch of open road ahead. Pete pushed it up to 110.

WHEN ZACK HAD BEEN IN HIGH SCHOOL AND college, he was in pretty good shape. He worked out often and ran about three miles every other day. Back then, the run took him somewhere between twenty and twenty-five minutes.

Today, he had about fifteen minutes to run three and a half miles, which was impossible. And it wasn't exactly a clear track to Justin at the Esplanade. Throngs of people strolled along the sidewalks and walked right down Storrow Drive, which the cops had blocked off to traffic. There were bikers, and skaters, and baby strollers everywhere. Zack was running through holiday pedestrian traffic like it was a gigantic, organic slalom course.

He wasn't exactly dressed for the Olympics, either. Luckily, he was wearing sneakers, but he also had on jeans and a T-shirt, and a light red jacket and a blue Red Sox cap, more to keep him protected from the sun than for warmth. He was sweating freely after only minutes. As he turned onto a side street he started to notice his breathing. It was too hard and too fast. How was he going to keep this up for another thirteen—twelve—minutes?

Zack had thought about telling the cops about the attack, but he knew they wouldn't be able to do anything in time to protect Justin. By the time they checked out his story and decided whether they bought it or not, there would be absolutely no chance that they could evacuate the Esplanade. Zack would never see Justin again.

He dodged around a skater who was running his dog on a rainbow-colored leash.

No, if Zack were to have any chance of saving his son from this attack, he was going to have to do it himself.

And then he saw a cop running toward him from the right, already intending to intercept him. He looked quickly to his left. Another cop was closing in. Shit. Zack accelerated toward a space between two children and crashed right into their father, who at the last minute had lunged to avoid a bee.

By the time he'd gotten untangled from the father and a handful of balloons, the cops had him.

Zack lay in the street, gasping, his mind racing to a full panic.

In eleven minutes, some fanatic was going to launch a terrorist attack. And Justin was still two miles down the road.

EL AMIN PULLED INTO THE AIRPORT WITH NO problem and drove right to the hangar where his plane stood ready for him. He climbed aboard with his cargo of deadly grenades and placed them carefully, so that they would be easy to reach while flying. Then he climbed back down and opened the trunk of his van.

He'd had to rent a larger vehicle than usual this time, because he'd wanted to be certain that he loaded as much of the explosives as the plane could handle. He began moving the fertilizer over to the plane. He had pulled a muscle loading the van, so everything was going to take longer than he originally planned. He wasn't going to get to begin his attack at four o'clock, as he had hoped to do.

But as the cargo area of the plane began to fill up with the ingredients for a spectacular bomb, El Amin checked his watch and contented himself with the knowledge that he would take off right around four o'clock. He would be in a position to start dropping the grenades about ten minutes later.

God would understand his tardiness.

"IS THERE A PROBLEM, TROOPER?" ZACK STRUGgled to catch his breath as one cop hauled him up from the ground by his right arm, while another gripped him by the left. Stay calm. Stay calm. If he lost it, they'd cuff him, and he'd never see Justin again.

"Tell you what," right-arm cop said. "How 'bout you just cool off for a minute and come over here with me and let's talk about your big hurry." He turned to the left-arm cop and said, "I got him, Fred." He was about twenty-six years old but was trying to sound like he was as bored as a fifteen-year veteran. Great. *I've heard it all before, so don't even bother explaining what's going on. We'll take it from here.*

Trooper Fred drifted away as the other cop led Zack to the side of the road, where a couple of state police vehicles were parked and a handful of cops were standing around, talking and ignorantly watching the good people of Boston head to their deaths at the Esplanade. Zack had to get out of this, fast.

"Trooper, I'm an attorney," Zack said, hoping that whatever this cop wanted, he could give it to him quick. "I'm sorry I ran into that guy back there, but he jumped right in front of me. I told my five-year-old son that I'd come get him—he's down at the Esplanade—and I'm late, and the poor kid gets freaked so—"

"So you're an attorney," the cop said. Somehow, incredibly, he sounded more smug than before.

"Yes," said Zack, reaching into his jeans pocket with his free hand and holding out his wallet to the cop. "I've got ID," he offered.

This was a situation that the trooper was real comfortable with. "Take your license out of the wallet, please," he said coldly. Zack pulled his driver's license and bar registration card out and handed them to the cop. The other troopers watched. "That's my bar card," Zack said, hoping that overcooperation might free him. "I practice out in Northampton."

The cop looked suspiciously at the second card, compared it with the license, and then looked back at Zack. "Wait here," he ordered, walking over to the other cops with Zack's ID.

Foot traffic had been steadily growing, and a huge throng of pedestrians was coming down the street—maybe the former passengers of another trolley. It was five minutes to four. Zack looked over at the cops. The one who had stopped him was in one of the cruisers, probably checking to see if Zack had any warrants out for his arrest. The others' attention had been diverted by a tan young woman wearing cutoffs and a bright pink bikini top.

Zack peeled off his jacket, dropped it with his hat by the curb, then dove right into the middle of the crowd. The cops would be mad, but if they tried to chase him, they'd be looking for the red jacket and the baseball cap. It wasn't likely they'd find him.

Time was running out.

* * *

IT WAS ONE MINUTE BEFORE FOUR O'CLOCK when El Amin finally finished loading the plane, started the engine, and taxied out toward the small runway. The added weight of the ammonia and fertilizer was going to slow him down a little, but the plane was easily able to handle it.

About fifty meters from the runway, he thought he heard a strange whining sound from the engine until he realized that it was a siren. A police vehicle was speeding toward him, emergency lights flashing. He had been discovered. He increased his speed. He had to get the plane to the runway and into the air immediately.

WHEN ZACK RACED AROUND THE FINAL CORner to the last stretch of road to the Esplanade, he was soaked with sweat and gasping for air. He pulled his cell phone out and tried his sister's number again.

No answer.

His heart sank. It was already a minute after four. He was going to have to fight his way through thousands of people to get to Justin. And in the very unlikely event that he actually found him quickly, there was virtually no way he'd get him out of here in time.

Terry had said he'd call as soon as he had good news. He hadn't called. The terrorist was on the way. If Zack failed, Justin was going to die.

His chest was burning and his legs felt like rubbery lead, yet still he started to try to run around and over the picnic blankets that people had spread on the grass. But the partiers were so dense that he could barely move faster than a walk. And then a giant fist grabbed him by the shirt.

"Hey, Jer, look, it's that lawyer!" bellowed an oversized teenage thug who smelled like he'd been drinking since dawn. "Break any scumbags out of jail today, Counselor?"

Zack, desperate for breath, bent at the waist, put his hands on his knees, and looked back for Jer, but saw only four stupid-looking young men, haphazardly lying around in a variety of athletic jerseys, shorts, and sunglasses, getting sunburned. He turned back to the idiot who was clutching the shoulder of his T-shirt.

Zack had to do something, but there was no way he could overpower this guy. "What do you want?" he wheezed.

"Want?" The kid snickered. "I want your autograph, dude. You're my fuckin' hero."

Zack was out of time. He gathered the last of his strength, yanked himself free of the drunk's grip, and staggered toward where Justin had to be.

Then he heard the sound of an airplane engine.

PETE WAS GOING SO FAST WHEN HE HIT THE exit off the turnpike that he almost rolled his cruiser. And the best he could do between the exit and the entrance to the airfield itself was 55. It was 4:02.

He was sure that he was too late, but he raced the cruiser through the entrance anyway.

Where he saw a small plane taxiing to the runway.

As Pete closed the gap between his car and the plane, he saw two things. First, the registration number was XD4437. And second, the pilot knew he was being chased. Either Pete stopped this guy from taking off, or there was going to be a catastrophe.

The moment that the wheels of Pete's cruiser touched the runway, the plane was a hundred yards away. Pete turned to the left to try to cut it off.

He was fifty yards away now, and getting closer. Suddenly the pilot bent down and threw something out of the plane. It bounced on the tarmac as Pete sped directly toward and over it. Then Pete heard an explosion behind him. Jesus *Christ.* He had just driven over a grenade. If the pilot had timed it better, Pete would have been dead.

He was twenty yards from the plane now, and here came another grenade. Steering clear of it threw Pete another ten yards out of his way. The grenade exploded harmlessly to his left and behind him. But it had been much nearer than the first.

Now Pete was directly behind the airplane. He had only a few seconds before the plane would be in the air. He lowered his window, drew his service revolver, and pulled alongside the plane, hoping to take out a tire. Keeping one hand on the wheel, he shot, but just as he did, his tires bumped over a crack in the tarmac and the car lurched slightly to the right. His shots missed.

The plane was going too fast. He was out of time. There was only one sure way.

He turned his cruiser toward the rear wheels of the plane just as he saw them lose contact with the tarmac. With one last surge, he rammed the front of the car into the plane's wheels. They skidded up over the hood of the cruiser, punching a big hole through the windshield and cracking the rest of it into a gigantic spiderweb. As they dragged and banged across the roof, Pete swung hard to the left, slammed on the brakes, and watched as the plane wobbled forward into the air. If it straightened itself out, there was no telling how many innocent people would die today.

But then, without warning, the aircraft abruptly tipped forward and dove into the runway. It skidded onto its nose with a horrible scream of metal on concrete, and then it cartwheeled. A wing snapped off as it flipped, landing on the fuselage, and then exploded into a tremendous ball of flame. A half second later all the windows in Pete's car shattered into a million pieces, and he actually felt the car lift off the ground and bounce down again, as if it were a giant toy. Even though the plane was dozens of yards from the car, the heat from the blast was intense. Pete's face and neck were instantly covered with a slick layer of sweat. He pushed himself out of the cruiser and ran.

It was only when Pete put his hand up to wipe the sweat from his forehead that he realized it wasn't sweat.

It was blood.

THE AIRPLANE NOISE OVERHEAD GREW LOUDER. Zack was out of time.

His breathing sounded like barking now, his legs felt numb, but none of that mattered. He saw the handicap area that his sister had mentioned, and shoved past the last of the people in his way, ignoring their curses and protests.

Somebody's cell phone was bleating. Zack stumbled and then fell, just missing a little girl who was blowing bubbles. He scrambled back up to his feet and staggered forward.

And then, there was Justin. Zack dropped to his knees and his son ran into his arms.

"Daddy!" Justin shouted over the din of the plane, but Zack could not answer. He could only hold the little boy tight, so his last moments wouldn't be filled with terror but rather with an embrace from his father—reassurance that no matter what, everything was going to be okay.

That cell phone kept ringing. Wait. *His* cell phone

kept ringing. He pulled it from his pocket and held it up to his face. He had so little breath he could do little more than exhale into it, and he could barely make out Terry's voice on the other end. But then he looked up.

What he had heard wasn't a plane. It was a jet. Lots of jets. Fighter jets.

Justin was safe.

TWENTY-EIGHT

President to Address Nation Tonight on National Security

President Matthew Ferguson will deliver what White House officials are describing as a "major address" on the topic of national security and terrorism in a special television appearance tonight. The President is expected to reveal more information regarding the aborted Independence Day attack in Boston, as well as other details . . .

(*Boston Post*, July 9, page 1)

July 9—Worcester, Massachusetts

PETE HAD TO STAY HOME FROM WORK BECAUSE of the stitches he had in his face and neck. Which was just as well, since he still had some symptoms from the concussion he'd received from the explosion.

Vicki had videotaped all of the news reports of the airplane explosion, and Pete's interviews, but what Pete liked doing was watching the part of the news that came after all of that stuff. The footage of the fireworks at the

Esplanade and the huge crowd of people who were jammed into the park to take part in the celebration.

And as he watched the thousands of people enjoying their national holiday in safety, for the first time in a long time Pete took pride in his work. He'd shown up that day, just like he showed up every day, and put in a good shift. And that had been enough. Because he'd done his job, a disaster had been avoided, and innocent lives had been saved.

He really had made a difference.

Northampton, Massachusetts

CALVIN THOMPKINS WAS STILL GETTING USED to just driving around.

He had spent so many months in jail, and so many years before that in a fog of vengeance, that just taking his rented car around for a drive on a nice summer evening with the windows rolled down was a bit of a novelty.

On a whim, he had looked up the home address of Zack Wilson, and had decided to drop in on him and thank him—again—but as he approached he saw that Zack was playing with his son in the front yard of his house, and Cal was reluctant to interrupt them. He pulled over to the curb across the street and a few houses down, and parked.

The trial had been so surreal, it was hard to accept that it had even happened. But then, afterward, when it was learned that one of the six victims hadn't been one of the terrorists he'd thought, Cal had really been rocked. It was bad enough that he'd decided to play God with the lives of terrorists. Had he killed an innocent person in his haze of revenge?

Like so much of Cal's life, that question was likely to haunt him forever.

It turned out that the sixth victim was actually a cousin of Ahmad El Amin, the one who ended up dying in that small plane explosion on July 4. And although the government had nowhere near as much evidence that the cousin was a terrorist, they strongly suspected that the dead man had been a relatively recent recruit to Al Qaeda, and that he'd been involved in the planning of the Boston Independence Day attack.

So had Cal gotten away with murder? Had he thwarted an attack against thousands of innocents, or had he merely perverted an already severely challenged justice system?

As he drove away from Zack Wilson's house, Cal knew he was going to have to spend a lot of time figuring that out, or accepting the fact that he'd never know the answers.

ZACK AND JUSTIN WERE PLAYING "I'M BEING Somebody" before bedtime again.

But this time, Justin was standing, fully clothed, in front of the couch, just moving his head back and forth and smiling. Occasionally he'd sing tunelessly. "La la la. La la la." Then he'd shrug. And then start in again with the head movement and the smiling.

As usual, Zack was stumped. "I have no idea." Justin kept on doing his thing. "Justin?" he said, trying to get his son's attention. And then the little boy stopped what he was doing and opened his eyes and mouth wide. "Justin?" Zack said again.

"Daddy!" he shouted, rushing over to jump up onto

the couch and into his arms. "That's the right answer! I was being *me*! Justin!" He was laughing and bouncing rather painfully up and down on Zack's chest. "You are the winner! The luckiest big winner in the whole world!"

And, hugging his son, Zack had to agree.

About the Author

ED GAFFNEY took ten years of work as a criminal lawyer, added an overactive imagination, and came up with a new career as a novelist. This has led to an unexpected number of requests from his softball teammates to appear with Terry and Zack in future books.

Ed lives west of Boston with his wife, *New York Times* Bestselling Author Suzanne Brockmann, their two children, and their anxious, but ever-loyal dogs, Sugar and Spice. PREMEDITATED MURDER is his first novel and he is currently at work on his second.